ALSO BY M. N. COX

The Dora Hermansen Series:

The Strange Brew

The North Queensland Vampire Mysteries:

The Red Line

T0362668

THE RED LINE

A NORTH QUEENSLAND VAMPIRE MYSTERY

M. N. COX

THE LONG
HOT SPELL

Published by The Long Hot Spell.

Written by M. N. Cox.

Book cover design by Rocking Book Covers.

Epub ISBN: 978-0-6454922-3-1

Paperback ISBN: 978-0-6454922-4-8

In memory of my Nan and Pop.
I was fortunate indeed to have known you for so long.

PROLOGUE

A sticky line of blood traced the contours of his neck and disappeared into the deep hollow of his armpit. It pooled there before trickling on the floor. He groaned but was too weak to put up much of an argument.

It took just a heartbeat to overpower the man, even though he was in his prime. Was there a human alive who could fight me off? Not alone, for sure. I had speed too. He'd had no time to scream.

My teeth were deep in his neck as I gulped rhythmically.

Stop, Sarina, or you'll drain him.

I forced myself to pull away from him. It was the only way my little set-up, my "special project", could work. Discipline. Or prison—or worse—awaited me.

I stood up. The man's butt rested on the couch while his top half jutted over it. I'd positioned him like that to avoid staining an otherwise lovely chaise of beige leather. I could still smell the cows. Yet treacly red drops had ruined it anyway ...

Red wine still sat in a goblet on the coffee table. My face puckered at the fragrance. It had been four years since anything besides life-blood—blood from humans—had passed my lips. It was all a vampire needed.

He lifted his arms. They lingered unwieldy, unable to help him. It always disappointed me that bottom-feeders' survival instincts were the same as other, more worthy people. They, too, will fight to live, even though they add little to society.

Pricking my ring finger with my canine, I squeezed a few drops of my blood into his wound and watched it close up. The regeneration process was so magic.

'Come now,' I said, talking down to him as though he were a child. 'We have to get you cleaned up.'

Once I'd tidied the scene and the man, I left him sitting neatly with fresh clothes. From the kitchen, I brought a small knife, a camphor laurel chopping board, and a block of cheddar. The timber smell was pleasant, but I tried not to inhale as the cheese repulsed me.

With no cheese knife, nor any cheese you'd bother setting out for guests you cared for, I pushed a paring knife towards his wavering hand. It didn't matter. It was enough. The man's hand closed reflexively around the handle. I held his fingers in position and "helped" him stab the crease of his groin through the light canvas of his shorts. His femoral artery spurted, soon leaking through the fabric.

He made sounds like he was trying to argue. Pissed off about how things had gone that night, I guessed. He'd expected to have his way when he opened the door to me.

Instead, I was putting him out of action. Forever. He would never overpower another human female again. He was done.

I manoeuvred his thigh over the couch to cover the earlier droplets with more blood. There went the thousand-dollar couch. When his body grew heavier, I let it slip to the tiles. Blood pooled underneath him as I switched the air-conditioning onto high and started for the balcony with a plastic bag containing his soiled clothing.

Before I closed the sliding door behind me, I paused. 'You should be more bloody careful, mate. Wine and cheese nights can be dangerous,' I said. Then I disappeared over the railing into the humid darkness.

CHAPTER

ONE

The following night, I arrived at work at eight thirty p.m. I worked for the semi-confidential Department of Home Affairs branch in the After Dark section. It was a combination of basic policing, border control, and criminal justice. My job was to find and kill vampires. That's right —my kind. As an After Dark Detective, tasks included finding and taking out those vamps who were criminals or unregistered. I didn't *love* killing, but sometimes it needed doing. I was pragmatic, and besides that, I was good at it.

If *all* my friends and family knew the truth about my secretive life, I'm sure it would have shocked them. So I killed vampires *and* humans. It was complex. You'll have to trust me.

The receptionist greeted me on my way through. 'Evening, Sarina.' After a pause, she added, 'Watch out for Mike, honey. He's on the warpath.'

'Thanks,' I said, tapping my code into the panel beside the door. It gave me access to the main floor, where each staff member had a desk with a computer. An advantage of my employment was the innovative technology. Of course, we didn't brag about that publicly. As force members, we weren't supposed to draw attention to ourselves. But it was fun that outside, ordinary people lived in 1997 while we had access to so much futuristic tech. I even had a number, like James Bond. Not as catchy as 007, though. Four, five, three, nine, B. Oh, well.

'Sarina!' yelled my boss, Mike. 'Get in here now.'

To an outsider, it would sound as if I had messed up. But that was just Mike. One of the oldest vampires in Standfort, he was pushing a hundred. Something pissed him off decades before, and he still wasn't over it. On days when his whinging droned on, I fantasised about bumping him off, but I always let the feeling pass in the end. After all, I knew little of his rough character beyond our professional relationship, except that he was married to a human woman. And possibly the most exciting thing—they were the first interspecies couple in the state of Queensland to be allowed to adopt a child.

'Evening, Mike.' I tipped my head to him, then rested my shoulder against the doorjamb.

'When did you last attend a booth?'

Uh-oh. Perhaps Mike's mood *was* about me.

'Only a day or two ago.' I shrugged, then started re-tucking my light blue pinstripe shirt into my slacks.

'Don't shrug me off. You got a problem I need to hear about?' His face wore a rusty flush of anger. Vampires weren't always pale as marble. They are full of blood, after all. It's handy to know if you're a human.

'No, Mike.' I looked at my Doc Marten's, so shiny on the toes. I just wanted the problem to disappear.

'We can't have a fucking anorexic working for us.'

'I'm not—'

'Well, if you're not using the booths, the only other explanation is that you're getting blood somewhere else.' He stared at me until I looked up at him. 'Is that what's happening here?'

'No. God, no,' I said. I even opened my hands at him as if to say, '*Not me, Mike. Never.*' I stopped short of batting my eyelids at him.

'You know full well none of you can shirk off. The Health Department knows where and when you're eating. So get down to a booth before sunrise.' His office chair bounced a little as he leaned back in it, confident his management of me was complete.

'Done,' I said, as glad as he was to be finished with the conversation. 'Now, what else is on?'

'You're off beach duty and on a case. I need you focused on this one,' Mike said, lips pursed. 'It's important. Donny'll fill you in.'

Excited, I slapped my leg and flashed a smile at Mike to show that I appreciated the break.

On the way to my desk, I thought about how many shifts I had been stuck on that damn shore with its sand, salt, and Donny.

Beach duty was the Task Force's version of a stake out— boring as a M*A*S*H rerun. We sat night after night, waiting for vampires to walk right out of the ocean. Then, if we did our job correctly, we would nab them. With no need for oxygen, any vamp in good health can move through the water or swim from a neighbouring country wholly submerged. All they needed was a long sleep beforehand and to travel deep down where the sunlight couldn't reach them during the daylight hours. Weights came in handy for that. Well, that's what I'd heard.

I always thought I wouldn't mind trying a country-to-country trip one day. It was on my bucket list, along with skydiving and learning Swedish. If you're surprised I kept a running tally of goals and events I wanted to complete, think about it. My existence is eternal.

'Hey, Don. What's the deal, then?' Donny's desk was beside mine.

'We snagged a beauty, mate. About time, too. Here's the story.' He hunched toward me as if letting me in on a thrilling secret. 'There's a new kid out there somewhere. Unlicensed. But get this. The mayor's son is missing. Two weeks now.'

'So *you* think it's him?'

'Not just me. Sounds like it could be the kid.' He shrugged at me. 'But this came down from above. The mayor herself or someone else high up. Some chick saw the kid—Steve—and recognised him. We've got her name and place of employment but don't have any other names or leads yet. Nothing but what's in the report.'

'You're right. This *does* sound good.' It's important to give credit where it is due.

'No sand, baby!' Donny stood grinning at me, arms open. His hair was greased back like it still lived in the '50s, and his signature white Hanes T-shirt hugged his pecs. Not that I was interested.

'No sand.' I offered my hand for a high-five as I snatched the file off his desk and started reading the details.

CHAPTER
TWO

By nine thirty, Donny and I walked the Standfort Esplanade. We were seeking a woman who knew something about a bloke who'd 'been seen' with the kid. That explanation of the mission alone was worth an enthusiastic eye roll.

The report said he was a James Cook Uni student and an all-around good guy. Weeks ago, he had been out with his mates when he met a girl and went home with her. Since then, he'd neither returned to the unit he shared with two friends nor attended his engineering classes. Plus, his bank account had been cleaned out.

The esplanade was pumping. Hanging heavy in the air was the fishy, fatty odour of seafood platters, hot chips, vinegar, and meat—not my sort of meat. That was there, of course, in the sea of people listening to live music, milling outside the noisy bars, sitting at tables laughing with friends and strolling the timber promenade. A few stood watching the moon rise over the water.

Vampires shot into public life in the late eighties. Since

then, nightlife had increased for readily apparent reasons. Youths, drunks, and tourists loved all-night parties. Now vampires had joined the revellers and capitalised on it by opening nighttime-only bars and restaurants that offered food and drink for humans.

A couple of large establishments had additional licencing for vampire feeding booths. Like the pokies, which began popping up in pubs in 1992 and 1993, booths were controversial but brought in cash.

'Where does Treemer work again?'

'Macks,' Donny said, turning his head away from me to watch a group of women pass. The naïve would assume he was a run-of-the-mill, hot-blooded male. But I knew he was also interested in the thick life-blood pumping through their bodies.

'When did you last eat?' I said. Vampires couldn't go over two to three days without food, or a distinct lack of energy and vigour would set in.

'Yesterday.'

'Me too. Stop by Grove Street on the way back?'

'Grove Street! You and Marinda and that dingy shit bucket,' he scoffed.

'Leave Marinda out of it. Anyway, I prefer routine. What do you care? You gotta eat, right?' I returned the punch.

'You really wanna pleb for every single meal? It's like going to Macca's when you could choose a fine Italian restaurant.'

Said the Italian. I ignored him.

'We got a description?' I asked as we entered Mack's.

Donny's face lit up as he listed, 'Blonde, tall, indigenous. Nice.'

It was more info than we'd had other times. I shrugged.

I saw a waiter who lived in a shared apartment in my building. 'Hey!' He stopped and moved closer with vampire speed on full display, a tray and two empties in his hands. 'We need to speak with Ruby Treemer. Tall blonde. Works here.'

'Ruby. She's...' He scanned the floor. 'Must be on a break.'

'She smoke?' I asked.

The waiter nodded and swung his head at the rear of Mack's in answer. 'She in trouble?'

'Nah,' said Donny, continuing his walk-through as though he owned the place. We headed straight for the back, into the 'staff only' section.

As After Dark detectives, we wielded similar power to the police. It was an influence no vamp would have had in pre-vamp society. When I showed my badge around town, it was worth something. Vamps knew us—many humans, too.

Standfort had just over fifty thousand, taking tourists into account. So Donny, me, and the other Task Force members rarely went about our business completely unknown.

I felt the eyes of the bar and wait staff on me as we marched to the back. But no one stopped us. I'd be lying if I said I didn't enjoy the power. But you probably guessed that about me already.

Three waitresses and busboys were startled as we pushed through the saloon doors. 'Ruby?' I asked.

A human tilted her head towards a door almost hidden by boxes of spirits and corn chips. What do humans want after beer or cocktails? Nachos. God, I was glad to be undead. I mean, I wasn't happy about *how* I'd been made. It was my reality, and I accepted it, even enjoying my new life. But there were now a lot of mortal ways that turned my stomach.

The door was unfastened, so I used my foot to push it open, scanning quickly. Only one person was there. She was leaning against a rusty skip, eternally long legs stretched out in front of her, and her mind elsewhere.

'Ruby?'

The girl nodded.

'We gotta ask you a few questions about Steve Gorman,' said Donny

'That guy who's missing?' She swallowed lightly. Her hot pink painted nails had no chips.

'That's right.' Donny stepped forward, lifting his leather boot on to an old crate near her to rest. What a pathetic himbo.

'What can you tell us?'

'Nothin' really.'

'That's not what we heard.' Donny hooked his thumbs into his belt loops and stared expectantly at Ruby.

She lowered her face, scanning the ground littered with cigarette butts.

'Look,' I said. 'This isn't about you. It's the Gorman boy who we think's in danger. No one's seen him for weeks.' I paused and gave her a moment. Ruby remained silent, staring back at me with shiny brown eyes, so I added, 'You realise he's the mayor's kid, right?'

'I don't know anything,' she said, holding my gaze momentarily before taking a drag on her cigarette. There was a pause, an exhale of smoke followed by, 'I just overheard something. That's all.'

I widened my eyes to show I expected her to keep talking.

Ruby gave an angry sigh before she spilled a bit more. 'It was less than a week ago. I was working, and this vamp was chatting me up. John Martin. I get sick of him. He's real pushy, you know? No offence...'

As if I would be offended. I may be a vampire, but I wasn't out trying to crack onto humans every night. Wait, I thought suddenly. That comment was probably aimed at Donny.

'Then this other guy comes in. Kinda tall—and I'm tall.' Ruby's eyes widened as she considered the guy's height. Good looking. Short, dark hair. Asian. He was talking to John about a "Steve". It hadn't been on the news then—'

'Vamp, or not?' I said.

'I dunno. Sometimes I can't tell. He wasn't interested in me, though. That's for sure.'

Vampires almost always know who is human. They smell entirely different. Humans have a mixed, earthy tone, while vamps have a more singular one based on blood. Plus, the way they move is so distinct that it's hard for us to make a mistake or to be "unsure". Unless we only see someone from a distance, I suppose. But even with vamps out of the coffin, humans remained so damned naïve. No wonder they were so easily duped. Centuries and centuries passed. They never worked it out until the last decade.

My feelings about mortals were mixed. Sure, I'd been one. Yet, pity and frustration over our differences seeped into my psyche once turned. It turns out that most people were never satisfied, vamp or human. Right then, my frustration with Ruby was palpable.

'What were they saying, these two blokes?' I asked, careful to modulate my voice. I wanted to sound like a friend.

'Only that someone had taken the boy. They looked grave, y'know?'

I nodded.

'So who did John and this other dude say took the boy?' asked Donny.

'If they said that name, I can't remember. Sorry.' She gazed at me doe-like. I thought she might cry. Ruby appeared genuine.

'Okay. Fine.' Donny slid a card out of his wallet and gave it to the girl. 'If they come back in or you think of something you've forgotten, gimme a call. Anytime.'

Was he hitting on her? I held back an eye roll.

I handed her one of my business cards as well. She seemed like a sweet kid and didn't deserve the Donny treatment.

We turned to leave.

'You're wrong, you know that?' Ruby said.

We stopped and looked at her again. The girl's face was awash with a sad mix of fear and resignation.

'I *am* stuffed. If word gets out that I spoke to you. I'm a goner.'

I softened. 'Phone. Okay?' I pointed toward the card she was wringing in one hand.

'You'll be the death of me,' Ruby said under her breath. But then she nodded, and we left.

CHAPTER

THREE

H e was hard but soft at the same time. He gently grabbed my hair and pulled me towards him. Torn since the turn, I didn't feel I belonged in the human realm.

Could I ever belong to a mortal?

But I let him draw me close, so close. I heard his heart beating and smelled his humanity. It wasn't the same as the ones I fed off. Emotion was the key to the difficulty. If only I could just bed down with him—or eat him—or both. But with Will, there would *always* be feelings involved.

I nuzzled into his neck, the thump-thump in his artery distracting me. A whisper of his hair brushed my face—a sense of home. I opened my lips a little and kissed the dent between his collarbone. He pulled his fingers through my hair, guiding my head back to look into my eyes.

'I missed you,' he said, sincere as anything.

'You too, baby,' I replied, trying to muster his mortal earnestness.

He brought his lips down to mine and kissed me. I kissed

him a little in return. Then a lot. It was natural and irresistible so long as I didn't overthink. So, I pushed all my thoughts aside. Senses were all I needed right then. And the sensation was captivating. My skin prickled with anticipation the more he touched me. My shoulder, my breasts, my thighs.

I groaned and placed my hands underneath his shirt, running them against the curve of his chest. I undid his top buttons and lifted the shirt over his head. Will wasn't a muscleman, but those telltale signs that screamed male were delicious.

Sinking, my body relaxing as though a Valium was kicking in, I kissed his chest, his stomach, his...

Will moaned before grabbing my waist and throwing me onto the bed.

It took seconds before he opened my legs and entered me, causing us a deep groan of pleasure.

We'd known each other for many years already. We both knew what to do. Not that we rushed it. Will drew it out long enough, like a virtuoso, building until neither of us could wait.

Lying there afterwards, the usual pang overcame me. A pull to remove myself from the confusion I'd lived in since becoming vampire.

I was a different being, not the person he'd known. For one thing, we didn't require protection, given vampires can't procreate through sex and few diseases cross over. Vampires were incredibly grateful for that, given the AIDs epidemic that reared its head in the years preceding vamps coming out of the coffin.

But those facts further highlighted that Will and I weren't the same species anymore. It didn't matter how well we meshed in bed or how much we'd connected emotionally before. I'd changed. I was a vampire.

If I had been of good moral character, I would have been

strong and broken it off with Will. But I wasn't. I was a cad who kept returning for more, even though I sensed it was wrong. It only worked as long as I acted through the physical. Easy during the act. But as soon as I used intellect instead, the anxiety crept right in and ruined every goddamned thing.

Will wrapped me in his arms, but I pushed away. He looked hurt, yet I couldn't let myself feel it too much. A good man, Will needed someone to build a life with. Children. Marriage. Someone to love him the way he deserved. Profoundly and honestly—and with a future.

That wasn't me. I was dead—dead inside and never returning to life.

'You don't have to push me away,' he said for the hundredth time.

'I do, and you know it.'

'Well, why do you keep coming back, then? You know you like being here. You want me. Why fight it?'

'You've got no idea what you're talking about.' When did I become such a ruthless arsehole?

With that, I cleaned myself and threw on my pants and shirt.

Will lay supine on the bed, looking sad but hot. He had one arm folded behind his head, his bicep prominent, the sheet *just* covering his waist.

I wanted to scream about everything. From the human life taken from me to the dead-on fact, we'd become different species. Things would never be as we intended. We had planned to be together, but it was all fairy floss bullshit by then.

Looking down at Will, gorgeous on the bed, I thought of Donny. Bloody Donny. Backward and chauvinistic. It occurred to me that if I couldn't do right by Will, I might end up just like

Don. I hated that idea and noticed my eyes turn hot and scratchy.

I threw myself at him before Will could ask if I was okay and how he might help. My sadness vanished amongst the lust unleashed as we became one again for that short time.

An hour later, he was sleeping, and I was beyond peckish.

Will had asked me to apply for an arrangement with him many times. 'I want you to feed off me,' he'd told me, his face steady and caring. I brushed him off, even though he attempted to commit to me. After everything that had happened! He wanted to be mine.

I may have been out eating around—and don't worry, it isn't always sexual. But sleeping around, I was not. Yet, knowing Will's mortality would separate us soon enough, I couldn't bring myself to settle down. Our lives had become so messed up.

I quietly dressed and left behind the man and life that should have been mine.

CHAPTER
FOUR

Since I'd ignored my bosses' instructions and met with Will instead of feeding, it was no surprise I was ravenous afterwards.

I entered Five Grove Street and asked to see Marinda. There was a twenty-minute wait. Checking my watch, I saw I was pushing it with sunrise coming, but I thought I could eat and still make it home before the first rays. Settling on a squishy vinyl chair, I felt thankful I no longer sweated as a human did. No one raised in Queensland could ever forget the stickiness of car seats against their thighs during the summer.

A few vamps came and went as the receptionist, Sam, sat behind the glass panel, flicking through Dolly Magazine. His nails were dark red, like the deep claret of old blood. Sam was a smart kid. He'd started at Standfort State High School just before I finished year twelve.

Ten minutes in, a vamp arrived that I didn't recognise. With short brown hair, stark against his white skin, his defined features reminded me of Ruby's description. What had she said? Tall. Good looking. Dark hair. Asian-Australian. Check, check, check, check.

The vampire paid through the glass window and sat on the bench beside me. He wouldn't wait long since he hadn't requested a specific human. He looked me over intently and with a faint smile. Either he recognised me as an After Dark employee, or he was slimy like John Martin, the bloke Ruby Treemer had mentioned. Or Donny.

As expected, he was called over the crackly loudspeaker well before I was. When I passed him ten minutes later on my way to my assigned booth, I was careful not to look *too* interested. I continued down the broad hall, lined with small windows approximately two metres apart. Behind each sat a human. Donny was right. Grove Street was dingy compared to a few of the other booths. Its decor had an overall grey appearance, stained here and there, and there was a smell like a carpet that had seen better days. But it had something the others didn't. Marinda.

Booths were how most of the undead were expected to get sustenance. Unless you were monogamous with a human and had applied for a government licence to eat from them—and only them. There were stiff penalties for those who ate outside the law. But the booths weren't so bad. At first, humans with haemochromatosis worked at them. It's a disorder creating too much iron—handy for vamps. However, science soon came to the rescue with a pill that allowed increased blood production in other humans.

'Hey, Mar.'

'What's happening, gorgeous?'

'You know. The usual,' I answered stiffly. Marinda sat on a chair behind a glass window with a circle cut out of it large enough for a vampire to feed through. Her hair, a mousey brown with natural highlights that made me think of the bark on a eucalyptus tree, was pulled back into a ponytail.

'So, Donny, then.' Marinda chuckled, blue eyes wrinkled lightly at the outer corners as she smiled, and that big grin dazzled me. After sleeping with Donny not long after I began my work at After Dark, she'd never forgiven herself. Nor had I forgiven Donny, who'd gone home with her twice before he stopped calling.

I reckoned he was like that before the turn. To his credit, though, he was always the same, no matter what situation he found himself in. No pretensions at all. That would have been more positive if he weren't so damn annoying. Still, he was an excellent partner. I had to give him his due. At work, I could count on him. He had my back, as I had his.

Wiping her neck with alcohol, Marinda followed it with a water wash that was supposed to remove the odour and taste of the alcohol. It never worked. Vampire senses are powerful, and it would take hours before the minuscule traces were unrecognisable. You got used to it.

I leaned in as she pushed herself towards the window. I drank for a few minutes before detaching, but then I stayed in place to appear as though I was still feeding. That was how it had to be. Sometimes I'd drink a lot, sometimes a little, other times none. But to everyone, including the Health Department, it seemed like I was getting my entire sustenance through the booth, as I was supposed to.

When I began my special projects, Marinda thought up the cover idea. If I were regularly hunting criminals, I'd have been silly to let that delicious life-blood go to waste. But if I drank it down, then I no longer required blood from the booths, making the risk of being found out very real. I couldn't see how to avoid being caught until Marinda started working at Grove Street to put herself through uni and voilà. I had my cover. I could eat or simply pretend to eat at the booth. Whatever I required at any time.

At that part of the morning, quiet approached. Humans, vamps, and all their bustling noises were dying down. The booths took on a desolate feel. I knew I had to make a move to be home before sunrise, so I acted like I was disengaging from Marinda's warm neck and sat up, wiping my face with a damp throwaway napkin. Had I been drinking from Marinda all that time, the wound would still be open and oozing. But I hadn't, and so it had dried up. I only needed a quick prick of blood from my index finger—vampire blood, the great healer—to close up the already dry puncture marks I'd left on her.

Even Grove Street complied with government regulations on cleanliness. Marinda began applying the disinfectant, causing my nose to wrinkle.

She smiled at me.

'How are Mum and Dad?' I asked quietly. Yes, Marinda was my younger sister. My only sibling.

'They're fine. Missing you.'

I shrugged.

'You should come over more. I'm serious.'

'Maybe. It's so hard to find things to talk about.'

'I 'spose. I'll help, though.'

I was already standing, ready to leave, but I opened my wallet, the metal Guess symbol glinting under The Grove's fluoro lighting. I withdrew a red twenty for Marinda. She knew not to refuse my tip and instead smiled in thanks as she pinched the brand new plastic note's corner between her thumb and pointer finger. She was doing me a tremendous favour, after all.

'Did you hear the new Savage Garden song? It's the bomb!' She pursed her lips cheekily, adding, 'Not as good as *To the Moon and Back*, mind you. That's the one you need to listen to.'

My brow furrowed as I tried to work out what she meant. Clearly, Marinda was having some go at me, but I didn't have time for her teenage drama, and she knew damn well I rarely listened to music.

'Talk to the hand,' I said humorously, offering her my palm and an eye roll as I stood to walk away.

Marinda giggled, and we said, 'Over and out' simultaneously. My mind was already on the tall hunk from the waiting area. Who was he, where was he from? And did he know me?

As I approached the back exit, I could hear my sister singing something about daddy issues and someone who had a problem with making emotional connections.

I felt irritable as I drove home, the sun on the horizon threatening me.

CHAPTER

FIVE

'Here she is,' Donny chimed across the open office space as I walked in. 'Finally.'

'I'm only three minutes late!' I frowned.

'Wrong side of the bed, eh?' Donny sat on the corner of my desk as I threw my oversized vinyl tote bag beside him. I kept up my glare, though. I'd told him a hundred times to keep off it.

Eventually, I gave up and plopped myself on the chair beside him. 'I've got good and bad news,' I said.

Donny wore a big smile. How was he so darned happy? Some days, I couldn't stand it because I was sure he was only so joyful because of his mental state as a prize prawn. I'd always thought people like that were just naturally cheerier. Yet he *was* a solid detective—he really was. He found connections others would miss, plus I knew he was reliable. So I guess he was an idiot *except* in his career, where he excelled. Inexplicable. And infuriating!

Pushing my distractions aside, I told him, 'I've got a lead. But there's also something we've missed.'

'What?'

'I don't know.'

'Oh, well, that is mighty helpful.' He gave me one of those looks that went right through me.

'It's just ... I can't grasp it.'

'It is our job to *find* the leads, Miss Sarina. Let's concentrate on that.'

I flopped forward, momentarily resting my elbows on the desk, head down. The lead from Ruby Treemer the night before was so-so. She said she'd only 'heard' some guys talking about a kid called Steve. She hadn't seen him. Right? *But the report, the report...* It niggled at me.

I flew back to life. 'Gimme Steve's case file, Don.' Donny reacted in mock surprise.

He sang the blues as he walked to his desk to get it. 'She's got an idea, yeah-eah she has. She's got a thought, yeah-eah, she do.'

Despite the time I spent cursing and ridiculing Donny's personal life—not to mention his habit of providing a soundtrack to what we were doing—there were plenty of worse partners I could have been paired with. Marcus, who only wanted to discuss his so-called "stomach issues," for example. Yes, a vampire with a dodgy alimentary system. Don't get me started. Or Mike, my boss, the tetchy yet eternal "victim" of everything from his human wife to the filing cabinet under his desk that he fought with half of each day. Or Janette and her "relationship". If I had to hear about her incredible mortal love even one more time, I might rip his head off during the next work function. Those were the people who *really* drove me insane.

My personal issue bubbled up directly on cue—the option of applying to turn Will. With him in my mind's eye for a split second, I noted luminous skin and cheeky fangs peeking through those lips. I stuffed the idea down again real quick.

'Give it,' I said, snatching the folder from Donny's hand and opening it on the desk. 'Someone *saw* the kid, right? That's what you told me last night, and, like morons, we forged ahead, forgetting that important fact.'

Donny stood with his eyes scrunched to half closed, looking up at the ceiling, brain working overtime. 'I guess,' he replied.

'Here.' I tapped my finger on the handwritten notes. 'Ruby bloody Treemer. That girl didn't exactly talk straight with us...'

He grabbed the file and read. 'Witness, Ruby Treemer, overheard Steve Gorman's name used in a conversation between two men at Mack's Bar & Restaurant. One said the man had "been taken", but as they left, Treemer saw both men meet up with a couple near the menu stand at the entrance. One guy said, 'So, you're Steve?'

Donny's brow furrowed as he turned to me. 'Bitch lied to us.'

'Don't call her that, Donny. It's unnecessary.' I pulled out my notebook from the night before. 'The second guy. She said he was tall, had short dark hair, and was good-looking. I don't think she knew him 'cause John Martin chatted her up. Right? He'd pestered her before. I mean, he's bothered half the women in Standfort.' I made a mental note to look into Martin when I had the chance. It wouldn't have surprised me if he turned out to be the kind of predator I liked to take care of in my spare time.

'But this second guy, she described him,' I said.

'Your point?'

'Well, last night at Grove Street, waiting to see Marinda, a vamp with just that description comes in. He sits by me for 30 seconds before the next available.'

'C'mon, though. Could be anyone.'

'True. But you know, let's check it out on the way back to

have a serious chat with Ruby. Cos if Steve Gorman was at Mack's, then the mystery guy, Martin, or Ruby Treemer, should be able to give us more information on it.'

I found a photo of an innocent-looking Steve Gorman in the file. Posed post-game in the university rugby league uniform, his hair was plastered in a slightly unflattering style to the front of his head while the rest stuck up like a fluffed-up rooster, ruffed up by teammates, perhaps. He didn't look big, so I guessed he played in the halves. I wasn't exactly a sports fan.

'So young,' I said to Donny wistfully, holding up the passport-sized picture for him. I stowed it in the pages of my notebook, grabbed my keys, and we were out the door.

AT THE GROVE STREET BOOTH, Sam sat in reception again. We'd always got along okay, which was a positive. As a detective, you're off to a better start if you have a pre-existing, amicable relationship with someone. Anyone can lie to a stranger, but it takes something extra to deceive a friend. Or an acquaintance, in this instance.

Sam had worked there for a couple of years. Operating a booth was a respectable job requiring a three-month TAFE-acquired qualification. Honesty was imperative, as the government needed control over where the vampires ate—and who they ate from. It was understandable. No one had spoken of war. Not publicly, at least. But if vamps decided on it, mortals would have a fight on their hands. We might have been a minority, but our skills and strength would be hard to beat. Then again, humans had infrastructure and a lot of weapons. So, who knows?

Each booth visit got recorded in a ledger, and no vamp, not

even ones Sam recognised and knew, could pass through without showing their identification and following all the rules set by the government. Marinda would do prison time if anyone found out about our arrangement. Me? At the very least, I would lose my job, but being put to death was not out of the question for a fraud of that extent. If my body hadn't run naturally cold, it would have turned frigid, thinking about the repercussions.

Sam ran his now black-painted fingernails down the pages of the register. 'Here,' he said finally. 'Immediately after you. Damion L ... la-you?'

I spun my finger in a circle in front of Sam until he swivelled the book around so I could read it. Damion Lau.

Sam told us that Lau had entered Grove Street many times since the previous month, with the address noted on his I.D. as 39a Mary Street. But I wondered *how* Lau had been in town all that time without coming to the After Dark Department's attention. I also questioned if his ID was government-issued or a clever copy.

'Shame we don't have a picture of this Damion dude to show to Ruby,' I complained when Donny and I returned to his Commodore.

'My girl's got a gut feeling,' he said in a low voice to himself as he pulled out of the park straight into a red light. He was right, though. We were onto something. I was sure of it. I braced for Donny to sing about us driving back to The Esplanade.

CHAPTER
SIX

When Donny and I arrived, we found the floor of Mack's crazy-busy. The manager saw us—though he clearly wished he hadn't. I flicked my head and waited for him to deposit the plates of food on a table and come over.

'We need to talk to Ruby again.'

'Well, you're out of luck. That girl hasn't been in for her shift tonight. No call, nothing. She won't be coming back. I can't run Mack's with staff like that.'

'When'd you see her?'

'Last night. When you were in here.'

I looked at Donny, giving him my best "this better not be how it sounds" look.

'Well, we believe she's got more to tell us. So we'll need her contact details and to speak to those two who worked the last shift with her. They here?' Donny asked.

'Yeah, fine. Head in back. I'll send 'em in. But please don't cause a fuss in here, ay?'

Heading for the saloon doors, one of the other servers flanked us. I recognised her from the previous evening.

'Rube's was pretty pissed off after you left. Maybe that's why she hasn't turned up tonight. Probably afraid you'd come in again asking all these dangerous questions. And here you are,' said the girl argumentatively. Dressed in the Mack's uniform of a basic black A-line skirt and a short-sleeved blouse in claret, her brunette hair pulled back neatly into a ponytail.

I explained, 'We're not here to get anyone in troub—'

I turned to Donny, my nose twitching.

'Yep. We've got a problem, alright,' said Donny.

I told the girl to let her manager know we didn't want staff coming through the swing doors.

'How're we gonna serve customers?' she asked.

'Not my issue,' I said, turning away from her to open the haggard back door leading into an alley. The skip reeked, and not only with rotting food.

Donny leapt onto the thin edge of the metal bin, balancing there impressively and searching the contents with his eyes. He couldn't see what he needed, so he leaned over, holding himself across the top of the skip, using one hand while reaching down and lifting a few bags and other pieces of God knows what.

A moment later, with a flourish of movement, Donny stood back on the ground before me.

'Yeah, it's Ruby,' he said solemnly. 'She's long gone. Damn it! Call it in.'

'You're sure?'

'Same hair colour, skin tone, nails... it's her.'

Mack's manager's nightmare became real. The restaurant would crawl with police, including forensics, all night. There would be no more food and drink served until it was sorted.

Of course, it was also my nightmare. I thought of Ruby's

parting comment, 'You'll be the death of me.' My gut lurched, and anger pumped through me. 'God damn it!' I said, thumping my fist loudly on the metal skip. 'We should have taken more care.'

'How could we know?'

'We should have. We just should.'

Donny slapped my back.

Harden up. Harden the hell up.

I was vampire. Human death happened so easily. I understood it and sometimes took responsibility for it. But I aimed for the bottom feeders, the stalkers, the abductors, and the controllers. I would never turn on a young woman like Ruby, with her whole life ahead of her. She only copped it because Donny and I asked her a few questions.

'The staff need questioning.'

'You!' Donny pointed to the girl who claimed to know so much about Ruby's feelings before pointing his thumb towards the back room.

'What's your name?'

'Kimberly.' Her face, round and pretty, was tear-stained.

'We're appalled by this, too,' I said as soon as the saloon doors stopped flapping to and fro. 'I'm sorry. Really. I can tell you were good friends. That's why I need you to talk to us. We have to work out why this occurred.'

'You got her killed. That's what happened. Plain and simple.'

'We're just doing our job, miss,' Donny said smoothly.

'We already know Ruby eyeballed the abducted kid that night. The quickest way to get justice for your friend and to remain safe is to tell us anything you can to help find the killer.'

Kimberly pivoted her head to check the swing doors. 'I wanna stay alive, too, for fuck's sake!' She huffed. 'Look, Ruby re*ckoned* she'd seen the missing bloke. At the front, where the menus are kept. Two men who came in...'

'Right,' I said, hanging on to her words.

'John Martin was being a pest last week. He always tried to hit on the girls. Oh my God, do you reckon it was him? I wouldn't put it past him.'

Well, one thing was sure: if it was Martin, I could arrange justice for him from within After Dark or outside it.

She continued. 'But Rube's said another guy came in. Much nicer. She described him as cute. Tall, chiselled. Not in a body-builder way. Thinner, but still manly and fine. She seemed keen on him.'

'Did you get a good look at him yourself?' asked Donny.

'Nah, I barely remember him. Except that he dressed pretty swish. I sorta noticed cos he was smart. For around here.'

'What, like in a suit?'

'Shit, no. Suits don't come to Mack's. Maybe suit pants, but not a full suit. Dark-coloured—like slacks. Yeah, slacks and a bright blue T-shirt. So bright. I noticed that from a distance. Reckon he shoulda left that ugly shirt in the eighties.' She chuckled before the dire situation hit her again, and she cut it off.

'Aren't the bright colours on their way back in?' Donny asked.

I waved the question away with a hand movement. I wasn't there to discuss fashion. 'Could be the guy I saw.' Donny nodded slowly. 'You heard the name Damion Lau before?' I asked Kimberly.

'Nope. Not that I can remember.' She pursed her lips. 'But Ruby...'

'Ruby, what?' I encouraged her.

There was a long silence as she wrung the edge of her

apron between her fingers. Then she said, 'Ruby reckoned someone new was in town.'

'Someone new?'

'You know, running things. With you lot.' With a look of fear, she leaned in and added quietly, 'Vamp business.'

'Criminal vamp business?' I asked, surprised at the turn the conversation was taking.

'I don't wanna get in trouble. I've got no problem with you.'

'You don't have to mince your words. We're detectives charged with keeping vamps legal around here. You're not telling us anything new when you say there are criminal elements in the vampire community here. Okay?'

She nodded and tucked her fringe behind each ear.

'So tell me more about what Ruby said about this new someone.'

'Nothing else.' Kimberly shrugged, letting her arms come to rest lightly on her sides.

I sighed. *Great.* I noticed she was playing with the hem of her apron again. Nerves. Her friend had turned up dead. That would be enough to give any human anxiety. But what if it was more?

I moved a little closer and spoke in a hushed tone. 'Right now, you are the only person who can help your Ruby.'

Her eyes darted from side to side a few times.

'You really think it's John Martin?' Donny asked her, trying to get the conversation going again.

The girl screwed up her face and appeared to be pondering the question before finally she lowered her voice to a whisper and said, 'Dunno. But someone's taken over managing the illegal vamps, and word on the street is they're an up-and-comer. Ruby was excited to tell me, but I'd heard that goss before. Heaps of people have. You can't tell anyone I was the one that told you, though. Or I might end up dead like Rubes. Right?'

Donny and I glanced at each other.

So maybe that's who Damion Lau was.

'But no one said 'Lau'?'

'No. But do you think it was him?' the girl asked us back.

'I dunno, kid. You're meant to give us intel, but we'll find whoever did it. Okay? Now, what did Ruby say about Steve?'

With a frown creasing a straight line right across her forehead, she said, 'That night John was here, and the other bloke—'

'Lau,' suggested Donny.

I flicked him a look. 'We can't be sure yet.'

The girl nodded and continued. 'Well, they were leaving when this young bloke arrived with a girl. They all stopped to talk for a minute or two. Ruby overheard the tall, cute one say, 'You're Steve.' She was interested in it. She came and told me straight away 'cos we'd heard about him on the news earlier that night. She hoped it was him.'

I turned to Donny. 'So it *had* been on the TV, and she'd seen it before that lot arrived at Mack's.' I shook my head. 'So, did she report it? Or did you?' I asked Kimberly.

'God, I'm not in trouble, am I? And no, she didn't. She got scared.'

Though frustrating, it wouldn't help my cause to frighten her with the possibility of prosecution.

'Nope. We need leads, that's all,' I said.

'What about the girl?' asked Donny.

Donny's question made the corners of my mouth curl down.

'I didn't see the boy, Steve. But I remember her 'cos I recognised her. My brother went to school with that chick. Standfort River High. Lindy someone. Lindsay, maybe?'

'Lindsay Jenner?' Donny spat it out.

'Not sure. I need to go home.'

'Describe her,' Donny said, his face taking on a weariness, his eyes sad.

'Shortish. Shorter than all the men she was standing near. She was wearing jeans and a white T-shirt. Cute hair, like the chick off *Friends*. All bouffy and that. Light brown colour.'

Donny was nodding with a severe countenance.

'And when did you last see Ruby?'

'Well, that was it—last night. We were on the shift together. You came in. She worked a bit more. But I don't remember her leaving. It was near the end of work, and often we'd have a drink after, you know? To relax. Not here, though. Stuff, working all night and then staying on at Mack's. We'd usually go a few doors down to the SeeSaw. That bar with all the mismatched tables and chairs. It's cooler than Mack's. But Rube had left before I finished my clean-up, ready for the next shift's staff to take over. I thought she had.' Kimberly's face dropped into her hands.

'Did Ruby say goodbye, or where she might go?'

Wiping her cheeks quickly and taking a deep breath, Kimberly said no. 'That's the thing. Not a word, nothing. It was weird she'd leave without talking to me first. It probably happened while I was refilling sauce bottles and the serviette dispenser or something. I can't take it! To think she could have been in trouble while I was just...'

Kimberly cried again. I noticed a flicker of movement from Donny like he might step forward to comfort her, so I did it myself. 'I'm sorry for your loss,' I said. 'We appreciate the help you've given, though. You've done well.'

She looked up at me with red eyes, tears welled and about to fall. 'How you gonna make me safe? I could turn up dead, too, and it'd be your fault. Ruby thought that good-looking one wouldn't muck around.'

I handed the girl my card, a repeat of twenty-four hours earlier with Ruby. 'We know you've put yourself in it. Keep my card—our cards—handy, alright? But this is important. Do not tell a soul that you gave us any information. Pretend you had nothing to say. We'll back you up when we interview the others.'

The girl nodded and turned, leaving the saloon doors thwacking again.

Extra police arrived to secure the scene, and the forensic team started working, setting up lights in the alley. Donny and I stayed to interview any staff members who knew Ruby. However, Ruby's friend Kimberly was still our number one witness by the night's end. True to my word, we mentioned casually to other staff that we'd come up empty to lessen the heat on her.

Finally, Donny and I called it quits. Standing on the dock overlooking the ocean, Donny opened up to me. 'I know her. The girl.'

'That's every woman in Standfort, Donny.' He didn't smile.

'I went out with her for a bit at school. Lindsay Jenner. She's a good person. What do you reckon she's doing mixed up in this?'

'She's not vampire?'

'Shit, no! My family keeps in touch with hers. I'd have heard if Lindsay got turned.'

'Unless she'd been made illegally.'

Donny paused, looking out over the bay before saying, 'Nah. I'd have heard then, too.'

He was right. Most info filters through the After Dark Department pretty quickly, especially if it's about locals.

CHAPTER
SEVEN

T he following night, when we arrived at the office, Donny had only made two calls before he had Lindsay's current address scratched on a small square of paper. Soon, we were pulling up in front of an old weatherboard house. It was dimly lit, as though the entire house lacked power and only had one candle. Donny stared out into the night.

'Are we going in?' I said.

There was a pause. It seemed like an eternity. 'Yeah.'

'What is she, the one who got away?' I said.

Donny's face looked ready to crumble.

'Jeez. Sorry, I didn't know.'

'Cut the mushy stuff,' Donny said, attempting to cover up his vulnerability. 'Let's go.' He headed for the house, slamming the car door roughly.

With a loud bang on the security screen, it was only a few moments before a figure moved up the hall. The timber door had been opened to allow the evening breeze to filter through the home—typical for the tropics.

'Oh, my God. Donny?' Enormous eyes shone from underneath layers of hair. *Friends*, I remembered. Kimberly was right, and it *was* a Rachel cut. Except the fringe layers had slightly fallen onto the human's round face.

'It's been a while.'

'You're not kidding. What's going on?'

'We need to talk to you about a missing person, Lin. Can we come inside? My partner, Sarina Massey.' His pointer finger aimed right at me.

'So you're still working for that government place? 'Spose I have little choice then, do I?'

'We'd rather you didn't look at it that way. Someone's gone missing. Surely you want to help?' I said, earning a subtle frown from Donny.

Lindsay said nothing but eyed me while she unlocked the screen for us. I smelled bong water, candle wax, and fake cheese in the lounge. Humans, I thought, feeling disgusted. The distaste for the texture and smell of most human food comes quickly after turning, and you never get used to it again.

A bag of Twisties sat open on the low coffee table. Two candles burned on a black stand sat next to the snacks. There was no television or couch, only a few cushions and a large cardboard box in the corner.

'You just move in?' I said.

'Not really.'

'Did you or didn't you?' I asked in a harsh tone. Then I remembered Donny. 'Look, we're searching for a young guy, that's all. It would help if you could give us straight answers,' I said, forcing a smile.

She looked back and forth between Donny and me, seemingly lost in some stressful inner decision-making process.

My partner didn't seem like he was going to step up. It was

strange to see him this way, hamstrung by his own emotions. Perhaps we had more in common than I had imagined.

'Lindsay,' I said. 'Do you know a man called Steve Gorman?'

'I... I've heard of him,' she said, followed by a breathy, inaudible, 'Maybe.' Except Donny and I had immortal-level hearing, so we heard. Vampires really lucked out compared to humans with the senses. We could beat them on all five.

I glanced at my partner. *Come on, Donny.*

Not even the worst detective could miss that Lindsay wasn't playing straight. His mouth rolled a little to the side. Finally, Detective Donny checked in.

'So you *do* know him, then? How are you involved in this, Lin?' he asked.

Lindsay kept a good, silent watch on the beat-up linoleum floor.

'That's as much an answer as anything.' Donny sighed. 'You could be in danger, Lin. We need everything you know. We can help you.'

At that, she stepped back and leaned on the peeling plaster wall. Dropping her head to rest in one hand, it jerked a little, her long fringe like a swinging curtain for a moment. She was in pain and had no way out. We knew, and she knew.

In an instant, she was on her knees, hands together. 'Donny, Donny, please. Please don't tell them.' Lindsay was hardly blinking as she turned to me. 'I can tell you're a caring person,' she said, getting me wrong. 'Please, I'm begging you. You don't have to tell anyone about this. You could pretend you never found us.'

'Us?' I blurted out.

Donny grabbed her firmly by the arm and guided her upright. 'Stop.' He shook his head. 'Just stop.'

Then there was all out bawling from Lindsay. I wasn't too

fond of the sound when I was human and had grown less fond as a vampire. Being able to smell the salty tears from metres away didn't help.

'How are you mixed up in this?' asked Donny.

The question was met with scrunched-up, moist red cheeks.

'We haven't got all night, Lindsay. Unless you want me to take you into the After Dark office,' I offered, knowing it would feel like a threat to her.

'Go easy,' Donny warned instantly.

With a roll of my eyes, I asked her, 'What about Damion Lau and John Martin? Do you know them?'

Lindsay tried to pull herself together while shaking her head. Wiping her eyes on her boxy, midriff-length tee, she inhaled a few times. Being dragged into the Department was the last thing most humans wanted. It seemed unbelievable that she would not admit to knowing the rest of those men. She was there in Mack's with them!

'I know Steve. We've been dating for a while. About three months.'

'He's still alive?' I asked.

Tears began leaking from her again. 'In a way,' she said through the stream. *Eew.*

'So he *has* been made vampire. He's the dead kind of alive?' I turned and stared at Donny. *It was true.*

'Let's hear the complete story first, eh?' He indicated to Lindsay to talk again.

'It's not his fault. He did nothing wrong. Someone made him, and he doesn't know why. It might have been, like, some revenge thing or making a point of some kind. I don't know. He won't tell me the full story. Honest. He *never* wanted this.'

I rested my hands on my hips, a deep sigh escaping me. 'Who made him?'

Her shoulders shrugged. 'Steve's never said. Because he loves me, he says it's not safe for me to know. Please. It wasn't his choice. I know him. He would never... He's the sweetest guy. I need him, Donny, please!'

'We have to report it, Lindsay. If what you say is true, he should be okay,' I said.

'You know that's not true.' Lindsay eyed me.

I did. The illegal ones get snatched up by the likes of Donny and me. Some never return. I'd been lucky to be earmarked to work at After Dark instead. They keep a close eye on the department and are always looking out for individuals who might be good employees. They seek a range of skills and character traits.

'Please, Donny. I love him. I'm *in* love with him. I can't live without him. Please help me. Help us.'

'Oh, Jesus, Lindsay. Fuck.' Donny hunched over and held onto his knees for a few seconds. Maybe he was thinking. But it appeared he'd taken an emotional punch to the gut. It was shaping up to be a strange night.

'Sarina?' Now Donny also looked like he was pleading with me.

'Oh, you must be joking, Donny. Outside. Now!' I ordered Lindsay to stay where she was.

In the darkness of the verandah, I told Donny it was a bad idea. 'You realise that by keeping this to ourselves, we are going against our job description, risking a fine or even our jobs?'

Given my out-of-work pastimes, the irony of my words was killing me. Fortunately, Donny didn't know that.

'Just for a short time, Sar. Come on. Let's dig around a bit and try to find out what happened. Then we call it in. It's not like we're covering it up, just delaying writing it into the notes on the case.'

'Keeping info from the Department is playing with fire, and you know it! And for what? An old girlfriend's new love? Get a bloody grip, Don!'

'I'm begging you, Sarina Massey. I'd do this for you. If I could see what you were doing was important. I would.'

Oh, you would, would you? Interesting indeed.

'I dunno, Don,' I said. 'I need to think it over.' Meanwhile, my extra-curricular activities kept pressing forward in my brain. Would Donny support me in *that* if he knew? Ultimately, though, Donny and Lindsay asked nothing compared to what I kept from After Dark, my partner, and everyone else—barring Marinda.

'Where is Steve, by the way? I notice you haven't pressed her on that yet,' I continued.

I knew Donny was a soft touch, as well as a rogue. But for him to ask me to keep information back was out of character for him. 'Look. Let's call it quits for tonight, head home, and I'll think about it. But if I wake up tomorrow night and decide not to keep your little secret, we call it in. No arguments. Okay?'

'Fine.'

As Donny walked away, I called after him. 'Ask her again about Martin & Lau, too!'

I reached to turn the key in the ignition as Donny spoke to Lindsay at the door, but I let my hand drop back into my lap so I could listen to their conversation instead. Despite my excellent undead hearing, I wouldn't have heard them over the engine idling.

'Come on, now. What are you doing with a vampire, Lin?'

'Oh, please tell me you're not playing that card. Silly vamp, you.'

'I am a vampire, and I know what we can do, what we're like. He's new, so there's even more danger.'

'I love him, Don. He's *the one*.' Though I couldn't see

Donny's face, I saw Lindsay open her hands up as though suggesting it was fate, and what could she do?

'I don't like it. But I'm sure that means nothing to you.'

'Why should it? What's good for the goose is good for the gander, right? We agreed not to be like that with each other, didn't we? I'll be careful. I promise.'

'Look, Lin, there's some serious shit going down around this case. Whoever did this to Steve isn't mucking around. You're not to tell anyone this, but one of our witnesses has already turned up dead.'

In the passenger seat, I mouthed, 'Bloody idiot.' I couldn't believe he just told her that.

'I'll be careful. I swear it,' Lindsay replied to Donny.

'One more thing, though. John Martin & Damion Lau. You sure you don't know 'em?'

'I know of Martin.'

'Does your boy know him? Has he mentioned anything about him?'

'Nothing.'

'Okay.' Donny was slowly nodding.

Lindsay looked happy, then, and even threw her arms around him for a quick hug. At that point, I turned the car on and could no longer hear them, but the girl listened intently. Donny probably told her to hide Steve because we might call for him the following night. Oh well, it wasn't my problem.

Given *my* extra-curricular activities, I couldn't be angry at Donny for wanting to bend the rules. But I was now more interested than ever to know if he would turn me in to authorities or cheer me on should he discover what I'd been hiding. It would be best if that situation never came to pass.

I'd managed to buy myself the rest of the night off work, and I planned to use it.

CHAPTER
EIGHT

It was unusual for me to have two 'special projects' going simultaneously, let alone to have both lined up and ready. I needed plenty of time to ensure that I took out guilty parties only. I wasn't in it for the violence, despite how it seemed.

But the bloke who'd met his end on the poor man's "wine and cheese night" had given me a tip without realising it. Early on, while I was still watching him and digging into his background, I'd overheard him tell someone about a guy he knew who took drunk women home from the pub, finding them an easy target. I called him the "Oaf".

But now I was also beginning to mull over John Martin. Being a vampire would make a John Martin project more challenging to complete. He'd be more difficult to overcome physically. But vampires didn't receive a get-out-of-jail-free card just because they were life-challenged. Not in my world. They could do more damage than a human, too. Perhaps I'd start digging around and see what more I could find on him.

Rumours had swirled around him for years. Yes, I think it was time to know for sure.

And so, John made two. What a lucky vamp I was. There is so much evil to choose from!

It was primarily men that I investigated and dispatched during my little extracurriculars. Only the dense or ingenuous would argue female rapists were a problem *on par with* male rapists. Still, I had encountered that breed of woman several times and handled them precisely the same way. Sexist, I was not.

Donny and I drove back to the department to leave the work vehicle in the lot that night. After ranting about God laughing at our plans, he took off in his Commodore. I switched to my car and drove home to change quickly into a dark but figure-hugging dress. Less than ten minutes later, I arrived on the outskirts of Standfort and parked two streets away from my target's house.

Though I hadn't planned to complete everything that night, things were falling into place for that possibility. I had gotten lucky—I knew the Oaf's wife was away, staying with the man's brother and sister-in-law. They were two of the few people his wife was "allowed" to socialise with, and they lived nearly an hour away, heading west of Standfort.

I'd already established the man's guilt. He'd even been charged with an assault against a woman in Central Queensland in the eighties. He'd gotten off on a legal technicality. There seemed to be a lot of 'legal technicalities' when it came to violent crime. But the Oaf hadn't stopped after getting lucky that one time. Wine and Cheese told me that this guy still cruised for women at bars. Such an honest creature was ol' Wine and Cheese. But I'd followed the Oaf and had seen him attack a young woman with my own eyes. Intervening, I'd grabbed my umbrella to hide my face and then knocked on the window of his car, asking for directions. That put the wind up him. After he thought I'd gone, he rolled the inebriated woman out onto the curb, leaving me to find out where she lived and take her home. No one can say I'm a complete monster.

His marriage was a debacle as well. The Oaf's wife was allowed to go out for shopping and other errands, but he always had to know where she was. Her social connections were few, seeming to exist solely of a few family members—mainly his! But all of them of his choosing. A little digging had established that she rarely saw her own family. One night, I created a conversation with her sister in a theatre and learned that the wife's family missed her terribly. They couldn't understand what had gone wrong. There was some bitterness towards the Oaf, but they remained unsure of the full extent of his involvement in their sister's isolation.

Soon, my hands were gripping the brickwork outside the house. My nimble fingers quickly pulled me up the few metres I needed to sneak a look through a large living-room window. I'd have made a terrific rock climber with my super-strength. But who had the time? Between full-time work and my special projects.

Inside, the man drank a stubby of beer, resting it conveniently on his spherical gut between each sip. Since it was past ten o'clock, I estimated he'd had a few already, and the half-dozen tins on the table backed up the estimate. He lifted a cheek and farted loudly. Vampires have strong stomachs, but we also have robust senses. The smell made me glad he would soon meet his end.

I took no chances on establishing guilt nor making sure no innocents were harmed. So I dropped quickly to the ground and slunk around the back to confirm his wife was away. The curtains were wide open, so the casement windows could catch the breeze and direct it inside. No other living creatures were within, and with that established, I jumped down again, heading straight for the front door.

I knocked gently and then once more. Footsteps, slightly off-balance, started for the door.

'Who is it?' came the gruff voice.

'Sorry to bother you. My car broke down a couple of doors up. Your light was on and...' I paused as he opened the door a crack to squint at me. I made myself look small, standing on the cement porch in my short dress and bob all teased up in a way I wouldn't usually be seen dead with. 'I just wondered if I could use your phone?' I said.

The door opened wide as the Oaf invited me in, his voice taking on a syrupy feel. 'Of course, no problem,' he told me, ushering me through.

'I was just having a few beers. Sorry about the mess.' He quickly gathered the empty beer bottles from the floor beside the couch, placed them in a plastic bag, and smiled at me.

'The phone,' I said. 'I'll leave money to cover it, of course,' I reached into my pocket, pulled out some coins and searched through them.

'No, don't worry, love. Do you want to have a drink first, though?'

And there it was. Would any young woman want to sit and drink with that Oaf rather than call roadside assistance to come and help get her car working? I honestly doubted it.

'Sure,' I said.

He turned for the kitchen, and before he reached the doorway, I had my hand over his mouth, and my arm curled around his neck. There was a minor struggle—his legs stiffened, and his arms tugged at mine, unable to remove them—gasping and then quiet.

I slumped him onto the couch and found a pen and a sheet

of writing paper. By the time he regained consciousness, I was well-prepared.

'Don't make a sound, or you won't live through the night,' I whispered, keeping my tone serious and eyes on him.

He shook and nearly fell off the couch.

'Ah!' I said sharply, putting my finger to my mouth and telling him, 'Shhhh.' I looked deep into his eyes, holding his gaze.

Trancing, sometimes called glamouring, was a calming technique that vampires had at their disposal. In the past, it had helped vampires feed without killing a human, which in turn aided vampire's ability to stay hidden for so long. It was still used, but it wasn't so important now that we had legal options for sustenance. I loved trancing humans, though. It might have been my favourite vampire skill.

Honing my focus, I continued the eye contact, not letting up even for a second. It felt like I was becoming one with him, connecting through an invisible cord as though I could communicate without saying a word.

His eyelids became heavier with each passing second, closing, encroaching on his light blue eyes. But they didn't close completely. He remained awake and looked right at me. But an empty, glazed look hinted that he was now entirely transfixed and under control. My control.

'You're going to write a pleasant letter for your wife,' I told him.

'Yes,' he followed my verbal instructions, nodding gently.

Placing a pen in his hand and a sheet of white bond paper from a stationery drawer in front of him on the coffee table, I asked, 'What do you call her?'

'Mimi.'

Hearing his affectionate shortening of his wife's name broke my heart a little. It was a shame he hadn't been sweeter to Mimi. But I pressed on. 'Write this,' I said. 'Dear Mimi. Comma. New line. I can't do this anymore. Full stop. I have treated you terribly.' I urged him, 'Start writing!'

He began enthusiastically copying down my suggestion, word for word. His head bobbed lightly as though he thought it the most marvellous proposal—to write this apology and goodbye to his dear, long-suffering wife. As though he welcomed the process.

'Then write, I don't know if I can change, and you deserve better. Full stop. Please have a wonderful life without me. Full stop. Never look back. Place an exclamation mark after 'never look back.' I paused a moment for him to catch up. 'Then, on a new line, sign your name.'

When he finished writing, he looked at me as if I were his mother and would be thrilled with his excellent work. *Yeah, a gold star is coming your way, buddy.*

I folded the paper in half and left it on the kitchen table, already laid out for breakfast. Since I doubted the Oaf had done the place setting, Mimi must have prepared it for him before she left. One place, ready for brekkie the following morning. The placemat had an English country cottage scene on it.

'Now we're going on a little trip,' I said, returning to the lounge. 'It'll be fun.'

To cause a trance state looked easy as pie, but getting a human to go under like that took a lot of mental energy. That's why I'd overpower them when I could. Trancing wasn't usually worth the effort, despite how fun it could be. But that night, I needed him to write the note, and the last thing I wanted was for him to yell out before I was ready.

Since the Oaf was already under my spell, it made sense to make the most of it. Instead of waking him, I led him down the hall. 'Come on, wobbly boot,' I whispered, taking him by the hand.

Passing an open door, the study caught my eye.

'Stay,' I said and entered the study out of sheer curiosity. I scanned the walls, then shuffled the papers lightly, fingertips swiping each sheet away, seeing nothing of interest. The man was a plumber, and the paper pile was mostly invoicing for his company. I peeked at a few, my eyebrow-raising when I saw Mike Thompson's name on one.

Even vamps require plumbers. Still, it piqued my interest.

But a photo completely grabbed my attention. Moving the stack of invoices, I saw someone I recognised staring back at me. I squinted at the man in the hall. His feet stood in place, though his trunk oscillated lightly on the spot with a natural sway, exacerbated by the number of beers he'd consumed. He certainly took no interest whatsoever in what I was doing. But I took a renewed interest in him.

I looked back at the picture. *Steve.*

Why the hell did that doofus cut a big picture of Steve out of the newspaper to keep?

CHAPTER
NINE

It was easy to transport the Oaf out to the state forest. Still in a trance, he followed me to the car and got in without a word.

I was desperate to learn about his connection to Steve. After walking a kilometre into the forest, I kneeled him down in a clearing and lifted the hypnotic state with the smell of pine all around us.

Although trancing makes humans docile, their minds are not the sharpest in that state. It may be a bit like truth serum, but you couldn't be sure you were getting the *complete* truth when they were under. Missed information from someone tranced was regular.

The man panicked as he returned to reality in the forest's darkness. They often do. Waking up in a new place with a stranger was frightening. Holding his shoulders tight, I explained, 'You are a man. I am a vampire.' I flashed my canines at him, which caused a moderate panic—as it should. But I squeezed his shoulders to alert him to my strength, too.

Then I whispered in his ear, 'You can run, but you won't get away. I'm too fast and too strong. Do you understand?'

He nodded as his body shook. I gradually released my grip until I was sure his actions matched the nod of agreement that he wouldn't do a runner. I hadn't been joking. That brute wouldn't leave the forest unless I allowed it. That was a fact.

I knelt in front of him so I could see his face. He was pasty white with a slight flush of rose on his cheeks. No anger. Only fear. His eyes darted here and there, avoiding me, the source of his fear, and hoping for a way out.

'Why are you doing this?' he cried, his face a good replica of innocence.

'Aww, of course. You ignorant petal. Well, I know about those women you assaulted. The ones who were too drunk to say no. Or too drunk to stop you.'

'No, you've got me mixed up with someone else. I'm not a dangerous man. I love women.'

'So that bloke who looked exactly like you, bundling an out-of-it girl from a bar in town into your car a month ago, wasn't you?'

That got a reaction. The Oaf's face froze.

'Yes, I've been watching you. Remember the woman holding the umbrella?'

His face went even whiter than I'd expected—and I'd seen a lot of scared humans in my brief life as a vampire.

'What did you say to the girl when she murmured, "Please, I just want to go home"? Hmm? As I remember it, you said...'. I touched my chin with my hand to dramatise my thinking. 'Oh, that's right. You said, "I'll take you home. No worries." Remember that?'

He looked around in the clearing, looking for a way out.

'Shut...up,' I said, sensing he was about to scream. I placed my finger on his lips. 'Your game's already up. There is an easy way out, though. I need to know why you cut out a picture of Steve Gorman and kept it in your study?'

I waited ten seconds and heard only the sounds of nocturnal mammals and the rhythmic call of a storm bird.

A sudden loss of patience caused me to throw him a few feet onto a bed of pine needles. I just as quickly pushed my stretchy dress up to the top of my thighs and launched myself over him. I landed with my limbs creating a cage over his supine body. I was sick of his pathetic attempts to cover up his violence. Hell, I was sick of all of them. Plus, I needed a show of strength to make him crack open and tell me what he knew. Crack open metaphorically, of course. The literal cracking would come later.

A squeak came from frightened lips, which were taking on a purple shade in the chilly air near dawn.

'It was ju...just that, well, I wanted to help find him. You know, to help the poor kid. After what happened to him. I'm a dad myself.'

I leaned in until I was inches from his face. 'Liar.'

They had no children. He didn't even have children from any past dalliance. Not that I was able to find.

His face screwed up. He continued. 'I just wanted to help rescue him.' I could see him gaining confidence in his own bullshit, then.

'No. You didn't.'

'I don't know. I honestly don't.'

'What? Rubbish! You had the picture there. Why?'

With my face just a ruler's length from his, I made a show of my teeth again to remind him he wasn't dealing with some weak human he could play with.

He blubbered and spit sprayed from his mouth. I stood to get myself out of the line of fire. He sat up and looked around, clearly considering trying a run.

'No.'

I placed a foot on his leg and pressed hard enough to remind him he had few options.

'Why?' I repeated.

'The Red Line,' the Oaf said, his teeth chattering lightly.

The Red Line.

'What about The Red Line?' I asked. 'What's your connection to *that* place?'

'I never knew what they were up to! I didn't,' he blurted out, followed by more blubbering. 'Only went there a few times. For the girls. I didn't know they'd do something like steal the mayor's kid.'

'You reckon Steve Gorman's disappearance had something to do with The Red Line?'

He nodded vigorously. 'I saw 'im there. At least, I think I did.'

My head was tipped slightly. One eyebrow arched as I took in the rather exciting information the Oaf was offering. Finally, I said, 'You think? Or you know?'

'Promise me you'll let me go? If I tell you.'

'I'll let you go.'

'It was him. I'm sure of it.'

'What was he doing?'

'I only saw him for a second. I passed him in the lounge near the front.'

'But was he fighting? Did he look like he needed help? Or was he there as a customer?'

'I dunno. He looked alright to me, but then...' The Oaf paused, a flush of worry crossing his face momentarily. 'Well, no one saw 'im after that, did they? He just vanished.'

The Oaf was in an excellent position to lie about any connection he might have to it all. The Red Line was a brothel on the outskirts of Standfort, and I knew precious little about the business, the running of it, or any broader community connections. Yet something told me the human had given up all he knew. My senses for those things were good. I wasn't chosen to work for After Dark simply for my vampire prowess or patience with Donny.

I knew The Red Line never seemed to get closed down. I didn't even recall hearing of raids there. It wasn't my specific area of work, of course. As a team, Donny and I focused on the cases and tasks Mike gave us. Nothing more. A dodgy brothel wasn't our business unless Mike said it was, and he had never mentioned the place.

But The Red Line was, then, very much in my view.

I looked down at the Oaf. It was his time.

I flew towards him, landing on top and crunching him back into the ground cover as I pierced his neck with my canines. He barely had time to scream before I was sucking the life-blood from him. Delicious. His pulse was fast at first. After all, he'd had a terrible fright. Gradually, it slowed until I was pretty sure his heart would soon stop. I kept drinking.

Afterwards, I dug a hole with the spade I'd brought from the boot of my car, placed him inside, and filled in the trench. Covering the fresh grave with pine needles, I smoothed my stretchy dress downwards to cover my legs again and headed home.

This time, the sunrise was a mere promise on the horizon as I turned my key in the door. There was still plenty of time to chop up the tropical fruit—the only human food I had in my apartment—for my little possum friend, Missy. Able to climb the balconies from a tree below. She'd begun visiting me the week I moved in. That night, I sliced up a cavendish banana and left it on the balcony for her before retiring for the day. After that, I couldn't get rid of her.

CHAPTER

TEN

When I got out of bed, I dialled Donny's number to let him know I'd be late for work. 'Family drama,' I said.

'But are you going to do it?' he asked.

Was that the *only* thing on his mind?

'I still can't believe you're even asking me this, Don. Jeez. She's in love with someone else, mate.'

There was silence, and I felt like I had pissed Donny off, so I finally came out with it. 'Why are you so into her? I don't get why this girl is causing you so much angst.'

'You really want to know?'

'No, Donny. I'm asking because I want to stay in the dark. What do you think? Dickhead.'

An irritable grunt moved through the phone's cordless handset to my ear.

'We went out in high school, and I thought she was the one. She was *so* cute, and she loved me, you know? She wanted to stay together, get married, and build a life, high-school-sweethearts style. But I wasn't ready to settle down. That's how I am—or was.'

'Mmm,' I said, getting stuck on his use of was. I couldn't be sure *that* was a correct assessment, but I did him the favour of not disagreeing with him since he was opening up to me. We didn't often go deep and meaningful, so I wanted to give him space.

Donny sighed. 'I sowed my wild oats, and it wasn't until she got sick of it and moved on that I realised what I'd lost. It hurt me and made me wonder if something was wrong with me. She's a good person, Sarina. Lindsay would never knowingly hurt anyone, not the Lindsay I know. So she doesn't need bad things to happen to her. And I said I would *never* do anything to hurt her again.'

There it was. Donny carried regret around like a ball and chain and wanted to make up for his actions. 'I get it. I'm sorry,' I said.

'Eh! It's my cross to bear.'

I felt as though I understood him better. 'Look,' I said, 'I'm not inclined to keep their secret—I don't even know them. But I haven't decided yet.'

'Fine.' He was impatient. I ignored that and hung up the phone.

I had plans for the evening.

Opening my blinds to enjoy the deepening Prussian blue of the sky, I looked beyond the manmade landscape to the ocean. I was on the fourth floor of my building, so I had a good view. Not that I'd know what it looked like during daylight, except for memories of the general area from before my turn.

I had fallen on my feet for a girl who'd been turned so unexpectedly and violently, an experience I tried not to focus on. I had a good job, a hobby that enthused me—and made the community safer if my opinion counted. The upmarket unit looking right out across the water was like the icing.

The entire block had been built especially for vampire residents and included all the security necessary. You must understand that not every human accepted or even tolerated us. So, while we slept, we had to ensure we were protected from human attack. My building provided the strictest security, and the ability to make it light-tight for use during daylight hours was built into the initial design.

I went and opened my closet to scan the contents. Something that didn't scream, 'I'm an undercover cop,' and was distinct from my typical attire was what I required. I didn't want to be recognised by anyone, so I decided on a dark tan suede mini-skirt. I bought it from the Pacific Shopping Centre, which opened several nights a month to service clients like myself who couldn't come in during the day.

The skirt was a purchase I regretted the moment I got it home. I'd just been too lazy to return it. With a light sigh, I removed the tag and paired it with a loose cotton top, a boxy style in maroon. There was nothing wrong with the blouse, but the colour had been a mistake. I'd only worn it once to a work function, and the moment Donny admired it, I told myself I'd never wear it again.

There was little space in front of the bathroom mirror, so I pushed all my lotions and potions to the back. Vamps like their beauty products, too, even though we don't have to worry about ageing. You won't find a more excellent anti-ageing procedure than vampirism itself. No wonder so many humans will take a chance on being made illegally. Some humans would risk *everything* to stay young and for the slightest possibility of eternal life. People like that rarely consider the flip side. That death being so intricately wrapped up with life can be depressing. You'll never see the sunrise again, for example.

Then the kicker: forever can be "too long" for some. Many a vamp had succumbed to depression over the never-ending life that they're given.

I emptied my makeup bag onto the counter. I rarely used more than a little red lipstick, but I planned to go all out that night. Once I cleaned my face, I began applying foundation, powder, and eye shadow—the lot. I pasted it on thick. As I applied the finishing touches, I saw a straight-up clown staring back at me in the mirror. But that was okay. Plenty of women, and even a few men, went overboard with the makeup. It would help my disguise.

Then I started on my hair. I kept it in a short, blunt bob with a long fringe. My hair was darker than Marinda's, a medium-dark brown, though it could almost appear black at night. In other words, all the time for me. At the risk of sounding rude about Marinda, I looked more like her with all the makeup I'd troweled on.

Marinda was fun and young and loved to follow fashion trends, while I had become set in my ways. She and I had always been close, and my sister was the only one who knew what I did outside of work hours.

The fact was, she'd kicked it all off. In her late teens, she was invited out on a date with Dave, who she'd known from school. He'd been part of the "cool" group, and Marinda couldn't believe her luck. But the night soured when Dave turned on Marinda and raped her in his flat after she'd agreed to a coffee.

And there I was—a new vampire at the top of the food chain. It seemed wrong to sit by and do nothing.

So Dave got clumsy, just like the Wine and Cheese guy would later. It wasn't difficult for me to get a date with Dave myself, and after a few drinks, he took a nasty tumble and ended up in the drink down at Dolphin Cove. Okay, fine. So I'd "helped" him with a solid push. Anyway, his body washed up several days later with chunks missing from sharks having a go. Marinda was "suitably horrified" but somehow got on with her life. Wink.

Come on, now. Dave had his chance to be a pleasant human, and he wasted it. Was I supposed to feel bad for a rapist who'd attacked my sister? Trust me, she wasn't the first person he'd mistreated, but once I'd taken care of him, well...

I looked hard in the mirror, spritzed my hair with a little water and applied a styling product. I pushed my fringe to the side and pinned it with a small diamanté clip.

Taking one last look in the full-length mirror, I saw I looked ridiculous. Perfect.

ELEVEN

Forty-five minutes later, I was in my car diagonally across the road from The Red Line. I felt concerned that I hadn't told Donny what I was up to, but I brushed the anxiety away. Donny had involved himself too heavily in this drama by wanting to cover up what he'd learned from Lindsay. Plus, these feelings Donny had for Lindsay. The whole situation plucked at something inside me I couldn't put my finger on.

No, I couldn't rely on him that night.

I wound up my windows and made sure the car was locked. My high heels—a far cry from my usual work shoes, a combat boot style—clacked on the bitumen as I approached the security staff at the front door. They were two burly blokes, one human and one vampire. So, straight off the bat, the vamp would know I was his kind.

'I'm new,' I said, offering a flirtatious smile. I felt foolish. I rarely needed to try on my wiles during After Dark work. In my extracurriculars, yes. But that was a private affair that no one knew about. At work, I commanded respect for my position, badge, strength, and seriousness about the job.

As the vampire opened the door for me, the opulent interior promptly struck me. It wasn't freshly done, but the rich red furnishings still looked more luxurious than the usual decor you see in Standfort.

'How can we help you tonight?'

I turned toward the saccharine voice to see a middle-aged woman with blonde highlights and a feathered fringe. She held a clipboard, which gave off a more work-function vibe, but her outfit matched the decor in opulence, not colour.

'Hi. I'm a bit nervous,' I offered straight up. 'I've never been to one before.' I bet every damn person says that.

'We'll take care of you.' She smiled, and it reminded me of a cartoon villain. 'I'm Shey. Madame Shey.' She looked rather pleased with herself as she held the clipboard out for me to take, her deep red talons wrapped around the edge of it and one well-defined brow arching.

So that's *the* Madame Shey, I thought. I'd heard about her. Her eyes were bright and hazel-coloured, and she didn't look away. Instead, she kept my gaze as though she had zero fear of vampires. Curious for a human.

'Thank you,' I said as I took the clipboard. Scanning, I saw a services list as long as my leg—and my legs were pretty long. Always were. It's not a vampire thing.

The menu contained the classics, of course. But I did a double take when I noticed the place offered humans to vampires. The section for vamps included a "special". A human male or female. While it wasn't made explicit, I had to imagine that being able to feed on them was an option. I don't know whether it was still my proximity to being human—after all, it had only been a few years compared to hundreds, possibly even thousands of years for some vampires—or my relationship with Will, or that I still had a human family left. But my stomach soured as I read the menu. I couldn't imagine that any human in that place would have an easy time of it. I may have been a killer when I had my reasons, but mistreating and torturing innocents wasn't in my vocabulary.

Plus, it was an absolute no-no, given the government was always trying to legislate for human safety. I did my best not to show any surprise as I read further down the list. Of course, on the next page was the fine print involving a lot of legalise but essentially saying, "We're not responsible for anything that might go wrong on the premises". Comforting? No. Though funny when their entire business was operating illegally, anyway!

Donny had sworn he'd 'never been there' one day when we'd talked about The Red Line. But we already knew, word-on-the-street style, that The Red Line was popular with humans *and* vampires. I wasn't the first female to enter through the front door. I knew that. Not that I expected they'd make a roaring trade with human females, but vampires tended to be less moralistic and, though I wouldn't say I liked to dwell on it, more self-centred. In defence of vampires, relationships can pose a problem for some—especially when they involve a vampire and a human, à la Will and I. So, I could imagine that more female vamps than female humans might walk through The Red Line's front door as clientele.

'What do you recommend? It may be my first time here, but I'm up for anything.' I gave her a broad grin, hoping my response would help this Madame Shey person do the work for me and suggest the special. That would look less suspicious than asking for a human myself, and it also seemed like the best way to get the information I wanted.

'Well, a woman like you deserves the best.' Madame Shey gave me a look up and down that many might have missed. 'I think you'll be popular here whatever you choose. But I recommend the special.'

There it is. I felt hatred surging through me. I drew a sharp moral line at what was going on there.

'The special it is.' I nodded. 'I'll take a female, please.'

A young woman, elegant in a mushroom-coloured dress with sparkly butterfly clips holding back her hair at the front, showed me through to a lounge. From there, we walked down a hall with several doors before I was finally deposited in one room to wait.

The room itself continued the luxuriance of the entry and lounge, except the decor was rich green instead of red, still with a gold accent. It contained a bed, a washbasin and shower, and a TV—of all things. It was like an uncanny valley designer had come in to work on a prosperous honeymoon motel renovation.

I sat on the edge of the bed, my hands tucked between my knees, trying not to touch anything. While used to human and vampire gunk and goo, The Red Line was outside what I was accustomed to.

Elevator jazz piped through speakers into the room. There were no windows to the outside, but the room had air-conditioning running, or it would have been too hot for humans. Despite the recycled air, it wasn't stale. Of course, that was a vampire opinion. We didn't need to breathe, but we did inhale and exhale to speak, sigh—and I did a lot of sighing—and importantly to use our sense of smell.

When, eventually, there was a ginger knock on the door, I was startled. I had just relaxed and was deep in thought about why the man I'd killed the night before knew about Steve. My heart slowed again when I saw the girl. She was a tiny human—short and skinny—wearing forlorn like she was born into it. It was a pitiful sight, even with her dressed in a rich purple silk pencil skirt and matching top.

'I'm Sherri.' Only Candy would have been a more stereotypical name, surely?

The girl smiled and came and sat beside me. She smelled like honey and apples, which was oddly pleasant.

'Have you worked here long?'

'A few months.' Sherri smiled at me and shrugged. 'Would you like to start with a massage?'

'Actually, Sherri, I'm not here for that. Do you think we could talk? Just between you and me, you know? You don't have to mention it to anyone else here.'

'I don't mind so long as it's not weird stuff—S'your money,' she said, a hint of ocker entering her voice.

'Great. Where are you from?'

'A cattle station in the west. I left as soon as I turned eighteen. Had to get away, you know? Went to Brisbane and left all that dust and backward shit behind me.'

I should have done that. Instead, I stayed in Standfort and was made a vampire. Then again, this girl had done just that and ended up here all the same.

'How old are you now?'

'Nineteen.'

'So you didn't stay long in the capital?'

'Honestly? It wasn't what I thought it was going to be.'

'Things often aren't,' I told her, attempting to offer mature advice.

'Are you a vampire?'

'I am. Does that bother you?'

'Are you going to bite me?'

'No.'

'I don't mind. I mean...I prefer it when they don't. But it's my job.' She shrugged like she'd long given up on having opinions on many things. As though she didn't believe she had a right to say no. It damn near broke my vampire heart.

'Sherri, I need to ask you about someone who may have come here to The Red Line.'

She nodded.

'I need to know if you met a boy named Steve.'

The girl's brow furrowed immediately, and she looked towards the door.

'I won't say anything to your boss. I promise you.'

'I can't answer your questions, miss. How about I give you that massage?'

'I told you, I'm not here for that. Steve is why I'm here. Youngish - early twenties, average height, brown hair. Was he here?'

Sherri looked stricken, then. There were a lot of scared girls getting about, and they all seemed connected to this case.

'So, he *was* here then,' I said.

'I can't talk to you about this.'

'I won't mention it to anyone here. I swear.'

'They'll hear. They'll know.' Her voice raised a little, and she grabbed for her mouth, covering it with her hand like a child.

'Can you nod in answer? An honest answer is all I need. Nod if he was here,' I said, hands splayed like what she needed to do was easy.

I took a slight head dip as a yes and proceeded. 'Thank you.'

Sherri nodded, her brown eyes wide like a confused doe.

I whispered, 'Is he still here?'

She shook her head.

'Was he made vampire here?'

'Stop,' she said. 'For God's sake.' She threw herself on the bed face down like she couldn't take it anymore.

I felt for her, and I worried for her. So I left it briefly, and we sat watching the TV. The cube-shaped set was attached to a metal swing on the wall. Its speaker was subpar, distorting the voices that blared from it.

Steve got a mention when a news update came on during a break from some boring sitcom episode. Sherri stared at me, eyes wide but stone-faced, willing me to remain quiet. And I did. The newsreader reported Steve had been missing from a nightclub on the north side of Standfort for several weeks and that he was Mayor Raquel Gorman's son. They also mentioned the mayor's divorce from Steve's father. That information about a female mayor was still newsworthy in the small towns in the nineties.

A timer went off, and Sherri began preening and tidying the room even though all we'd done was talk and sit on the bed. When a knock came on the door, she said noisily, 'Nice to meet you. Hope you'll come back and see me again.' But as she brushed past me near the door, with no one else in the hall, she leaned in and added, 'Someone here knows. Not me, but someone does.'

I grabbed her arm a little too roughly but quickly loosened up to correct my mistake. I put my finger to my mouth to signal her to keep quiet about what happened between us.

Sherri glared at me before rolling her eyes and walking down the hall.

CHAPTER

TWELVE

Donny and I had gotten through the next few nights of work without fuss. I told him nothing of my visit to The Red Line, and it helped that I had finally agreed to keep the story about Steve and Donny's ex, Lindsay, quiet. It didn't sit well with me, but more than anyone, I understood the expression "the law was meant to be broken". Besides, Donny wanted it so much. Though it shouldn't, it stung. But I also wanted him to be happy.

Agreeing to Donny's wishes had a spill-over effect I was not entirely happy with, however. We were working on the case, yet we weren't. You didn't need a colossal intellect to guess it pissed me off. But Donny agreed we would spend the time following up on some loose ends from previous cases. Stuff we'd never had time for. It was nothing ground-breaking, but it helped dispel that feeling of running on the spot.

Look, I was a vampire. Immortal. All I had was time, sure. But I couldn't have a family and raise children, so what else did I have to spend my time on? I threw myself into my job, and in my spare time, I had my little project to help keep the homes and streets of Standfort safe. It kept me looking forward.

My next night off was a Tuesday. I parked my little Toyota on a cross street near The Red Line. I'd arrived as early as a vampire could manage. Once, I'd tried to start my day just as the sun receded below the rainforest's canopy to the west. It had been a mistake. Not that I would have burned up. I don't think so, anyway. But it was incredibly uncomfortable. My skin itched and burned like I'd rubbed against a Stinging Tree in the rainforest.

Settling in for a long one, I wished I could snack or perhaps drink gritty black coffee like detectives were supposed to on a stakeout. But vampires can't ingest food or drink. I could have continued smoking. I'd been a smoker before the turn. But afterwards, nicotine had no physiological effect on me, so I couldn't be bothered anymore.

I let myself slip down the seat and continued staring at The Red Line's entrance. Plenty of people were coming and going, and I noted all of them. However, none of the people involved looked critical to the case. I wondered about the staff. Where did they come and go? It didn't seem to be from the front entrance, so I risked losing my parking space by driving around the building.

Sure enough, a door in the back opened into a car park. At that point, I wished I had my usually faithful partner, Donny, there. I didn't want to miss anything at either door, but I was one vampire. We had many skills, but being in two places simultaneously wasn't one of them.

I watched the staff door from a well-placed park for a while, where I could see the driveway and the back door. A couple of women—one human and one vampire—plus a vampire man arrived, entering the door using a code. *Very modern.* Security was important to the management. Noted.

Two security guards stepped outside at around eight p.m. and flanked the door. Despite only rising hours before, I had been fighting sleep for a half hour. But that sure woke me up. Within minutes, a minibus passed my little old hatchback and turned into the car park to stop just outside the back door. The bus partially obscured the door, which was inconvenient enough that I got out of the car and slunk into the yard of the next business. A human-oriented company based on the fact it was closed, their frontage and bushes made it easy to avoid detection as I stood there.

When the minibus door opened, a pool of humans streamed out. Of course, I knew they were all human. Some passed greetings with the door staff, others entered The Red Line head down, and a couple appeared to be in a daze. It didn't feel right. My vampire gut was screaming. Arriving together like that raised the possibility of trafficking. Combined with the strict security, it certainly helped confirm that The Red Line was up to no good.

The workings of this nasty little business were bumping up against my case. 'Steven Gorman,' I gently exhaled as I pondered it all.

The night slowed so much once the busload was inside that I lapsed into a meditative state. It wasn't sleep but was a common way to get some rest. Perhaps akin to a human mid-afternoon nap. I only returned to my senses when the minibus sped past me around four a.m. Roaring to life, I turned over the ignition but didn't switch on the headlights. Unlike humans known for their terrible eyesight, I could see plenty well, especially in low-light situations.

The minibus wobbled with each turn before finally reaching the main road out of town. A few kilometres north-west, it turned and travelled ninety kilometres per hour past several sugar cane fields before slowing and entering a driveway in front of an old weatherboard house.

I pulled over and parked. Entering the cane field next door, I slipped this way and that on the uneven soil. It was hard to hear anything from within the cane. Insects rang and blared, and the leaves of the sweet stalks swished together despite little breeze. Nearing the edge of the cane, which butted up around the yard of the house, I slowed down and stepped carefully.

'You know the drill. Come on, come on,' I could hear a burly dude with a black t-shirt and cargo pants telling the passengers. The young men and women were climbing from the bus one by one.

The Red Line provided humans for vampires. I had already proven that for myself. That it was allowing them to feed off the humans had been established by Sherri when she asked me if I was going to bite her. Undoubtedly, these humans looked peaky or, dare I say it ... 'drained'. The whole situation seemed worse by the minute.

Large spotlights clicked on as the group lumbered single-file from the bus toward the front steps. I stepped quickly back into the cane and stood like a statue.

The humans likely wouldn't have seen me, but the vamp minders...perhaps. The powerful floodlights illuminated a solid twenty-metre arc at the front. I scanned the house for anything else unusual and found cameras. Why would an old farmhouse, stuck out there in the cane, need security lighting and cameras? The Red Line? It made sense. Banks and all-night petrol stations? Of course. But that was just a little ol' house ... except I was starting to think it wasn't.

Once everyone was inside, the front door locked and locked and locked. There must have been three or four solid locking devices on it.

The driver then parked the bus in an open shed on the western side of the house. He didn't enter. Instead, he sat on a milk crate near the front door. I heard the click of a metal flick lighter, his face illuminating for a second as he lit his ciggie.

Beginning a stealthy 180-degree walk around the back of the property, I kept myself within the limits of the field. That's when I saw *every* window was security screened. Either someone didn't want anyone getting in—or, more likely, they didn't want those humans getting out. It was like a prison.

I stepped gingerly out of the cover of the cane in the direction of the house, avoiding the front and listening intently. I picked up some voices and conversation snippets. It was mostly chattering about the night. The humans were tired, hungry, and resigned.

But then I caught the voices of two who spoke in hushed tones. I focused in.

'...if we run, though, where to? We don't even know what's out there. What about crocs?'

I couldn't argue with that. A river infested with crocodiles lay barely a kilometre or two to the west. Even I wouldn't want to take on a croc.

'You're right. Plus, snakes in the cane.' I imagined the girl's body trembling a little as she said it. Then she continued, 'So I think the best spot's the smoking area at The Line.'

'Exactly. From town, we can run until we find somewhere to hide. A yard in the back of a nearby business—anywhere. Then we just have to wait until morning. It'll be safer to look for a way out of town once the vamps are asleep.'

'There's no such thing as safe anymore, Jen.'

'Not completely. But it's the best of our options.'

'What are you whispering about?' A third female voice entered the conversation.

'She's okay. We're getting out.' There was a moment of

silence before she added. 'When we're smoking in the court-yard at work. That's the best spot, I reckon.'

'Well, I want in,' said the unfamiliar voice. 'I'll die if I have to stay here. If John comes at me again, I... Ugh. He makes my skin crawl,' she sobbed. I wondered if John could refer to John Martin, but I knew it was a stretch, given that the name was so common.

'I'm concerned we'll all die here, hon.'

'So, when?'

'I don't know. But as soon as we can...,' she said, followed by sniffling and the muffled sound of someone with a tissue trying to control their sadness.

As a customer and a faux customer at that, I hadn't been privy to the smoking courtyard at The Red Line. It must have been some inner area. Would they need to scale walls and escape onto the roof? The main takeaway, though, was that my suspicions had been correct. These were not humans who *chose* to live and work there in Standfort nor at The Red Line. No. They wanted out.

With dawn approaching, I returned to the sugarcane just as the girls' conversation turned to their guards.

'He looks like an over-inflated bike tyre. He might have muscle, but I doubt he could run far.'

Both girls laughed, and the corners of my mouth curled up with them.

'That's the key, then. We have to be prepared to run,' I heard one say as I took off into the cane again.

CHAPTER

THIRTEEN

Red dirt tamped down under each footstep as I traipsed back through the cane. I mulled over the ramifications of what I'd just learned. At the very least, *some* humans weren't there by choice. Not holed up in that house, and certainly not being put to work at The Red Line. And if some were captive, didn't it make sense that they all were? Men *and* women held against their will. Slaves. Or, at the very least, they were kept working through some coercion or threat I had yet to discover.

Pushing aside cane plants already taller than me, I moved through them towards the west, where I'd left my car. This new information would rip the case open, not only because of the gravity of it but also because of Steve and Lindsay. Donny and I couldn't just ignore this one. However, I wasn't looking forward to telling him that. I worried he was suffering from some nostalgia with the way he appeared so stuck on Lindsay's request and, frankly, so attached to her. Nostalgia was a terrible affliction for a vampire. Perhaps akin to depression in humans. It could be fatal. It would be a first for Donny if that were the case.

Just two metres shy of the road, there was a roaring noise.

Confused, I found myself on the ground, looking up. The tips of the sugarcane stalks swayed back and forth. Beyond them, the sky was a deep blue decorated with twinkling pins of light. I could have laid there all night gazing up at that. It was beautiful, except for a few roots and hardened pieces of soil digging into my back.

Yet ... something wasn't right. It seemed like time had slowed—or was that just me? I touched my face gently, my fingers slipping on its wetness. It felt like a hot mess.

Blood. I felt its pleasing stickiness and smelled that sweet metallic scent...and then I saw him as he launched himself at me. I was under attack.

Seeing him coming that time, I tried to roll out of the way. Unfortunately, my plan didn't work. There just wasn't enough room with the plants sown solidly together, especially at that stage of their growth. I tried to drag myself around a couple of stalks but didn't get far before he came down on me with his elbow straight into my chest. Winding isn't a thing for vamps, given that we don't need breath. But it sure hurt.

Curled up like a baby to protect myself, I saw him coming again out of the corner of my eye. This time, he held a stake in his hand. I turned my back to the dirt again, and as he brought his arms down, his face contorted with his total weight behind it, I raised my legs and pushed out at him. The vamp, a good 120 kilograms, went flying. I heard the repeated thwack of the stalks flicking out of the way as he passed through the cane and landed with a thud. Plus, the sound of the sharpened timber landing just a couple of metres away.

I didn't wait to see what would happen next. I got up, wove around three plants, grabbed the stake, and started running.

Sure, I could have stayed to fight, but there was no guarantee I could overcome a male vampire of that height and muscle mass. Any human male on the planet, yes. But I couldn't ignore the edge a male vamp would have over me.

Instead, I ran, weaving in and out of the cane stalks. I didn't look back until I reached the middle of the field. Then I crouched and listened. The only sounds were rustling and a few animal noises—and the distant tinkle of female voices carried from the house.

I stood up and began running again, this time to the edge of the field. I needed to make it to my car. Then I could be out of there. But a smell reached my nostrils that stopped me in my tracks. Despite better judgment, I turned and moved closer, looking for the odour. I couldn't help myself. I was a vampire, a detective—and I smelled a dead human.

It didn't take me long to find it, either. I'm sure I would have picked up the smell earlier had that lumbering vamp not attacked me. I couldn't be sure why I missed it on the way in. Perhaps the wind direction had worked against me.

As I approached, the odour was strong and rank in the air. I first saw a pair of blue slip-ons that you might wear to the beach or a shared shower facility. They rested against swollen feet.

Standing over the body, I saw the woman wearing an oversized t-shirt, maybe something she would wear to bed. A tainted muddy red, it would have been a light colour originally. Her hair was muddy, also, and my heart skipped a beat. Lindsay? I kneeled, trying to ignore the mix of rotting flesh with human excrement, and leaned down to see her face, which was as bloated as her feet.

I felt instantly gutted to realise that I knew her. It wasn't Lindsay. Instead, it was Sherri, the girl from The Red Line.

My mind ticked over like a movie projector, rerunning

anger and regret. Sherri had to have been killed because I'd questioned her that night. It would be too coincidental for both girls to turn up dead just after I'd asked them about Steve Gorman's abduction and turning. We should have taken more care of these kids. Still, what could we do? There wasn't enough to warrant placing full-time protection on Sherri. Besides that, my investigation had been off the books.

I mouthed, 'Why?' and rested my face in my hand momentarily as I kneeled there in the dirt beside her. After ten seconds, I realised I had to return to my car. I *had* to raise the alarm.

Like a dog, I tipped my head and listened again. In one direction, I heard the vamp fumbling through the cane. Fortunately, he was a distance away. I had size on my side. I wasn't short, at five feet eight inches, but I was tiny compared to him. Using that difference to slink quietly towards safety seemed my best option. The fact we were both in the cane field would prevent him from gauging my whereabouts by smell alone—and me his.

I crouched down and moved as lightly as I could. I twisted my body around the stalks rather than pushing them aside and kept listening. Before I knew it, I had reached the edge of the field. One step more, and I'd be on the shoulder of the road. I'd be near my vehicle but out in the open—a dangerous position. I found my key and had it ready before I dashed towards the car. With my heart racing, I turned the key in the ignition and tore off the shoulder onto the road just as my solid, undead attacker spilled out of the cane. I watched in my rear-view mirror as he erupted into anger, his face distorting and fists banging his sturdy thighs.

'Bye-bye, mofo,' I whispered, pedal to the metal.

THE AFTER DARK DEPARTMENT had cutting-edge technology, which meant I had one of the smallest mobile phones available then. It almost fit in the palm of my hand. We kept the phones in the glove compartment. But only in the Department's work vehicles. Of course, I was using my car for my off-the-books investigation.

As I drove, I decided it was better to keep things anonymous, anyway. I didn't need questions about why I was out there without telling the Department. Instead, I stopped at the first phone booth and made an anonymous triple zero call.

'There's a body in a cane field out on Grovers Road. Looks like a vamps work,' I told them hurriedly, deepening my voice a little as I spoke. It didn't look like a vamp's work, but I wanted to sway the case towards After Dark since I felt it connected to my case. Then, I mentioned a few landmarks so they would find poor Sherri.

Letting go of the receiver, I felt overcome and kicked the phone box wall before leaving. But Steve was pushing his way to the forefront of my mind. Something deeper was occurring with this case, and I felt strongly that Steve wasn't safe.

FOURTEEN

'**G**od damn it, Sarina. I thought I could count on you!' Donny's frown had taken over his entire face. I hated to see him like that, but I had to be strong.

'I know what I agreed, and I know I'm going back on it. But this is bigger than we thought. You don't know the half of it, Donny.'

'Fine. All of what? Go on.' He flopped down onto his futon couch with a thud. Why were futons so damn popular when they always seemed to have the comfort level of a brick?

After the disturbing morning in the cane fields, I'd gone straight home to beat the sun. When I woke that evening, I drove to Donny's. It was my second night off, and I couldn't let this go a moment longer than I had to. Besides, we couldn't have this conversation at work. Not now.

'I get why you want to help Lindsay, and I wanted to as well,' I lied. 'But I... I.' Oh shit, I thought. I hadn't decided where to tell Donny I'd got my tip. It wasn't possible to tell him that a human male I'd killed a few nights earlier had told me to check out The Red Line concerning our Steve Gorman case. Nor could I say anything about Sherri.

'I overheard some information when I was at the booths.' I finally lied, my body able to relax again. 'That led me to check out The Red Line. I went in—'

'Sarina went to The Red Line,' Donny perked up. 'Well, well! You didn't have sex with anyone, did you?'

'Why? Do you think I don't care about sex, Donny? Do you think you're the only one getting any in Standfort?' It came out sounding more bitter than I'd intended.

'I just mean. Well, you wouldn't have to pay for it.' He looked me up and down, smiling appreciatively.

'No one *has* to pay for it,' I said, exasperated. 'Some people want to, though, for various pathetic and sometimes nefarious reasons.'

'I just meant ... Oh, never mind. You seem intent on misunderstanding me.' He couldn't leave it at that, though. A second later, he couldn't hold his curiosity, asking, 'Was it luxe, though? I've heard it's nice inside.' He looked like a little kid hearing about the most popular new toy of the season that their best friend got a hold of before the store sold out.

'Yes, mate, it's nicely decorated,' I said, exasperated. 'More importantly, I discovered a special menu for vampires.'

'Right.' Donny nodded his head like he hoped I'd get on with it. It seemed like he'd known already there was a menu just for the undead.

'So, you're sure that you haven't been there?'

'Yes, I'm sure. Do I seem the type to pay for it?' He pointed to his chest. He had a well-proportioned masculine physique that he wrapped in those body-hugging t-shirts all the damn time. Don't get the wrong idea now. I didn't *want* to notice. Donny just made it so difficult not to.

But it wasn't about looks. "The type to pay for it" was

about temperament and character, and while Donny loved his women, he *didn't* seem the type to pay for it. I had to give him that.

'I ordered a human from the menu, and the girl was scared, Don.'

'You chose a girl? I didn't know about that side of you, Sar.'

'I just thought a girl would be easier to talk to. Don't read into it.'

'Sure, look, of course, she was afraid! We're scary bastards if you're human. We all know that.' He flashed his teeth at me and smiled. 'It's a shitty industry. Hey, I learned a lot when I worked Vice. Things I didn't want to learn.'

'Yeah, but she was scared to talk to me because of the staff there. But ... she admitted Steve had been there.' Every word about Sherri cut like a knife, knowing what had happened to her.

'Lindsay's Steve?' Donny turned utterly serious then, his brow furrowing.

I nodded.

'What the hell would Steve Gorman be doing at a brothel? Did the girl say what happened? What was he doing?'

'That's just it. She wouldn't say. Too frightened.' *Rightly.* 'All I got was that, while he'd been there in the past, she didn't know where Steve had gone, and she wouldn't say if she knew anything about him being made vampire there.'

Donny held his head with both hands and tipped his head onto the back of the couch. His eyes were wide as he appeared to find the ceiling fascinating. His lashes, unfairly long and lush, twitched gently.

'She did say one thing, though.' Donny's head flipped up, ready to hear me out. 'Someone there knows what happened to Steve. Not her, but someone at the establishment.'

'Faaark,' he groaned in a deep voice.

'We can't ignore this. I know it, you know it.'

'But I gave Lindsay my word. We can't put her in danger.'

'I'd say she's in danger already with Steve being a new vamp. He could turn on her even without meaning to. But my biggest concern right now is that the people responsible for abducting and turning Steve—and murdering Ruby—may go after Steve. Or Lindsay, for knowing about him, or even both of them! Donny, we can't ignore this now,' I said again.

I would keep pushing him until I got him on board because high on my mind was that Ruby had been killed, and now Sherri. What was to stop Lindsay or Steve from being next? We didn't know why he was made a vampire, and whoever made him may well want to cover it up now that it was becoming such a hot case.

I wished I could further impress that upon Donny without admitting Sherri was killed.

Donny nodded in agreement, and I felt my muscles relax a little.

'Look, I don't think we need to write all this up in our notes yet. Let's keep Lindsay's name out of it. But we need to pursue it. It's our job, Don. It's what we do. I'm glad you see it.'

'Okay. Of course. I mean, you're right. Sarina Massey. Right again.' He sounded like an arse, but he was being resigned in a good-natured way.

I nodded, and my mouth curved in a down-turned smile. The best I could manage. 'I've got to get going. Dinner with the folks.'

Donny's eyes widened.

'Yeah. Wish me luck, hey?' I jumped into the driver's seat and rolled the window down.

'Good luck, partner. Try not to eat them.'

'Ha ha,' I said back at him. 'But I think you should check on Lindsay and Steve and tell them about the danger, Don.'

I got a nod from Donny. With the matter settled, I rolled the window back up, relieved to have handed off my duty regarding Steve and Lindsay's safety.

On the drive to my parent's home, I turned the radio on, swivelling the dial to find a station airing the news. There should have been an announcement to stay tuned for more details on a breaking news story. Ten minutes later, as I arrived at my folk's place, I'd heard nothing. Zilch! It didn't bode well.

CHAPTER

FIFTEEN

Even before I reached the door, I smelled roast meat. Not exactly my style. A roast was Mum's go-to for any occasion, whether Christmas (in the middle of summer, no less) or a family dinner. Especially one that didn't occur often, and family dinners had been rare since my turn. Since then, I had seen little of my parents, Tom and Susan.

At first, I was afraid of what I might do to humans. I didn't want to hurt my family, so I stayed away. I barely had anyone to help me through the change, so how did I know what to expect? It was like I had been "chosen" and thrown into the ring without training or support. Maybe that's why I don't like to talk about it much.

Once I got used to my new body, could understand its processes and trusted myself more, I tried to patch up my relationship with my mum and dad. But Dad was resistant. He wore the pants in our family, and his robust control over Mum and Marinda made it difficult for me to relate to him. Plus, it affected my relationship with Mum. Marinda was the only person I still had regular contact with, barring a few cousins who lived in Standfort. Marinda had been correct in suggesting I keep trying, though. Either I was going to give up, or I would keep trying. And I didn't want to give up.

It was Mum who answered the door.

'Oh, you look lovely, Mum.' She wore a dark red skirt suit with puff sleeves, a style she only dragged out of the eighties for special occasions. I smiled widely and wrapped my arms around her. Her hair gave off a faint whiff of perm solution, her new permanent waves tickling my cheek, and she felt stiff and uncomfortable.

'You're so cold,' she said, her face strangled with confusion.

'Yes. It's how I am now. I might be cool, but I'm living and have blood pumping through my body, just like you.'

'Yes, of course. I didn't mean... Come on in, darling.'

The house itself felt cool. I assumed the air con was on so Mum could cook without working up a sweat. Of course, it didn't bother me either way. Extremes aside, we weren't affected by temperature the way humans were. I could wear a coat around in summer if I wanted to, and I would not overheat. Likewise, I could visit the snow wearing jeans and a T-shirt. I'd have to stay in the cold long before noticing adverse effects. I wouldn't do that, of course. To do so would be like wearing a sign that screamed *I am a vampire*.

'It smells good, right?' Marinda said as I entered the kitchen.

'Amazing. You always made the perfect roast, Mum.' I curled my thumb and pointer fingers together at her.

'Except now you can't even eat it,' Dad said bluntly.

All three of us turned. Dad was leaning against the dining room doorjamb, a cigarette in his hand. His grey hair was a little wet around the edges, suggesting he'd been outside smoking just a moment before.

'Leave her, Tom.'

'I'm only stating a fact, aren't I?'

I heard Marinda sigh as she leaned in and hugged me. 'Glad you're here,' she whispered.

'It'll only be a few minutes now.' Mum switched on the exhaust fan to catch the steam from a pot of peas and green beans boiling on the stovetop. 'Sit down, ay? We don't get to see you much, so let's catch up.'

We took our places in the dining room. The table was set up exactly as it always was when Marinda and I handled the job. Little salt and pepper shakers in the shape of thatched roof English cottages, sauces, and a timber serviette holder on a checked linen tablecloth.

'Is this your work?' I asked Marinda, feeling a pang when she nodded. The pain of loss was not owned by humanity. It was early days for me, according to some of my vampire friends. But, like humans, their truths varied. Some had told me that the feelings of loss were worse early on. Others said that the pain grew. It would always be weighed against the positive, of course. Though vampires could be killed—simply, as it turned out—they did have the capacity for immortality. They were genuinely undying compared to any other living creature. Timeless. "That's a long time for the nostalgia for the human ways to fester," my colleague Marcus told me. He often seemed depressed.

Instead of—God forbid—sharing my feelings, I just smiled at Marinda.

'So, to what do we owe this visit?' Dad was sitting, arms crossed. He was always unaccepting, always judgemental.

'I haven't seen you for a while.' I stared at him and tucked my cotton t-shirt into my baggy jeans.

'Tell us what you've been up to, love,' suggested Mum. A flicker of concern washed over her but was gone just as quickly. I supposed she wanted the sanitised version, then. Who wouldn't?

'Well, I'm still working full time at the After Dark Department.'

Dad scoffed lightly. I ignored him.

'It keeps me busy and pays the rent.'

'Your sister's doing well at the uni. She's going to be a nurse. Helping people's an honourable profession. There's some good money in it now, too. Isn't there Marinda?'

'Yes, Dad, but Sar—'

'Marinda, she's working as well, you know,' Dad continued.

'Oh! Are you Marinda?' I smiled at my sister as she held back a giggle.

'At that bar on the esplanade. All the young people go there,' Dad continued. 'It's rough, but earning some money while studying is good. Hey, Mar?'

'Mm-hmm,' I said, trying not to appear sarcastic.

'I do all right there with the wages and tips,' Marinda said, flashing me that winning smile—all perfect white with just a little gum showing along the top.

'I bet you do. I'm sure you're friendly and professional with all your customers,' I teased.

Then I smiled and looked down into my lap for a moment. My hands were pale against my faded black Levi's. I twisted the ring on my finger. Will had given it to me back in the day when we were still a new couple. Fortunately, it was brass—vampires react badly to silver.

'But of course, Sarina's work is important, Dad. It's a government job and all top secret.' It always touched me how much Marinda tried to stick up for me. She was young, fun, and silly, yet she had a devoted, mature side. At her age, she shouldn't have had to pave the way for my father and me to have a relationship.

'Well, semi-secret anyway,' I corrected. Standfort and the rest of Australia knew the After Dark Department. Exactly what jobs we performed remained unmapped for the public.

'That's what concerns me,' Dad added, getting up for another beer from the fridge. His slight paunch caught a little on the table as he went.

'Don't worry, sweetheart,' Mum offered. 'It's hard for him when you can't say what you do. He imagines the worst. You know, now you're a...a.'

'A vampire? I'm not harming humans.' Okay, so that was a big, fat lie. But my *job* wasn't to harm humans, so I could kid myself I was speaking semi-truthfully. I would have loved to tell Dad that a big part of my job was catching and disposing of criminal vamps. To spit it right in his face. Instead, I said, 'He's got nothing to fear. But I'm not allowed to talk about it. I could get in trouble. Lose my job. Or worse.'

'I know, dear,' Mum said, scooping peas onto Dad's plate.

'What can you do, ay?' Dad sat back down roughly. Mum jumped up, remembering the green beans.

Fifteen minutes later, three Masseys were nearly through their roast meal. I had made two out of the three feel uncomfortable by not eating. Still, imagine if I had dragged a human in with me like a snack pack and began sucking their blood right there at the dinner table. Now, *that* would be awkward.

'So you'll eat afterwards, then?' said Dad pointedly.

'What do you want from me?' I stood up. 'This was a bad idea. You don't want me here, and frankly, as much as I miss you, I don't enjoy coming here and having you put shit on me the whole time.'

Mum acted shocked by my language, but I knew she said worse when annoyed.

'For God's sake, Dad. What do you want her to do?' Marinda cried.

'Sit down, sweetheart. We *do* want you here. We do, don't we, Tom?' Mum's eyes suggested to her husband he should be more supportive. But Dad always took my turning the hardest, and my anger about that had been building over the years.

'What is your problem, Dad? Do you think I wanted this to happen to me?'

'Some do, don't they?'

'Some. But I never went looking for this. You know that. So what's your issue?'

'You eat humans. You actually eat people.'

'Because I have to!' I screamed it at him. 'Do you want me to starve? Is that it? To show you I'm a good person, I should starve myself until I'm dead?'

Dad turned a pink shade. 'Of course, I don't want that. I'm your father.'

'So you're just being difficult to put me in my place?'

When it came down to it, he was just an angry man. He was mad that this had happened to me. Mad that it happened because I hadn't done exactly what I was told all those years ago. Then, he was angry that he couldn't turn back time or make it all better. He was furious that half of his children were no longer human.

Join the bloody club, I thought. But my dad had no one to direct his anger towards except me.

That's why I rarely visited anymore. *That's* what was killing the relationship between my parents and me.

CHAPTER
SIXTEEN

I earned little in the early nineties. I worked an automatic carwash while my best girlfriend worked at the local supermarket. Neither of us got paid much. Sharon and I had saved up for months to stay in a hotel in Cairns, see a Powderfinger concert, and go shopping the next day. I wanted to buy some CDs to upgrade the cassette tapes I'd been plugging for years. Plus, there were trendy clothing stores in Cairns that Standfort didn't have.

Inseparable since the first day of school at Standfort High, Sharon—or Shaz, as I usually called her—was my best friend, and we liked the same fashion and music. Even the same boys. It caused us to fight a few times, but we always worked it out. Ultimately, our friendship came before everything else. Then I met Will and had eyes for no man but him.

Cairns pumped that night. The air was thick with humidity, and a saltiness carried through from the ocean. It felt like everyone was out on the town for a big Friday night.

Paradoxically, Sharon and I had taken the time to achieve a perfect grunge look with our makeup. She wore a little floral mini dress teamed with a ratty leather vest and boots. I wore sandshoes with cut-offs that were short, very short. And a Ramones tee.

The night was fantastic. Powderfinger rocked, and afterwards, we went to the next bar on the main street, where we met up with friends and got sloppy drunk before returning to our room to chill out. The next day I bought *Nevermind* by Nirvana and *Everybody Else Is Doing It, So Why Can't We?* by the Cranberries. Plus, I got a new pair of Doc Martens boots and a flannel shirt that I intended to rough up before I wore it.

Sharon and I spent so much time going from store to store that day. Not wanting to waste a moment of our time in what was, for us, the big smoke, it was late afternoon by the time we left for Standfort. The road heading north out of Cairns was already streaked with shadows as the sun dipped in the west.

Dad had warned me to return home well before nightfall. 'We still don't know what these monsters are capable of,' he said. Vampires had only been known about for a few years. They wanted to live side by side with humans, they said. They wanted an everyday life, too, no longer having to hide in the shadows and move around all the time so humans didn't notice they weren't aging.

It all seemed fair enough to me. I couldn't understand why Dad insisted on thinking the worst of them. There had only been a few incidents of violence with vamps killing humans, and humans were quite capable of violence as well. So I promised I'd be home before sundown and set out to live it up. But time had gotten away from us.

Finally, on the drive home, we were listening to the radio. My new CDs were useless without a player in the car. We sang along to the top hits until there was too much interference on all the stations, and then I switched it off.

'Remember that vamp at Powderfinger?' Sharon started.

'Which one? I saw about five of them.'

'The gorgeous one,' she spat, as though I was crazy. 'John, I think he said his name was.'

'Yeah.' I saw him. *Who didn't notice him?* 'What about him?'

'Well, do you think they get more attractive when turned into vampires?'

I glanced at her. Black kohl was smeared underneath her eyes, flecks of hazel in her irises were highlighted by the setting sun, and she was picking absently at bits of skin around her nails.

'I dunno. Doubt it, Shaz. I think vampires just look how they looked when they were human. But a bit paler, you know? And colder.' I would learn later that many vampires *do* look more attractive. Vampirism offers a subtle glow or sheen to the skin. Once turned, you look healthier, if paler. Perhaps it's akin to wearing light makeup to highlight your best features. 'He seemed like a huge sleaze, though. You can do better.'

She ignored my comment. 'You know, that vampire said he was nearly three hundred years old. Can you imagine it? So weird, right? I wish more of them would move to Standfort,' said Sharon, starry-eyed.

'Your wish is my command,' I said in a funny voice, causing her to stop picking at herself and turn to look at me. 'Okay, you can't repeat this to anyone yet. Promise?'

'Yes. I promise.' I didn't see it because I was concentrating on the road, but I imagined her shaking her head lightly at me as though I'd asked her something stupid.

'Okay, well, Dad told me the government is creating some kind of vampire station in town.'

'Vampire station? Like a petrol station?'

'No,' I replied irritably. 'Like police or something. Oh, I dunno for sure. But there's gonna be more vamps in town soon.'

'As if!'

'I'm serious as a heart attack. There's gonna be a lot more of them in Standfort. That's what Dad said. I don't know what it's all about, but Dad knows through some contacts at the council. You can't tell a soul. You promised.'

I didn't realise back then that vampires had already been using Standfort—the most well-sized northern town in Queensland—as their entry point from overseas for some time. Possibly centuries.

Vampires can travel relatively long distances underwater because a long sleep enables them to stay awake for a few days, as long as they keep away from light. It's not exactly comfortable, but it's usually doable. Of course, to avoid the sun, they have to travel deep down where the sun's rays won't reach them.

Some who braved the journey would land in Cape York somewhere before travelling south to Standfort. There, they could meet up with other vamps who'd arrived before them, get the lay of the land and learn about the culture of Australia. But back then, they were hiding from humans the whole time, adjusting their accents, pretending to breathe, and using other ploys.

Other vampires arrive directly in Standfort to avoid the treachery of travel through the wild landscape of Cape York. Saltwater crocodiles are a problem when approaching the coast of northern Australia anywhere. While vampires can try to fight them off, there's no guarantee of winning. Salties aren't to be toyed with.

Still, those vamps who do make it through will often walk straight out of the surf in Standfort, where, if Donny and I were doing our jobs correctly, we'd capture them. It was impossible to police the entire coastline around the tip of Queensland, though. It's too vast. But it was part of our job to police Stand-fort's coast when we had time.

Staring ahead with the sun in her eyes, Sharon's mouth hung open for a few seconds. Lost for words. An odd occasion for her. Then suddenly, she pursed her lips happily and nodded.

We spent the next fifteen minutes discussing who from our school and post-school friendship group would make good vampires. Shaz volunteered first, and I agreed she would make a great vamper—one hundred and ten per cent. I was unsure about myself because I had an aversion to gore, but I ended up on our mental list because we didn't want to be split up, being BFFs and all.

'If I'm undead, you have to be as well,' she told me. 'We always stick together. Right?'

'You're right. I'm sure I'd get used to seeing so much blood, anyway,' I said. 'As a vaaampire. Raaar.'

We laughed as the darkness became complete, and we turned off the highway onto the road leading to Standfort. We were still twenty minutes out, so I switched the high beam on and off where I could. The route took us past sugar cane and other crops. Then, just past a well-known crossroads, we passed a car with its hood up. The driver was a woman who looked just a few years older than us. She was leaning against the bonnet with her thumb out.

'Damn,' I said.

'Don't,' Shaz said suddenly, knowing I was toying with stopping for her. It wasn't like Sharon to be more careful than me. She was right, though. I knew we *shouldn't* stop. Yet I felt that pull we all felt, wanting to help someone in need. Especially when it was a young woman like us.

'It's just one girl,' I said, screwing up my face.

'It doesn't feel right,' Sharon said.

I imagined the woman being stranded until a car full of hoons or a serial killer stopped for her. I couldn't leave her like that.

'Fine,' said Sharon, giving up.

I slowed my Corolla, took a U-turn, and pulled up a couple of car lengths in front of her green Mazda, which was even tinier than mine. 'It'll be fine, Shaz,' I said, my heart beating a teensy bit faster than average. 'As if a vamp would drive a stupid little car like that.'

'What if some guy is waiting in the trees or something?'

'Stay here.'

Sharon huffed as I exited and walked back towards the Mazda parked behind us. Glancing at the trees in the grove beside us, I saw nothing but leafy darkness. As the woman approached me, her blonde hair and full voile skirt fluttered loosely in the night air. The road was empty, and the only light came from the moon since my headlights shone ahead in the opposite direction.

There was a rush of air as the woman moved more quickly than I had expected. I screamed as she embraced me with icy arms and a hint of Samsara perfume. I used my hands to push against her face, but her mouth opened, and her canines suddenly dropped into place. They were sharp and glistening as she laughed.

'Run!' I screamed at Sharon as the blonde bit into my neck roughly. I struggled as she began sucking the wound, but I couldn't budge from her grip. Her strength was superhuman, or—as I realised—vampire.

The blonde removed her teeth and tipped her head like a dog to listen. I listened too and soon realised Sharon *had* run for it. I could hear her occasional shrieks and the crunch of leaves under her feet as she tore through the avocado grove next to the road.

Dragging me like a rag doll towards the trees, she dropped me on the edge. The vampire then bolted after Sharon while I held my neck, trying to stem the bleeding. So much blood, I remember thinking, my stomach so nauseous I could barely do a thing.

But I managed to call out again. With such a large wound in my neck, though, the sound was feeble. Meanwhile, in the distance, the trees sounded like they were exploding in the dark as the vampire moved through them, heading for my best friend forever.

'Go!' was my last feeble cry to my deepest, most loved friend.

A guttural scream rang out from the grove, followed by several seconds of silence. I lay on my back, looking at the cloudy sky beyond the avocado canopy. Serenity juxtaposed against the growling and moaning sound that started up. I tried to raise myself but found I couldn't. My best friend was being attacked, and I couldn't even get up to help her.

I wasn't sure how long I lay there. It seemed like forever, as those definitive times often do. But it may only have been a few minutes before a shadow crossed me. There, the blonde woman stood. Smiling. Her face was bloody yet waxen. Some leaves hung from the hair which she flicked over her shoulder as she stared at me.

'Is Shaz ... okay?' I asked, my voice still weak.

The vampire laughed deeply, flashing her teeth again—a frightening vision.

'I'm Marlene. You're so lucky, little one,' she said, crouching next to me so quickly that I hardly saw her move. She stroked my hair and whispered, 'So very, very lucky.'

SEVENTEEN

My father and I sat on the patio while Marinda and Mum cleared away and washed the dishes. The air-conditioning unit hummed nearby. Dad rested a stubby of XXXX, a classic Queensland beer, in a holder on his knee. He held a fag in the other hand.

'I don't want to be hard on you, Sarina.'

'Then stop,' I said, staring ahead, out into the darkness—which wasn't that dark for me, with my vampire eyesight.

'You've got to understand—'

I cut him off. 'I understand, Dad. But I'm sick of it.' I waved my hand about indiscriminately to highlight the ridiculousness of the situation and of being continually reminded of how I went wrong when it wasn't even my fault. But deep down, I knew why Dad wrestled with it. I had been out after dark against his advice. I was young. I'd made a mistake that I could never fix.

'I don't like that task force you're on.'

I remained quiet for a few seconds.

Finally, I said, 'What do you even know about it?'

'I know your boss.'

'You know Mike?' To say I was shocked would be an understatement. I was surprised he even knew Mike was my boss.

'He's in the Standfordt Business Association. So am I.'

'Ohh.' My mind was running a million miles an hour. The association was a big deal for many professionals in Standfordt. It provided peer-to-peer support but was also a social outlet. It was the only thing Dad did outside of his work running a successful electrician's business. He'd begun a trade at fifteen with one of his father's mates, and then he'd gone out on his own in his twenties. The company had grown until he needed half a dozen staff.

'What does Mike want with the SBA? I mean, he's in management. Isn't it more of an organisation for non-government workers?'

'I dunno.' He took a long swig from his beer. 'I don't like him, though.'

I looked over at my dad. He'd aged since I took my last hard look at him. How very human of him. I felt a pang to see his greying hair and a stronger paunch than he'd had. Humans were so fragile. So finite, so mortal. I looked away quickly, back out into the dark.

'Look, Dad, Mike's a bit of a dickhead, but he's alright.'

'Not from where I sit.' Dad pushed his hair back away from the sweat of his brow.

'Because he's a—'

'No,' dad boomed. 'No, not because he's a vampire, Sarina. I'm not an idiot. I know a dodgy man when I see one.'

I inhaled deeply. 'Mike can be a whinger. I'll give you that.'

'He took some members to a brothel,' Dad said suddenly. 'What kind of man does that, Sarina?'

I was reminded of my dad's good side—he'd always shown a robust moral compass even though he could be overly critical as a father. To hear that about Mike was a shock.

'It's a grubby den of sin,' he added. 'Don't you mention this to anyone, though? Promise me.' He looked at me seriously.

'I won't. Believe me! Wait. What place was it?'

'Red Link, or something.' My head started nodding unconsciously, which my dad noticed. 'About half a dozen blokes agreed to go with him. They were all old enough to know better. "My shout," is what Mike said.' Dad took a deep drag on his cigarette, his lips puckering into lines around his lips.

'Tell me more about what you know. Did the guys say anything about the place to you afterwards?'

'Why are you so interested? Does it have to do with your work? Someone certainly needs to be shutting these places down. I'd be happy to hear that was your job, Sarina.'

'Dad.' I paused, thinking about how much I should say. 'If you knew what I did for a living, you'd probably be shocked. But you wouldn't necessarily be upset. Can we leave it at that?'

'Well, I don't have a choice, do I? Once you became a vampire, I lost control over what you do and where you go.'

'To be fair, a parent is supposed to relinquish control over their children in the lead-up to adulthood. Perhaps you missed that in parenting class.'

As soon as I voiced it, I wished I hadn't. Not that I didn't mean what I said. It's just that I had felt Dad and I were on the cusp of a genuine conversation. Something that we hadn't done in years and which I'd considered might never happen again. Not to mention, I was interested in the intel on Mike.

'Still a smart arse, I hear.'

'Yeah,' I answered listlessly, kicking myself metaphorically.

'Like you'd know, anyway. You're not a parent, and you won't be able to be one now, will you?'

It hurt, but we sat silently for a few minutes, watching a

colony of flying foxes that flew overhead. Their black bodies and architecturally designed wings were just perceptible against the night sky.

Dad broke the silence eventually. 'So you can't go out at all during daylight, ay? You miss it?'

'At times, I do miss it. We get sick and can die if left out in sunlight.'

'Not exactly immortal then, are you?'

Ouch. 'I think we don't see much of each other anymore because you're so bitter, Dad,' I said.

'I'm a normal man, Sarina. A human. I don't know what you want from me.'

'You're still my father. At least you were. *That's* what I want from you.'

'That ship flew already. Like the fruit bats up there,' he said.

Strange deflection, but I ignored it and told him, 'That's been your choice.' I could have argued more, but I had something else on my mind. 'Dad, what else can you tell me about Mike?'

'Well, I don't like the cut of his jib. There's something off about him, and it's more than he's a dead man who could kill us all. It's his character. He's always trying to have things his way. To control everyone and everything. Threats...'

I frowned. 'Mike's always complaining at work. Like the world's stacked against him, you know?' I said.

'Doesn't sound like the same bloke.'

I scrunched my face as I sat in the dark, thinking about Mike, his strange ways, and why my dad might see him so differently than the way I did. Finally, I asked, 'Did he only take your members there once?'

'Maybe a couple of times. S'pose, he was trying to be a big man. Like being able to pay a prostitute is impressive.'

We both rolled our eyes. Finally, something we could agree on. It *did* sound ridiculous when he put it like that.

'I think the place is called The Red Line,' I said eventually.

'That sounds right. So you know it?' He squinted suspiciously at me, and I saw him relax visibly when I told him I knew it because of an ongoing case that my department was investigating. I immediately regretted offering that information, though. It was loose-lipped and dangerous of me.

'That has to be just between you and me, okay?'

'Of course.'

'I'm serious, Dad. Really. You must *never* mention it.'

'I know how to keep my mouth shut, miss. Don't you mention it to your mother, either? Even though I didn't go with them, she wouldn't be happy to hear that any Business Association members had been to a place like that.'

I nodded. 'Can you tell me more about what Mike has said about The Red Line? Or anything he's said that seemed odd.'

'I think you're the one that needs to leave it be, Sarina. Just stay away from him and be careful. That's the only reason I said anything to you.'

I didn't ask again. I knew my father well and could see it wasn't worth it. But a few seconds later, he added, 'Said it was a "nice" place, though.'

Dad looked at me funny, and we both grinned and shook our heads. *Nice indeed.*

'And he reckons he knows the manager. But he was probably talking rot. You know, big-noting himself.'

My mind shot to Donny. It was the combination of talk of big-noting and sex, I guessed. But Donny told me he'd never been to a brothel outside of work, let alone The Red Line.

'The woman who runs it?' I asked.

'What woman? You reckon a woman could run a place like that...'

'Dunno,' I lied through my teeth. Wouldn't Dad be surprised?

'Did he say *how* he knew the owner?' I continued.

'Not that I remember. Anyway, Mike seems like a bona fide artist of bullshittery, but one who could do some damage so—'

'So be careful and don't get involved with him,' I finished my father's sentence. 'Got it.'

He waved my cheek away, and I smirked. I'd missed how funny my dad could be since he'd hardly spoken to me in four years.

The scrape of the sliding door announced Mum offering coffee inside.

'I'm sure you'll enjoy that,' Dad said under his breath as we got up and walked inside.

CHAPTER

EIGHTEEN

After visiting my parents, I went to the all-night store for groceries. I bought laundry powder for myself, an apple for Missy, and a handsome-looking mango for Will. I remembered mangoes' taste—the creaminess of some and the stringiness of others. This one was ripe and perfect, and surprisingly, I appreciated its smell as it permeated the car despite being wrapped up in a plastic bag. Most human foods had become repulsive to me over the years. But mangos still smelled as good as the memory of their taste.

I knocked gingerly on Will's door. I'd walked out a week ago, and apart from a brief telephone conversation, we hadn't spoken since then. My heart was always in pieces for him, and I felt like a child on the floor trying to put those pieces back together. It differed significantly from my usual demeanour.

It took a minute before I heard Will shuffle over to crack the door.

'Let me speak,' I said, shoving the mango through the gap towards him.

He opened the door and ushered me through without a chuckle or a smile. He took that mango, though.

Will worked as an administrator for the Standfort Hospital. Once I was turned, he'd put his hand up for all the night shifts he could so that he was living on a similar schedule to me. Everything about Will screamed, 'I still support you. I still love you.' But instead of letting that buoy me, I hated myself for every bit of it.

In the lounge, I sat nervously, aware of the blood pulsing through my vessels. My body was cold and rigid. I wasn't used to talking about my feelings, not my real ones. I was better at the practical things in life: detective work, catching bad guys, revenge, and killing.

I swallowed loudly. Will, who looked tired and drawn, sighed and got up to put the kettle on.

Sometimes, it's easier to talk about the hard stuff while in action, doing something unrelated, like a teenager opening up to parents on a long drive. Concentrating on the road or bouncing a ball around makes the words flow easier. As a teen, I told Mum or Dad things on a long drive that I would never have said if they'd just knocked on my bedroom door and asked. In that case, I would have whined, said I had home-work, and put it off until later.

Except Will wasn't going to do the talking. I was. I was done putting him off. I was going all in this time. I was going to concentrate on him, just him.

'Will.'

He barely glanced at me before turning back to the kettle. It seemed to be about to boil, even though Will had been staring at it to avoid me.

'I ... I want to say that... Well, I just. I was wrong, Will.'

He turned to look at me just as the kettle started wailing. Removing it from the hotplate, he asked, 'Meaning?'

He was pissed at me. I could tell, and rightly so. He'd been offering me love in a genuine relationship for years. Me? I'd been fobbing him off and, in a sense, you could argue, using him for just as long.

'Will, you've been nothing but good to me since it happened. I know that, and I haven't responded to you as I should have. Certainly not in the way that you deserve. I won't go through all the excuses—'

'I've heard them all anyway.' He shrugged. Then, a wry smile crossed his face, and he poured hot water into a mug. The smell of coffee spread through the surrounding air. Gross.

'It's not like all of them were excuses,' Will said. 'I get what happened to you. Being made a vampire like that changed your entire life. You didn't ask for it, and I realise it was traumatic and confusing.'

'Yes, but that's not what I'm here for. I'm here for us. I was an idiot, Will. I should have taken you and loved you with everything I had years ago.'

He turned to face me, unsure of what I was really saying, but with hope in his eyes.

'I want us to make a life together. If you'll still have me.'

'If I'll still have you?' He chuckled. I wasn't sure if he was about to rebuke me or if his laughter was good news.

I stood still at the kitchen door, waiting for him to say something else.

'It's all I've ever wanted. You know that. But what are you saying?'

'I want to turn you. I want it, Will. I'm ready to apply for the paperwork. Am I too late?'

'God, no.' He was laughing now, though his eyes looked a little watery. I rushed at him and hugged him tightly until he made a squeaking sound to let me know it was too much. I'd held him *too* tight a few times. A vampire could *literally* love a delicate, precious human to death in a variety of ways.

Will hugged and kissed me back then. It was always like coming home in those moments. Before we knew it, we were in the bedroom, and he was undressing me, removing my T-shirt, and stripping me of my Levi's.

We'd have been fine together if only life could be built on passion alone. When he stood before me naked, I wished our lives could always be that simple. They couldn't, of course. But as he nuzzled me onto the bed, I succumbed to the moment.

It was different from being with a vampire. Will's humanity was never as stark and gratifying as when we had slept together. Then I could smell and taste him. I could feel his blood pumping through his body as he lay against me. So it was different but still physical, still carnal.

Almost an hour later, and not an hour before dawn, we lay together on his double bed. The windows were open, catching the breeze. It was cooling for Will, but I enjoyed the fresh air, too.

'After everything that's happened and everything you've learned about this life, Will...'

His head turned until he stared at me from barely a foot away.

I pursued it still. 'Do you still want turning?'

'You know the answer,' he said, lifting his head to stare at the ceiling. 'I love being with you, Sar. Why would I want to grow old, die, and be parted? But you've always made it about what you wanted. Or what you thought I wanted.'

I feared he might not love me as much as he protested. The lure of becoming immortal might have driven his regular suggestions that I could turn him to make it easier for us to be together. Believe me. That happened regularly. While some humans were squeamish—or moral—due to religion or other personal beliefs, others saw vampires coming out publicly as an opportunity. The idea of being made a vampire offered the prize of immortality. Humans have lusted for that for time immemorial.

But I'd known Will since I was a teenager. I hoped he couldn't pull the wool over my eyes that easily.

'So we'll do it, then. It's decided,' I said quickly, jumping to my knees next to him.

He sat up against the bedhead. 'So you mean it this time? You're going to make me vampire? For real?'

'Yes. It's time. One life. Let's walk through it together.'

'A pretty long one, once you're a vampire.'

'Yes, it is.' I smiled. 'You're ready for this? What about your parents?'

Will's parents had known about me since it happened, back in the early days of our relationship. At first, they'd been very concerned for him. Of course. What parent wouldn't be? But in time, they'd accepted me. Still, what they thought of me turning their son would have to be different.

'I can deal with them. I don't think it'll be much of an issue. Mum's pretty pro-vamp already, and Dad, well, he'll come around.'

With a lighter tone, I warned, 'You better eat up while you can. All your favourites. Burritos, stir-fry, steak. Are you ready to miss out on those for eternity?'

'To be with you, to *really* be with you, I'm ready for anything.'

'You're a romantic bugger, aren't you?'

'As charged,' he said, folding his arms behind his head with a smug look.

My eyes rolled, and I flopped down on the bed beside him. For a minute, we just lay there, thinking. Finally, I said, 'I've got a strange case at the moment. I think it's going to be something big.'

'You want to talk about it?'

'Actually, I'd better not. I don't want to drag you into it all. I shouldn't have mentioned it. Sorry. But I'll get your turning paperwork going as soon as possible.'

The corners of Will's mouth raised. It caused the cutest dimples on both cheeks, and I wanted to kiss them forever. And soon, I would be able to.

But right then, I needed to get home before dawn. I had been ruminating over Mike, which was not something you want to have on your mind before bed. I planned to follow up on that the next evening.

CHAPTER
NINETEEN

I tossed and turned in my bed as my body clock sensed sundown approached. A lot wasn't sitting right with me. The Mike that my dad described didn't sound anything like my boss. Taking Standfordt Business Association members to brothels? Not the stand-up, if brutally annoying, bloke I knew.

The fact that he was a Business Association member at all was odd. I know many vamps wanted to fit in with humans and be a part of the community, but really? It sounded way too dull for a vampire—even Mike.

My stomach rumbled, and I turned over angrily. I should have stopped by a booth on the way home. As nostalgic as the smell of Mum's roast was, it was useless for a creature of the night. But I'd had other things on my mind, hadn't I? The thought of Will eased the corners of my mouth upwards and settled my stomach. Confident I'd done the right thing, I was ready to commit and felt … happy.

As soon as I felt twilight approach, I flew out of bed. I wanted to catch Mike before the arrival of our co-workers and, definitely, before Donny arrived and stuck his nose into my business.

At After Dark, I found Mike arguing again with his filing cabinet. It made a repetitive flapping sound as he tried to force the drawer open.

'Bloody hell, Sarina. When are they going to fix this cabinet?' He looked haggard and drawn, which was partly just him. Mike had been in his forties when he was turned. It was back when the forties weren't the new twenties. His hair was grey and had receded in a pattern from the two corners of his forehead, leaving a tuft of hair in the middle that he made the best of. Of course, once turned, the balding had ceased. Vampire physiology was a trip.

'Dunno. When did you put in the request?'

'I didn't bother with the form, but I told maintenance several times.'

My frustration was palpable. Mike had answered his question since not a goddamn thing got done in the After Dark Department without the correct paperwork. He was the boss, so he would—or should—know that. I hoped he wasn't holding his breath—metaphorically—for the fix-it department to arrive.

I walked around his side of the desk and bobbed down to help him. 'So, Mike. This investigation on the Mayor's son.'

'Yes. I'm moving you to a new case tonight.'

'What?' I practically spat.

'There's been a murder in an apartment in town. It's already a week old, so I'm moving you and Don onto it. The plus side is it took so long to find the body because the air-con helped to keep it fresh.'

'But surely the Mayor's missing son is a vital case to solve?' I said. Then it dawned on me. 'This new case. Where was the body found?'

'Here.' Mike shoved a file my way. On opening it, I had to hold my expression steady. Never had it happened before. The fresh case was one of *my* murders. It was "Wine and Cheese". How the hell did that happen?

I'd never taken the time to consider how it would feel if one of my crimes was placed in front of me like that. I felt like stamping my feet and screaming that I didn't *want* the case.

'Steve'll get solved. Don't worry. I'll put someone else on it.'

Placing the new file on the desk, I went back to fiddling with the drawer to see if it could be easily removed from the frame. It couldn't. I started reaching into the drawer and trying to force my hand over its back edge to feel around behind its cavity.

Beyond my concerns about my crime having reached the notice of the After Dark Department, I remained perplexed at the Steve Gorman case being handed over to someone else in the department so soon after the investigation had begun. It all seemed very odd. Besides, who of our colleagues would do as good a job as Donny and I?

'So you're straight into this new case as of tonight.' Mike gave a nod.

'What's it got to do with us, though?' I asked, fishing.

'Looks like a vampire killed him and tried to make it look like an accident.'

'What?' I asked, looking up at him. I couldn't have felt more alarmed at that moment, and I hoped Mike hadn't noticed.

'You'll read it in the notes. On first blush, it looks like he slipped with a knife and cut his femoral. But someone reckons they saw a vamp go over the side of his balcony that night, so homicide scratched deeper, and now it's with us.'

'Mm,' I mumbled, like an absolute fool, my mouth drying

up like a dam in the dry season. I didn't stop there, either. 'Uh-huh, uh-huh. Yep. Okay.'

What in God's name have you gone and done, Sarina?

As though God was going to help!

I desperately tried to act casual as the total weight of what Mike told me settled on my shoulders.

Someone saw me. They saw me leave his place. Shit. SHIT.

Naturally, I'd always worried that this could happen. To prevent it, I took as few chances as possible. But you never knew what and how things could go awry. And that night, my worst nightmare was coming true. I saw the whole thing unravelling in my mind's eye for a moment, complete with my arrest.

I looked down to hide my horror as I stretched my arm into the cabinet again. Perhaps something had fallen over the back of the drawer. Inwardly, I continued to spiral.

'Great,' I said finally, my voice wavering before I got control. 'Well, Don and I'll get it sorted out.'

'Yep. I know you will. That Steve, he's a young kid, anyway. I'm sure he's got big dreams, and he's probably run off somewhere to live it up. What young 'un would stay here?'

'Erm, me? I see your point, though. But I'm sure the Mayor will still want answers.'

'She'll get her answers,' he said. I looked up at him briefly. He was standing well above me, looking distracted.

'I'd certainly take off if I were young and human like him. You know what kids are like, Sarina.'

I wasn't sure I did in that case. I wasn't so sure about anything Mike was saying.

'But at any rate, the murder is the more pressing issue,' Mike hesitated for a half second. 'It won't be long before the bloody media gets their teeth into this story. You know how they are when they hear a "murderous vampire" story. We'll never hear the end of it. So, that's where we're at.'

Raquel Gorman and Mike could be friends or acquaintances, at the least. Standfort wasn't a huge city, after all, and they both held positions of power, so presumably, their paths would cross. Mike would no doubt have some knowledge of what Mayor Gorman wanted and needed concerning her missing son.

My fingertips touched something, but my arm wasn't long enough to grip what lay behind the drawer.

'Who're the oldest vampires in Standfort?' I found myself asking suddenly.

'Well, there are a few,' Mike said.

'Yeah, but only a few, correct? There's that woman who lives out in the Daintree. She's a few hundred years old. At least. Then there's Rickie over North. He keeps to himself as well.'

'A lot of the oldies do, except for John Martin. He's got a few hundred on him, but he's pretty friendly.'

Too friendly if you're a woman, I thought. But I'd raised the question of age for another reason.

I thought back to the night before Sharon was murdered, when we'd been young and carefree in Cairns. When we'd seen a vampire about the same age as John—and with the same name. Had John Martin been lurking in the shadows longer than I knew?

Mike continued, 'Guess we all got used to the quiet life and the skulking. Not like those of you who were born living freely in the open. Amongst the blood bags.'

Blunt words from a man with a human wife. I felt a little offended by his attitude.

Continuing, he said, 'I guess I'm in between. I feel comfortable enough either way. Most of my life was spent in the shadows, of course. But this is good, too. It's different, I'll give it that.'

'But do you see my point? Even if you *are* young at a hundred years. Most of the vamps here in Standfort are young. Why is that?'

'Why am I young?'

Is he being purposefully dense?

'No. Why is Standfort's vamp population overwhelmingly young?'

'Have you looked around? It's not like we're living in a town to rival Paris or New York.' Mike was looking at me with a dumb expression.

'So you reckon we don't have as much to offer here?' I had to admit that it seemed clear.

'Think about it. All those with hundreds of years on them have seen many historical events occur. Cultures have come and gone, and so much change and development has occurred. I think that's why they probably don't all want to come and settle here in Standfort. It's also why I reckon that young man's just run off for an adventure.'

That made sense. Maybe Mike was right, but that meant that Standfort had little to offer, whether you were young or old. I briefly felt a flush over my face as I remembered my new case. I was working on my own bloody murder. What a night it was turning out to be.

Then, I managed to grip the thin card behind the drawer between my thumb and forefinger. It made a flapping sound, like a bird with a broken wing, as I brought it from the back, through the drawer, and pulled it out to give to Mike.

It was a folder without more than a few pieces of paper resting inside it. The name caught my eye, though. Written in a black pen on the file's label was TRL.

Mike was like greased lightning, snatching the file from my

hands. 'Thank you. You're a lifesaver,' he said as he placed the file on his desk and briskly placed an A4-sized diary on top. Then he opened and closed his filing cabinet drawer a few times. 'Good job. Well, I know who to call next time, eh?'

'What was the file?' I said.

'Oh, it's old, I think. Probably from before I was promoted. I'll make sure it gets filed properly in case it's still relevant to anyone.'

I smiled.

He was lying. I knew it, and he knew that I knew it. But did he sense I had any connection with the Wine and Cheese murder?

CHAPTER
TWENTY

I met Donny in the parking lot before he entered the After Dark office. Holding the Wine and Cheese case file in my hand like a grenade with the pin pulled, I told him, 'We need to talk.'

''Kay.' He leaned his solid frame against his driver's door with a thud.

'First, please tell me Steve and Lindsay were fine last night.'

'They were.'

'Good. This case... We're off it. There's been a murder linked to a vamp, and we've been put on that instead.' I paused to wonder how blunt I should be. It gave Donny time to be shocked, as I had been when Mike told me. 'Look. I will ask you something, and I need you to be honest. It's about Mike.' I grimaced and lowered my voice a little, worried it might carry further through the concrete lot than I expected.

'You know me. I'm an open book,' Donny said, opening his hands to prove his point.

An open zipper is more like it.

Bitchiness aside, though, Donny wasn't wrong. I'd always been able to rely on him.

'Mike,' I said. 'What do you know about his connection with The Red Line?'

'You serious? What connection.'

'Does it strike you as odd that he's moving us from one case to another?'

'Well, yes. But what does that have to do with The Red Line?'

'I've got a gut feeling. Something isn't right. Mike wants me to believe that Steve just ran off. It's like he's not taking it seriously.'

'Well...' Donny tipped his head wistfully.

Donny would love it if Steve ran off, I bet. Leaving Lindsay free...

I moved in closer. 'Donny, I think Mike might not be all he seems. There's something suss.'

'That bloke's straighter than they come,' Don retorted quickly, but he didn't make eye contact with me. Like a punch to the chest, I realised Donny wasn't quite the open book I'd considered him to be. How many more bombshells could I expect off the back of this case?

'As it turns out, I don't think he is, and I think you know he's into something, Donny Agosti. First, my dad told me Mike's a member of the Standfort Business Association.'

Donny's face had a sceptical look. 'I knew he was boring, but jeez!'

'I know, I know, but ignore that for now. That's not the point. So, Dad's pissed at Mike because he took a few of the guys to a brothel after a meeting a couple of times. Guess which brothel?'

'The Red Line,' Donny said, looking at the ground again.

'Correct. Second, why is Mike transferring us off this case? I'm a good judge of people, and he acted dodgy.'

'No. Nah.'

'Yeah. Three, I fixed that bloody filing cabinet drawer in Mike's room.'

'Good job?' Donny said, confused.

I sighed. 'There was a file stuck over the back, and I got it out for him. It was labelled T R L.'

Donny just squinted back at me and shrugged his shoulders.

'T. R. L.? The Red Line.'

Donny looked at me like it was a stretch.

'Oh, stuff you,' I said, leaning against the car beside his. 'I'm telling you I'm onto something here. I trust your instincts and expect you to consider mine at least.'

'TRL could stand for any number of things, though.'

'Could. But it's a bit of a coincidence. Don't you bloody well tell Mike anything about Steve and Lindsay? Please don't give him any heads-up. Not until we know more. I'll look into this, and the least you can do is not dump me in it with Mike in the meantime.'

'Uh-uh. No. You've got to give this up,' Donny said rashly, sounding nasty, before faltering.

Our partnership had always been just that—a partnership. Equal. So what was going on?

'You're such an arsehole. You know I can't leave it be. It's my job. If Mike's up to something, that's his problem, not mine, and surely not yours.' I stalked towards the stairwell door, the smell of concrete around me and my skin crawling with aggravation.

'I know you well enough,' he called after me. 'I know you'll follow this to its conclusion. But...' Then instantly, he was in front of me. 'I *need* you to give it up.'

That caught my attention. Donny's brow was furrowed. 'What is it?' I said.

Donny turned back towards the car and kicked the front passenger tyre. He looked like he was sweating, but I had to have imagined that because vampires don't sweat no matter how hot they get under the collar.

I moved in beside him.

'You don't know, Sarina.' His voice was quiet, then, and serious in tone.

'Oh, I know a lot, trust me. What do you know?' I squinted at him.

'You don't know the full story and what you're getting into here. It's best left alone.'

'I know that the young girl from The Red Line has been murdered too. Just like Ruby.'

'What?'

'Yeah. Her name was Sherri.'

'Along with half the whores in Australia.'

'Why, Donny? You don't have to use words like that.'

He ignored my chastisement and voiced his thoughts. 'That's two women. Two lives are gone.'

'Yep. I found her in the cane and called it in, but no one seems to be looking into it. There hasn't been one mention of it in the office or the media. It's like it's being purposefully brushed under the rug, and now, on top of that, Mike's switching us off the case. Come on! Ruby and Sherri deserve someone looking into this properly, Donny.'

'What the hell were you doing "out in the cane"?' he said harshly, then closed his eyes tight as if he needed a moment to think.

'You know more, and you've been hiding it from me. Here, I thought I had found information that meant something, but it turns out you've been on the inside this whole time. Well?' I grabbed my hips roughly and gave him a dry look. It seemed we'd *each* been lying to each other, but I wasn't ready to admit that.

Donny flicked his head towards the passenger door.

As soon as the car turned onto the street, he said, 'I had no idea about Sherri.'

'I could tell that. But what do you know that you've been keeping from me? And why?'

His face wore that look of someone reeling with genuine guilt. 'You don't know the half of it with Mike. He's not what he seems. A couple of years ago, I caught him in a lie. It wasn't even that important. He'd been skimming, you know?'

'Cash?'

'No, but the same process. He used his position to get something from the people in Standfort. You shouldn't know about it—'

'Oh, come on, man. Aren't we past that?'

'I'm thinking of you. You're a pain, but I like ya. What can I say?'

I felt both annoyed and cared for.

Oh, Donny.

'I'm right about The Red Line, aren't I?'

'Dunno. I know nothing about Mike and that place. But I know he's shady as shit, and we both need to be careful of him and anyone on his side.'

'Do you think he killed Ruby and Sherri?'

'No idea.'

'How did I miss this about Mike until now? I'm a detective, for heaven's sake.' It was disconcerting, to put it mildly.

'Sarina Massey, you are one of the best detectives in the department. After me, of course,' he said with a wink. 'But I learned about Mike by accident, and it was safer for you to be in the dark while you didn't suspect anything. I mean, what were we going to do about it? Mike'd be pissed off if he found out we were looking into him. I don't want to lose my job, but...'

'But?'

'Nothing. If you keep on this, losing your job at After Dark could be the least of your worries.'

'What?' I spat. 'What are you suggesting? Are you threatening me?'

'No! Of course, I'm not. But it's bad, Sarina.' We were stopped at a red light. 'I'm begging you to let this one go. I honestly don't know what he's capable of.'

'Skimming my white arse. It sounds like you dug up a lot more than that.'

Donny ignored me, and we quietly drove for a while as I considered the new developments. I had thought Mike was trying to play the big guy with his involvement in the brothel and taking the business association members out there. But the way Donny was talking, Mike's criminality went deeper.

I could have ignored what I'd learned, thought purely of myself and my career, and not questioned Mike's motives. But it wasn't my style.

'Well, our job is to find Steve,' I said.

'It was. I know.'

'So we'll keep investigating on the side—quietly. But I can't ignore what I've discovered. Someone has to do what's right for Ruby Treemer and Sherri.'

Donny was nodding in agreement, at least.

I voiced more questions aloud. 'What skin could Mike possibly have in this game?'

'Dunno.'

Ignoring him, I continued, 'We have to dig deeper. We can't walk away. It doesn't feel to me like that'll keep Steve safe. Maybe he will skip town, and everything will be A-OK for him.

But you know as well as I do this situation is a powder keg. We can't control it unless we do our jobs, which means scratching beneath the surface.'

'If we do our jobs, it might still turn out badly. For us.'

'But it might not.'

Donny screeched to the side of the road and put the car in neutral. He gave the headrest a couple of backward thumps with his head. 'Fine,' he said. 'But we have got to be the most stealthy detectives After Dark ever had.'

'Agreed.'

CHAPTER
TWENTY-ONE

Being inside Wine and Cheese's apartment that night felt incongruous. I'd never had one of my bodies found wanting. That is to say...found. Or found suspicious. My extracurricular activities weren't supposed to bleed into my night job.

My victims, if you could call them that, always disappeared off the face of the earth, or my crime scene set-up was so good that it was never suspected to be a murder, at least not by a vampire. As such, I was unbelievably disappointed in myself and tried hard to brush it off. I never realised the extent of personal pride I'd taken in not getting caught.

The smell of death inside the apartment was overwhelming despite the air-conditioning slowing decomposition. It bothered me much less than it would a human, but I still noticed. My nose wrinkled a little—and I took a fingertip of menthol balm at the door, applying it underneath my nostrils. Just because a vampire has a stronger stomach for death smells does not mean we *like* them. Fresh is always best.

There he was on the couch, exactly where I'd left him. A moulding chunk of cheese on the coffee table added a musty, sharp layer to the room's smell. I found myself wanting to look anywhere but at his body, but I took a quick peek anyway. His skin was mottled in a deep purple, and parts of him looked bloated, as though he might burst open. I hadn't completely drained him, of course. That would be too obvious. A long sigh escaped my throat.

'You 'right, Sarina?' called out a forensic technician.

'Yeah,' I said. 'Another day, another body.'

Excellent work, I encouraged myself. *Keep it up.*

I didn't feel bad about Wine and Cheese's situation. He'd practically begged for it with his criminal behaviour. But I wasn't used to being around my handiwork after the fact, especially while surrounded by colleagues and forensic staff who, though they didn't yet know it, were all there to try to catch *me*!

I took a deep breath and tried to push aside all my concerns. A moment later, I was in the fray, looking at the evidence before me and doing my utmost to throw my coworkers some juicy red herrings.

Then it happened.

'Sar, we should go and question the neighbours,' said Donny.

Please, no. No. Did my eyes widen enough to show the whites?

My blood was pumping. Donny's suggestion would include the neighbour who'd seen someone going over the balcony after the murder. And that *someone* was me.

'Right,' I replied, my voice weak.

Naturally, we knocked on *that* neighbour's door first. Why wouldn't we? That's precisely what I would do if I wanted to solve a case. As I waited for the human to open the heavy front door, I ruffled my hair, tugged on my shirt, and generally fidgeted in ways that ultimately would make no difference to whether this woman would recognise me.

Staleness wafted into the hall towards us as the door opened. A smoker. Behind her, I could see an ashtray on the arm of the lounge. It looked like a year's worth of cigarette butts had crawled in there to die.

'We'd like to ask you a few questions,' Donny said, flicking his head towards Wine and Cheese's apartment. It's not like the thirty-something woman standing before us wouldn't know why we were there. The unit next door was lit like a Christmas tree, with officials coming and going constantly.

Donny checked the little notebook he kept in his left pocket. 'Jennifer Gordon, yes?'

'Yep.' She ushered us in. 'You wanna sit?'

'That's okay, thanks. I know you've already explained to one of the other detectives what you saw on the night of the twenty-fourth. But could you repeat it for us, please?'

'You mind?' she asked, holding up an unlit Alpine cigarette.

'Not a problem,' Donny replied. I didn't want to draw attention to myself, so I continued to let Donny take the lead.

Jennifer flopped into the chair, and a moment later, there was a flicking sound as she sparked her lighter, lit the cigarette, and took a long drag. 'Shitty habit, but...' She shrugged at us.

'I know. It's a hard one to break. I get it. So, tell us about that night. Where were you? What did you see and hear?' said Donny.

Jennifer looked up and glanced back and forth between us for a moment. My heart skipped a beat, but finally, she began. 'I didn't hear anything earlier on. It was only when the woman left I heard her. Because I was out on the balcony.'

I took a deep breath and exhaled carefully to avoid drawing attention to it.

'Do you normally sit out there?'

'If it's hot, yeah. It was boiling that night. Bloody hell, I was sweating like a pig. The air con just wasn't cutting it that night. Stupid thing. It's never cold enough. I feel the heat more because of my weight. I've tried to get it down, but it's not easy.' She looked at me.

Say something. If you stay silent, that's going to look suss, too.

At that point, I almost regretted the hobby that had given my personal life meaning and focus since I'd been turned into a vampire. Not once previously had I experienced regret. But I felt it in that stale living room with its wonky air conditioner. The regret wasn't genuine, of course. I just didn't want things to end like that ... with me in prison. I enjoyed my life. I wasn't ready to give it up.

Finally, I woke from my fearful stupor. 'It is hard,' I said. 'The only thing that used to keep my weight down was being a workaholic.' I didn't expand.

She nodded wistfully.

I'd reached her.

Donny was all business. 'So, you're out on the balcony? Can you show us?'

Jennifer nodded and struggled out of the chair. I thought of offering a hand, but sometimes apparent pleasantries aren't pleasant. You could never be sure how someone would take offers like that, and besides, I was trying to stay incognito. Instead, I turned towards the sliding doors so she wouldn't feel like I was watching her. Also, I didn't want her watching me.

The balcony looked like Wine and Cheese's—a plain cement rectangle. Even the barrier was cement. Jennifer had placed a fold-up chair out there. A large paint tin sat beside it that I had to assume was at least partially full of cigarette butts based on her habits and the odour seeping around the corners of the lid resting on top.

'I was just sitting here, looking out, ya know? It's kinda

nice. You can see the sky and watch the flying foxes fly across sometimes, depending on their route.'

'What did you know about your neighbour?' I asked, careful not to let the words "wine" or "cheese" enter the fray.

'He kept to himself mostly, but he was single, so sometimes he'd bring home girls.'

'How often?' Donny quickly asked.

The thought, 'It's not a competition,' crossed my mind ungenerously and irritably before I chastised myself.

'Occasionally. He wasn't a looker. I mean, you've seen 'im, right?'

Yeah, I'd seen him. Right, you are, Jennifer.

Donny did well at holding the corners of his mouth stiffly. 'So you didn't know him well?'

'Shit, no. But I went in there a coupla times to have a few beers with 'im last year. I like a drink, but I couldn't keep up. He was pushing 'em, you know? I wasn't up for it.'

This is your chance, Sarina. 'Pushing the beers like he was trying to get you drunk?'

'Yeah. But I wasn't interested. That's not my scene, ya know?'

'Got it.' Jennifer wasn't into men. 'So you came home?'

'Yeah, I got a bit drunk, but I just left when he started sliding closer on the couch. Said I had to be up early for work.'

'Understandable,' I said. *Very understandable.*

It seemed Jennifer didn't know how clever she'd been. I turned to Donny and nodded. We'd worked together long enough that he knew it meant, 'There's a lead.'

She chuckled for a second. 'I only went back that second time cos I felt like having a beer, and he offered. I'd run out. I shouldn't have done that.'

'Why do you say that?' I asked.

'Just, well. You know. It was a bit cheeky of me, wasn't it?' She hung her head a little.

'So back to the twenty-fourth,' Donny asked, getting things back on track. 'You didn't hear anything next door? Voices? A woman, maybe? A scuffle or fight of any kind?'

'Well, I had the air conditioner running. You can hardly hear anything over that. But when I came out here, I closed the glass behind me cos I didn't want to waste what little cold air the bastard of a machine *does* put out—sorry! Sorry for swearing.'

'It's alright,' I said gently, looking around the cement barrier separating the two units. I liked the feeling of Jennifer being unable to see my face, so I stayed leaning out and pretending to focus on what was around the corner and down in the garden below. 'What did you see from here that night?'

'Nothing at first, but I heard someone come out on his balcony. I just thought it was 'im, of course. But there was, like, I dunno. It sounded a bit weird. Usually, he'd plop himself down on the chair when he went out there. I'd hear the sound of the plastic stretch a little, maybe hear him light his ciggie, take a drag. You know?'

I nodded.

'But that night, it sounded different. I'm not usually a nosey neighbour, I swear. I fuckin' hate those types. Shit, sorry.'

Donny laughed. 'Your nosiness that night is exactly what we need.'

Yeah, Donny. Great. Just great. Next thing, I'll be in cuffs.

Jennifer grunted in agreement and said, 'I just leaned over and looked towards his place. There was some woman, but she was already hitting the ground. Like, she didn't hurt herself or anything. I don't mean 'hit' like that. She landed like Wonder Woman or something. Then she stood up and walked off. At first, I was surprised she didn't hurt herself. I know she didn't cos I saw her walk just fine. Then she ran off towards the front of the unit block. I was watching her, but she was gone so quick. It was like she just disappeared into the dark. So, you know?'

Yeah, we knew. The woman was a vampire. Surprise, surprise.

God damn it!

'Can you give us a description?'

'Well, it wasn't like I got a clear look at 'er.'

That was the best news I'd heard all night.

'She had dark hair, shortish, like...' She paused. I looked over the balcony ledge again, hoping she wouldn't mention me. 'About the same length as yours.'

Crap.

'So chin length like Sarina's? What else?' Donny said.

'She was white. Very white.' She laughed. 'The clothes were dark, nondescript, really.'

Well, at least I got that right.

'The only other thing was...'

My inner dialogue was peppered with more swear words than Jennifer had managed. Here it comes, I thought. What the hell has she seen?

'I heard her mumble something. 'To be bloody careful,' maybe? Something like that. And something about cheese.'

Oh, no.

'Cheese?' said Donny sharply, with a glance at me.

'Yeah, weird. Unless I misheard. Maybe she said something similar, like please or sneeze. Knees, maybe.'

Dear God, stop.

'Got it,' said Donny.

'That's it. I really can't tell you anything more. Didn't see or hear more than that.'

Donny was about to thank her but asked one more question instead. 'Had you seen the woman before?'

'Nah. Didn't recognise her.' But then she glanced at me briefly, meeting my eyes.

Did that look mean anything?

I hoped to God—if there was one—that it didn't.

CHAPTER
TWENTY-TWO

The next night, Donny and I were in my car on the way to The Red Line. He always struck me as a man who'd drive a Monaro—or a motorcycle—but then, his souped-up red Commodore wasn't far off. Of course, a car like that would be too obvious for successful stakeouts and other important detective work now, wouldn't it? So that night, Donny and I were using my hatchback. Vampires need to get around, too, and a small car was a sensible choice for a woman at the time. It was also more affordable at the fuel pump.

'Something smells good in here,' Donny said, raising his thick eyebrows at me a few times. I ignored his comment, so he fiddled with the radio until he found the first station playing music. It was *The Macarena*.

'Stuff that,' he said brusquely, reaching for the knob again until *Gangsta's Paradise* rang out. Donny's head began moving back and forth, his lips moving gently as he sang in whispers.

I kept driving and thought of Will and our future. I'd made the right decision.

Donny started singing then about being a fool, which

seemed fitting. And about living on the edge. I let him have it and kept staring ahead. We passed near The Grove. Marinda crossed my mind. Was she inside that night or at home studying?

You Oughta Know came on.

'One for the angry girls,' Donny said.

'You'd know,' I whispered.

'If I didn't know better, love, I'd say you were taking me to The Red Line.' I could tell Donny had turned to face me. I knew him too damn well. I stole a look. His brown eyes weren't blinking, and he had no smile.

'Suck it up,' I told him.

'This is about the case we're no longer on, I presume? Isn't there a little murder we're supposed to be focused on?

'You'll understand soon.'

Once I'd parked on the street across the intersection from The Red Line, I could tell he was genuinely pissed about being railroaded. I understood. But it had to be done.

I handed him a small butcher's paper parcel. It contained what could only be described as vampire snacks: small animal organs that most humans would turn up their noses at. Vamps couldn't survive on animals alone. It was additional. I hadn't taken to it myself, still feeling a somewhat human revulsion toward the idea. But they say the way to a man's heart is through his stomach, which was undoubtedly true of Donny. His face lit up as he unwrapped the paper and breathed in the fresh, bloody odour.

'I'm going to tell you everything I know,' I started.

Donny sighed but unwrapped the plastic, took out a tiny heart, and began sucking on it. I had a captive audience for as long as it took him to get his fill.

'At The Red Line the other night,' I said, following super-quickly with, 'Don't say anything yet!' I didn't need his ridiculous jokes. 'As you know, I pretended to be a client, and something is going wrong at that place.'

'Yes, it's a brothel,' said Donny abruptly, followed by a sound I'd rather forget as he slurped the juice right out of another tiny organ. 'That ain't right.'

Donny, the moral man of Standfort.

'The vamp menu includes humans. If it were just sex, it would be illegal and concerning. Though not unsurprising. But I think they're doing more there. The second big problem is they are keeping human "workers" in some Fort Knox place on the outskirts.'

Donny stopped slurping and stared at me momentarily, so I pointed my thumb to the west. I had Donny's attention then, and his forehead creased firmly into three parallel lines as he considered what I was telling him.

He started wiping his mouth with a serviette, leaving smears of blood across it.

'Look, I questioned Sherri about Steve. He was there, alright. She all but admitted it. But she was scared witless and rightly, as we now know! She wouldn't give me more information, except he wasn't there anymore. That checks out since Kimberly said Ruby saw him at Mack's.'

It hurt to mention Ruby's name. I hated it when young humans got caught up in vampire business and ended up harmed. But my heart—yes, we have them!—was beating too fast because the moment was precarious. I was laying all the cards on the table with Donny, and if I had done the wrong thing confiding in him, well...

Since I realised Donny had kept information about Mike from me, it had sown seeds of doubt as to how much I could trust him. What if he was working with Mike? Or any other grave scenarios? But then I'd known Donny for years, and it was hard for me to believe he could live *that big* a double life.

Everything with him was always so upfront. All the good, all the bad.

Donny's face ticked with faint, erratic movements as if wrestling an internal demon.

'Damn you, Sarina,' he said finally, looking down at the scrunched-up, stained plastic bag and butcher's paper on his lap. 'Did anyone make you at The Red Line?'

'As an After Dark Detective? No. At least, I don't think so. I'm better than that, Don.'

Donny continued to look concerned. That wasn't something I was used to. Frankly, it knocked me off-kilter. Donny's confidence reassured me, and I had come to expect it.

He turned to me. 'Look, you don't know how serious this is. I know about Mike's activities. Lindsay told me. He's been taking cash from store owners, bribes and more. I don't know all the details, but he's in deeper than you know. We're up shit creek without a paddle on this case.'

'You mean we can't solve it? Rubbish. We can do this. Of course, we can!'

He rubbed his face roughly with his hands and said, 'You're playing with fire on this one. Jesus help us.' The car vibrated as Donny's knee jiggled up and down in the passenger seat.

'You can't possibly think we should ignore it. Let it go? Pretend we don't know this...no!'

'Stop.'

'Back down? Not do our bloody job—'

'Shut it!' he said.

So I did. I sat quietly, looking out into the street, lit only by a nearby street lamp and the neon glow travelling across the intersection from The Red Line's front.

After a short while, it occurred to me, though. 'How did Lindsay know about Mike's activities?'

'Well, she's an admin assistant. Maybe she knows someone who knows Mike or something. I dunno.'

'That's a rather vague theory. Didn't you ever ask her?'

'Yeah, but she said it was better if I didn't know.'

Many secrets were being kept for the apparent good of others ...

We sat in silence again, Donny's snack paper occasionally crinkling in his lap. 'You're right.,' he said at last. 'Something's going on, and we can't ignore it.'

I felt pleased to hear the words from Donny and not particularly surprised. He was—mostly—a good man.

'We're in it now, anyway. In the shit,' he said. 'The thing that concerns me most, though, is Lindsay. You were right. If Ruby and this Sherri girl have already been taken out, Lindsay and Steve might be sitting ducks. So what do we do?'

Donny was taking on a strange air of panic as reality hit.

'We need to get over there now,' he said, answering his question.

'I think we need to solve this case, Don and our best lead is this God-forsaken place here,' I said, nodding towards The Red Line.

Donny seemed to huff and puff next to me. Finally, he told me, 'No. We've got to get over there now!'

'But...,' I began but then thought better of it. Check it out, I thought. Donny was right. It couldn't hurt.

We arrived at Lindsay's place less than ten minutes later. The ground-level weatherboard looked dark inside, making me fear the worst. 'Wait,' I said to Donny, resting a flat palm on him to stop him from jumping out of the car. 'Let's do a little surveillance first, in case someone else is watching the place.'

I could tell it was almost impossible for Donny to stop himself from barreling in. Still, we sat for a few minutes, low in the seats, watching and checking out every direction. Then, when we saw nothing, we went to the house via the neighbour's yard, jumping the fence and knocking on Lindsay's back door.

My senses told me there was a human inside—a live one. After a short time with Donny continuing to knock anxiously, the door cracked to reveal a sleepy face. It was Lindsay.

'Oh, thank God,' Donny said, touching his hand to his solid chest.

'What the hell's going on?' Lindsay asked. 'Why are you here again?'

I almost chuckled but managed to head it off before the sound escaped.

'Let us in, Lin.'

Inside, Donny got straight to the crux. 'People who have information about this case are turning up dead, Lin. You're in danger.'

Lindsay herself chuckled then. A strange reaction to hearing her life could be in danger, I thought.

'You told me that last night, Don. Oh, sweetie, you thought something had happened to me? You don't need to worry about me. Steve'll never let anything happen to me. I told you that.'

'I think you may be underestimating this situation,' I said. 'Steve may be a vampire, but he's new and was made illegally. Something is happening in Standfort right now. Frankly, even Steve could be in danger.'

Lindsay's face fell. Her mouth opened a little. Even with my vampire sight, it appeared like a horizontal fissure in the darkness of the kitchen. Then she squinted at me, unsure of whether to take me seriously.

'I need to ring him,' Lindsay said suddenly, switching on the kitchen light as she reached for the wall phone.

'I don't think that's such a good idea.' Donny thrust his

hand out. It landed on hers as she reached for the receiver. 'I suggest you go into hiding until this is over, Lin. Can you do that for me?'

She peered at him, face etched with concern, her eyes darting from his to the phone and back again.

'I can take you to your parent's house.'

'But what about Steve?'

'We're on it,' I said. We're going to get to the bottom of this and find justice for Steve and...' I stopped myself. There was no point in offering her too much information. It would only make her less safe.

Lindsay didn't appear happy about it, but she agreed to pack a few things and let Donny and me drop her off at her parents' home. Within the hour, he and I drove back to continue our stakeout at The Red Line.

TWENTY-THREE

Parked in a side street, Donny and I settled in to watch. There was a lot of coming and going—The Red Line did a booming business.

Hours later, Donny elbowed me. 'Ow!' I said irritably, rubbing my eyes as I returned to life. I'd stayed alert for the first couple of hours. Then Donny took over so I could "rest my eyes".

Donny pointed across the road. 'A four-wheel drive just drove into the back. One like Mike's four-wheel drive.'

I turned the key in the ignition and put my little Toyota into drive, turning onto the street. Crossing the intersection, I drove past The Red Line's back entrance and made a U-turn.

'Like Mike, our boss's car?' I queried, the gravity of Don's comment hitting me, finally.

'Mm,' he murmured absently.

'Did you see anything else?'

Donny said nothing. His mind and eyes were 100 per cent on The Red Line and what might be occurring. I parked in the same spot I had when I'd staked the place out previously, and we sank into the cloth bucket seats to watch without being obvious.

'Yeah,' said Donny, as though finally answering my question from over a minute before. 'That's Mike's. The rego checks.'

Sure enough, there it was. Mike's ostentatious choice. It took his employees, myself included, less than two hours to get sick of hearing about it after the purchase. It got worse two days later when he found out it was a lemon with ongoing automatic transmission problems. But the situation wasn't all bad. For Mike, I mean. Because if there was one thing Mike enjoyed, it was complaining, and that car gave him ample material to work with. The man had made a true art of whingeing.

Two burly door blokes came outside as Mike stepped down from the driver's side, extinguishing any possible doubt. They opened up the back.

'What the...,' said Donny, and I saw it too. It looked like a body lying there, wrapped in a bed or canvas sheet. He reached his arm over to push me further into the car seat, nervous we would be seen.

'Are we just going to let this happen?'

'What do we do? Seriously? We're in a precarious situation here.' He sounded wound up and afraid.

The burly blokes reached in to grab the body as the bag sprung to life and began wriggling.

I jumped in my seat as Donny exclaimed, 'Dear God!'

Frankly, it was an understatement, given the person inside the bag in Mike's car was alive and had begun kicking. If we'd been closer, we might have been able to sense the life inside, but we weren't... One thing I could tell with a fair amount of certainty was that it was a human.

I reached for the door.

'No!' Donny ordered. 'We can't. We'll never make it out alive.'

The figure wrapped in canvas fought like its life depended on it. Despite my vampirism, watching it made my heart hurt, and my mind raced, trying to think of a solution—any solution —any way to help.

For God's sake, we were agents of Australia, part of a department meant to uphold the law. We couldn't just sit here and watch someone being handled like that, especially when they could be completely innocent.

That's when it occurred to me. 'Donny, you don't think it could be Kimberly? What if they brought her back here as part of damage control? They got Ruby and Sherri, after all.'

'Fuck!' Donny said as he sank back into the passenger bucket seat and slapped the meaty underside of his fist angrily on the dash. 'Damn it!'

We saw Mike return from the rear entrance and head for his car. I noticed another familiar face, too. John Martin. He was just inside The Red Line, and I only saw him for a second as he reached out to grab the door, which opened outwards, and pull it shut. I said nothing to Donny since I was beginning to think John might be my next big personal prize. Based on what I had learned lately, I was hardly shocked to see him working at The Red Line. I was confident it would be a perfect fit for him. All that unfettered access to women who found it difficult to say no. Besides, didn't one of the captive girls in the house by the cane field mention a 'John' in relation to The Red Line? I felt my face pucker.

'Here's what's going to happen,' Donny said. 'I'm going inside. You can't because they may remember you from the other night.'

I was nodding. 'So I'll head to Mack's to check on Kimberly.'

'Exactly,' Donny said, though he looked like he would prefer to go with me. We had little choice, though. Time was of the essence. God knows what was happening to that human inside.

Was it Kimberly? Even if it wasn't, Kimberly was in grave danger now.

Finally, Donny looked at me. 'Right. If anyone can manage it, you can.' I knew he cared.

'You take care as well. They could already know about you,' I warned.

'Possible.' He put his fingers in his hair and tousled it like that would help disguise him. 'Mike's leaving. Quick—take off as soon as he's out of the way.' Donny jumped out of the car and waved me off.

I got dream traffic, which was good because I didn't plan on waiting for all the red lights. At the Standfort Esplanade, I tore into a park, slamming the door behind me without even locking it. Inside Mack's, the floor manager rolled his eyes from across the room when she saw me. I couldn't be too upset, given during my last visit to the bar, we'd closed it down after finding poor Ruby dead.

I flicked my hand at her to order her to the back of the bar.

'Kimberly?' I asked.

'No. What?'

'Is Kimberly on?' I repeatedly, impatiently.

'She didn't come in,' replied the manager.

'What do you mean? Is she sick? Did she call?'

While waiting for answers, I scanned the bar to see who was there. Seeing no one suspicious, I turned back to the manager.

'Oh my God, is she okay?' Her eyes were wide, and her mouth hung open after she asked.

'Did she call?'

'No. She didn't turn up for her shift,' the manager said, looking stricken—the total weight of Kimberly's missed shift falling on her like a ton of bricks.

'Address, please. Hurry.' I wasn't going to bother with niceties. I wouldn't stand another innocent human's life on my hands. Because of what? Some dodgy vamps who wanted to turn a young man and picked the wrong one to turn!

I returned to my car within a minute and headed for Kimberly's flat. It was one of those refurbished sixties designs overlooking the water just a few minutes from Macks. There were huge windows along the front, and the curtains were open. I practically flew up the timber steps at the front. From the verandah, I could see right inside, and there was no movement, no life. But more reassuring was no sign of a struggle. That was positive, but it was hardly proof that nothing had happened to her.

Kimberly may have gone willingly or been taken by surprise without leaving obvious signs of a scuffle.

What on earth was the plan at that point?

The flat was a duplex. It took me a quarter of a second to jump the wall that divided the front verandahs.

The couple inside the other flat got the shock of their lives. They jumped up and moved away from the window where they'd been watching a movie on the couch. Neve Campbell was fighting off a guy with an enormous knife on the small TV. The VHS sleeve with Ghostface on the cover lay on the coffee table.

'It's okay,' I called with my hands up, trying to calm them. 'I'm looking for Kimberly, that's all. I'm worried about her.'

'Who are you?' the man called, shielding the woman behind him. They were dressed in track pants, and the man wore a faded denim vest over his t-shirt. The windows were closed, and the air conditioning was running.

The woman yelled at me, 'You can't come in here without an invitation.'

As though I didn't know that! Humans were so pathetic at times. The fact that vamps couldn't enter a human-only private residence without an invite had been the bane of my life during particular work-related and extra-curricular investigations.

I couldn't show them my After Dark Department badge. What if they called in to question it? Then Mike would know I was up to something.

As far as After Dark was concerned, I needed what Donny and I did that night to remain in the realm of never happened. That's how it had to be.

'I'm a friend of hers,' I said. 'I work with her at Mack's. She didn't come in for work tonight.'

Neither of the humans looked too sure as, through the corner of my eye, I saw Neve being stabbed and falling to the ground.

'Look, she left town. I don't know where to or why.' The man stared out at me, willing me to take the information and go.

'Did she go with someone?'

'I have no idea. Now, can you please leave us alone?'

'We don't know more. Really,' the woman said. 'We didn't even know her that well. She worked nights and slept late.'

Clearly, the couple didn't know more, so I jumped off the front balcony, landing softly on the ground.

Driving back to The Red Line, I hoped to catch Donny on his way out. But the Kimberly thing was playing on my mind. It didn't feel right.

I parked in a side street again, and it was another twenty minutes before I saw Donny exit through the front. When he moved away from the entrance, I flashed my lights to get his attention.

Approaching, Donny looked pale. He was a strapping, swarthy man despite the vampirism. Pale sat strangely on him and ill with me.

'So?' he asked, throwing himself into the passenger seat.

'Kimberly didn't show up for work tonight, Don. It feels bad.'

'Damn,' he said, catching his face in his hands as he let his head fall.

I felt an odd feeling in my stomach that I couldn't fully explain. Was Donny going to expand?

I stared at him. His thick brown, wavy hair, usually slicked back, had begun to fall stiffly towards his face.

He took a deep breath. 'Well, you're right about the trafficking. The bloke I chose—'

'You chose a man?!' I blurted, immediately aware and embarrassed that I was doing the same thing Donny had done to me when he found out I'd chosen a woman at The Red Line.

'To put them off the scent.'

'Fine,' I said, wanting the conversation to move forward.

'The kid can't have been much over eighteen, and I'm pretty sure he wasn't there by choice. You're right. There's something very corrupt about that place. Sinful even.'

'Aside from the obvious, you mean?' But for Donny to have brought up "sin", I knew then whatever he'd seen was terrible.

He nodded, still with his head held in his hands.

'What about the human in the bag, though?'

'You don't want to know, Sarina.' He looked up then, glancing at me for a second. 'I'm serious. You don't know the half of it, love. The kid they sent me sang like he was *Don Carlo*. Plus, I sensed some shit in there that's just...'

I paused, but when Donny didn't continue, I asked, 'So our boss is a human trafficker?'

'I don't know how deep he is in it, but he's evil. Sarina. I'm 100 per cent in on this now. God help us. We have got to be careful with this one. There's a lot at stake—everything.'

'Right. But you won't tell me everything,' I answered snippily, turning the key in the ignition. 'Look, we saw that bastard deliver a live person to the back of that shit-hole. What else could he have been doing? He's a trafficker. I get it.'

Glancing towards Donny, I nearly switched the engine back off again. He was usually jovial and can-do, but now his face appeared drawn, pummelled almost. But, we needed to be on the move and away from The Red Line, so I pulled out and headed towards the city centre. Donny was quiet, and once, when I glanced at him, I saw a tremor in his hand. It was hard to imagine what a vampire like Donny could have witnessed to elicit that reaction.

Donny was a rock. A vampire killer. Plus, he ate humans, for heaven's sake!

'I went to Kimberly's flat,' I began. Perhaps that would shake him out of his funk. 'According to her neighbours, she's left town. They don't know why or where to.'

Donny barely seemed to be listening to me. 'We have to do something...,' he started saying to himself as we drove along. 'The Mayor!' he exclaimed suddenly.

'What about the mayor?'

'That's our ticket. Mayor Gorman needs to know this is going on. It's the only way. Otherwise, we won't just lose our jobs over this. We'll lose our lives.'

'It's that serious?' The look on Donny's face was all the answer I needed. 'So how do we get to the mayor?'

'Lindsay is how. Let's go.' I turned off and followed Donny's directions to Lindsay's family home.

CHAPTER
TWENTY-FOUR

I parked my car a block away from the mayor's house. Every detail was worth considering. I didn't want my little hatchback to be seen there. Donny and I held back from the house, watching Lindsay's approach.

The Mayor's front door had two guards. It was an unfortunate side effect that with the discovery of my kind and taking our place beside humans in the community, humans had to take previously unnecessary precautions.

Lindsay's voice carried over the humid air that night. 'I need to talk to the Mayor about her son, Steve.'

Donny and I took off like lightning as soon as she engaged the two guards standing by the door. We ran, doubled over so as not to be seen, to the side of the house. I wasn't exactly dressed for sneaking around with my striped t-shirt and dark jeans, but we made it.

We scaled a tree there, enabling us to reach an upstairs bedroom window. It was locked, but being timber, Donny could jimmy it open. We paused for a few seconds to listen. If anyone *had* heard a noise, they didn't seem to be on their way to investigate.

In the house, creeping through the upstairs hallway, I began worrying about our plan. It may have been the only plan we could think of to keep us safe, but that was the case *only* if it worked. If the plan failed, we were stuffed.

My vamp hearing allowed me to pick up snippets of the conversation at the front of the house. Then, I blocked it out and concentrated entirely on sneaking up behind the mayor.

A flashy, boxy television flickered light through the room. It was about four times the size of Kimberly's neighbours. The mayor could afford the finer things. Sitting beside it was a stack of recent films she owned rather than renting. But Raquel Gorman wasn't watching one. She was dozing on the couch with some late-night talk show blaring.

I nodded silently to Donny as we jumped in, and I quickly covered her mouth tightly. I was on the Mayor before she knew we were there, and I felt terrible about it. I knew how frightening it would be for her. I could remember that much from my attack. There weren't a lot of options that night, though.

I leaned in to whisper in her ear. 'I know what happened to your son and am here to help. We want to put this right. But we need you to stay quiet to do that.'

Though I genuinely wanted to help, my canines began pushing and pressing at my gums, desperate to pop out and sink into the mayor's neck, which was ever so close. I was ravenous. I turned away a little. Not that it made that much difference. I could still smell her and feel her blood pumping through her body as I held her tightly. Her blood pumped faster as she panicked.

Within seconds, I started to loosen my hand from her mouth, reminding her, 'You scream, and you won't make it. Plus, you won't find out about your son.' Even though I didn't know the whole story of her son's abduction and turning, it was a way to keep her compliant, and I felt she understood me.

I took my hand off her mouth. Raquel Gorman, Standfort's mayor, snapped her head around to look at me.

'What have you done?' she said.

'Not us,' said Donny, lifting his hands in a show of honesty.

I told her, 'Not only do we know what happened to Steve— well, some of it, at least—but we need your help.'

Giving out bad news to a loving family wasn't my expertise. Still, I tried to adjust my face to give the impression of having many feelings about it. I *did* have feelings. But I was vampire. I was also a detective with After Dark. They hired me because I was tough, could stuff my feelings away, and hold my own in difficult situations. I was doing well in my job because I was strong, focused, practical, and could follow a lead and nut things out. It wasn't about "feeling".

'Mrs Gorman, I am so sorry to tell you that your son has been made a vamp—'

She began to struggle, and I knew she would call out, so I covered her mouth with my hand again. I leaned in and said quietly. 'He's a vampire, but he still lives. I didn't cause it, and I need you to get control over yourself. Can you calm down?'

She nodded.

'Good. Can you keep your voice down?'

'Mmhm,' she managed through my hand. I removed it.

'I am sorry for your loss. I *really* am. It wasn't Donny or I. But Steve still lives as a vampire. He's not completely lost to you.' My father came to mind, but I buried it.

She was teary and still appeared on the verge of panic. 'Steve seems like a nice kid. Donny and I work for—'

'Stop,' said Donny sharply.

'Does it matter now?'

Donny gave me a death stare.

'Donny, it's all got to come out if the mayor's going to help us. Look,' I began addressing her again. 'We found out he's been made a vampire against his will. It isn't right, but it wasn't his fault, either. We want to help him. Please stay calm because if you bring your security in here, this situation'll go up like a bonfire in the dry season.'

I felt Mayor Gorman's body relax just a little. 'Fine. I'll hear what you have to say. But stay back away from me. You've broken into my home at night, so I'm sure you can understand why I don't trust you.'

I could, and it was a precarious situation. Still, I loosened my grip on her, my biceps relaxing slowly. Then I stepped away. It wasn't the right time to tell her my standing back wouldn't save her if I did want to harm her. I could cross the floor before she was even aware I was moving.

'You'd better explain yourselves.' Mrs Gorman had gathered her strength and was trying to make a show of it. We often came across those plucky humans. Sometimes, it was inspiring. Other times, it was pathetic. Laughably so. But that night, I didn't laugh. I didn't smirk.

I addressed Mayor Gorman, occasionally glancing toward Donny—to keep an eye on him. 'I admit we don't know exactly who did what and why. Yet. We're going to find out. We need your help, though.'

'What help?' Mrs Gorman looked drawn, worried, and very suspicious of us. Fair enough, too. She should be concerned.

'We're from the After Dark Department,' Donny said, entering the conversation and showing me he was on board. We needed to bring Mayor Gorman into our plan and get her onside if we expected her help. I nodded at Donny.

'We need you. Not only will Steve be in danger if you don't cooperate, but my partner and I will be in danger, too,' Donny said.

I flicked my head in Donny's direction in agreement. 'Two witnesses in Steve's case have already been killed, Mayor. One more may be missing right now.'

'Oh, Lord,' she said. 'But you've just broken into my home!'

'I know,' I said. 'I'm sorry, but please understand we had no choice. Our boss is in on this, so we didn't know how to move forward without getting in more trouble.'

'Your boss?'

'Yep. This is a delicate situation, but we mean you no harm.'

Mayor Gorman nodded. 'Fine. I agree to listen. But you better not be playing me. I'm the mayor of Standfort. You won't get away with it if you kill me,' said Mrs Gorman.

'Absolutely, and you're right. See? We have a lot to lose here, too. Okay, here's what we know,' I said. 'Steve was taken to a place called The Red Line.'

Mrs Gorman looked suitably horrified. 'I knew that place needed shutting,' said Mayor Gorman, her face turning an angry shade of pink. 'I've been in a difficult position. It's not as easy to get things done as people assume.' She dropped her head down a bit, feeling defeated.

'We don't know yet what occurred at The Red Line—'

'Or why,' said Donny quickly.

I nodded. 'But we've heard that Steve was turned there. After that, he must have escaped or been set free for a reason we haven't established yet. But a couple of people have seen him, and ...'

'Where? Where is he?'

'He's in hiding.'

Mrs Gorman sat more calmly then. Her light pink lounge suit suited her currently flushed skin tone. 'So, he is out there alive?'

'Undead, yes.' I smiled at her. She grimaced back.

'Did you know that Steve has a girlfriend?'

'Yes,' confirmed Mrs Gorman seriously, glancing down as she smoothed out her lounge pants. 'Lindsay Jenner? Mm. Piece of work, that one,' said Mrs Gorman as though a lemon had touched her tongue. 'She's involved?'

'No,' Donny said emphatically.

I turned to see his incisors make an appearance. They shone bright white, even catching the light from the lamp and TV. No one could miss them.

Unfortunately, that can happen when vampires lose their cool. We don't always have complete control over it.

Mrs Gorman jumped out of her skin and I rushed to grab her, holding on tight.

CHAPTER
TWENTY-FIVE

'It's just a reflex,' I told Mayor Gorman. 'You're quite safe.'

Donny's flash of fangs *was* an auto-reflex. Brought on by hearing nasty words about his precious ex, Lindsay, I noted.

I let go of the mayor, aiming to calm the situation. 'Teeth away,' I ordered Donny.

I told Mayor Raquel Gorman, 'Lindsay Jenner seems a good person, so it might be helpful if we don't make too many judgments right now. She loves Steve and is doing everything she can to protect him.'

The Mayor said nothing but pursed her lips in a resigned fashion.

'I'm sure I don't need to tell you the danger Steve is in. Vampires who are made illegally do not fare well. You know that.'

'Can you help him?' she cried.

'I think *together* we can. Donny and I have put ourselves out there by bringing what we know to you. We want Steve to be okay, but we also want everyone to survive. That's where you come in.'

Mrs Gorman straightened up and put herself into the 'Mayor zone' to ask, 'I need your assurances that you aren't going to kill me. Or eat me!' she said, *still* stuck on the fear that vampires presented to humans.

It would be disingenuous of me to pretend she had *nothing* to worry about. Many vampires were happy to continue lying and picking off humans, as they had done while living in the shadows. I didn't want to be that kind of vampire from the outset. Thankfully, Donny didn't either, and many other vamps we knew were equally above board. But reality is reality.

'Again, that isn't what we're here for. We wouldn't have gone through all this trouble if that had been our plan. We'd feed from someone we could take off the street.' I was trying to help, but judging from the response on Mayor Gorman's face, I'd missed that mark by a mile.

'Or go to one of the booths,' I added, trying to save the failing conversation.

'We mean it. You're in no danger from us,' Donny said to help. 'We love our jobs, Mayor, and we love life. We don't want to do anything to jeopardise that.'

She seemed somewhat placated, if stuck between a rock and a hard place. It was something we had in common. If only she could see that.

'Right. That makes sense,' she said, though Donny still earned a stern glance.

Fair enough, I thought. I regularly gave Donny similar looks.

But I'd felt something in that last week. Donny's connection to Lindsay was like sandpaper rubbing against my skin. Why was that? It wasn't jealousy. Of course! Why on earth would I feel jealous of Lindsay? I had things she could never have as a human, and besides, I didn't "like" Donny. How ridiculous the thought was.

'Mrs Gorman,' I said, 'Lindsay Jenner is downstairs with your secur—'

She jumped up and made for the stairs to the entrance. 'Uh-uh.' I grabbed her. My patience was wearing thin. Why were humans so hard to deal with?

'But, you said she's the one that knows. We need to find Steve!'

'Yes. But we don't need to find him this instant,' I said quietly threateningly. 'I'm pretty certain he's safer where he is. Where none of us knows. Can you understand that?'

Her eyes bore through me like two blue moons. She was judging me. Determining how much she could trust me and what direction she would take.

I could feel my incisors tingle and loosen as I waited, hoping she would choose wisely.

'Look, if you care about Steve, this is how it's going.' I began taking control. 'No more arguing. No more trying to run off half-cocked. You listen, and then you do what you're told. Got it?'

The mayor nodded.

'You are going to go downstairs now, calmly and normally, and tell your security to send Lindsay away. Tell them, "She needs to make an appointment to see me tomorrow. At my office." Don't address her directly. She knows we're here— she's helping us. The plan is that when you send Lindsay away until tomorrow, she'll know we got inside okay. Once it's done, come back upstairs, and we'll get the next step sorted.'

Mayor Gorman went downstairs, leaving Donny and me to sit quietly and listen. I must have gotten through to her because she followed my instructions to a tee. Lindsay would now hide at her parents' home again until all this mess was cleaned.

Once Mrs Gorman returned to the lounge, I started on part two of the plan. That was where Donny and I were sitting ducks. We had to trust that Raquel Gorman would protect us. It was the only way forward.

Donny began, 'Our boss, Mike Thompson—'

'Mike?' Mayor Gorman repeated enthusiastically.

Damn. It didn't bode well that she knew and, judging by her enthusiasm, liked Mike.

I went on a limb, telling her, 'He's involved in this somehow. It would be best if you were wary of him. He placed Donny and me on Steve's case, but we discovered he has ties to The Red Line. I don't know exactly what ties yet. But it turns out Mike's not the clean-cut, above-board boss we thought he was. Now he's taken us off your son's case and...'

'Off my son's case? As in, no one is trying to find my boy?'

'Well, he's put someone else from our office on it. But Sarina and I are the best the department has to offer. So it's almost like he doesn't think it's the most important case to solve ... or he doesn't want to solve it,' said Donny bluntly.

Mayor Gorman looked grave as she considered what we'd told her.

'It all feels very dodgy and precarious right now,' I said.

I inwardly hoped for the best. Had I been religious, I would have been praying. Perhaps Donny was.

Finally, she said, 'What about Steve, though? He's been missing for weeks. Where's he been? What has been happening to him?' Her face creased with a mother's pain.

'Look, I'm sorry. I went undercover at The Red Line one night recently, and the staff were too scared to speak out. However, I got confirmation that Steve had been taken there at some point.'

Mayor Gorman went to speak again, so I gently raised my hand.

'This whole thing appears linked to The Red Line and Mike. So you can see the insecure position my partner and I are in. Do you understand what I'm asking?'

'I think I do,' Mrs Gorman said solemnly. 'You have my word that I'm on your side. I want my son back.'

'Then I need to know what you can do from your side that won't further endanger us all. The ball's in your court now, Mrs Gorman. Can you help us help your Steve?'

AS WE LEFT the Gorman home, morning light threatened the horizon toward the coast. I handed Donny the keys so he could drive. I was tired, but the plan, which all three of us had agreed upon, was the best we could hope for.

During the day, the mayor would make the necessary arrangements. Then, just after dusk the following night, Donny and I would join the police force Raquel Gorman raised that day to raid The Red Line. Before the raid was complete, Mike would also be picked up for questioning by detectives the mayor knew and trusted. It was far from foolproof, but it was all we had.

I let out a noisy sigh and leaned back in the passenger seat.

'You get the feeling this could be the end of us?' Donny seemed genuinely concerned.

'I don't want to agree, Donny, but yeah. I feel it.'

'Funny how you and I never...'

'What? Jeez, Donny. How do you go from fearing for your life to wishing we'd had sex?'

'I s'pose I have a lust for life, love. But I wasn't coming on to you. I was thinking,' he said, his forehead wrinkled.

'Well, please keep your lust for life and "thinking" to yourself. We'd make a terrible couple, anyway, because you're an idiot, and I'm not,' I told him, expecting a laugh.

But Donny's face remained serious for a few seconds before finally he said, 'You have to admit at least we'd be a good-looking couple.'

I nodded slowly, my mouth giving him a half grimace without even meaning to. 'Looks aren't everything.'

We were getting all the red lights Standfort had to offer. At one stop near the Central Police Station, I started worrying about our safety again. We had no more proof to back the Mayor's promise to provide us protection than we did to assume she would serve us up on a plate to Mike and anyone he was in with.

'Don?' He was tapping the steering wheel irritably, willing the lights to turn green.

'Mm?'

'I think we should bunk at Will's for the day. He's set up for it, and we're not safe at either of our homes when we don't know that Gorman'll keep her word.'

The lights changed, but Donny said nothing and just sat there.

'Donny!' I slapped my hands together, a foot from his head.

'Yeah, I...'

My face scrunched up as I looked at him, trying to understand. Again, his lovely swarthiness was overtaken by that odd paleness.

'What's going on, Donny Agosti?'

He finally put his foot on the accelerator.

'So, Will's?' I said. It was met with silence.

'Take me to Will's,' I said and sat, aggressively picking a few fluff pieces off my jeans.

Instead, Donny pulled to a stop outside a Pizza Hut restaurant. It was closed, but the neon lights remained glowing along the front.

A surge of nerves overtook me. I was unsure of the issue, yet I sensed something big was up.

Taking off his seatbelt, he turned to me, looking grave. 'Sarina, it was Will.'

'What?'

'At The Red Line. They had Will.'

CHAPTER
TWENTY-SIX

I don't remember deciding on how to proceed. It all happened organically as my vampire instincts took over. Reaching roughly for the keys, I pushed Donny back in his seat. He didn't want me to have those keys, so he moved his body forward to block me. Then, we began to scrap inside the car.

I pushed his face back using the heel of my hand, but he was grappling with me until he finally reached over and opened his door. We fell onto the street with rough thuds followed by agile moves taking us from the ground to a standing position, ready to square off.

'You know damn well I couldn't do anything.'

'And so you kept it from me? Half an hour, you sat there with that knowledge,' I spat back, punching out towards him but missing by an inch.

Donny got the upper hand for a few seconds, toppling me to the pavement and spinning me over so my back scratched the bitumen. Then he loosened his grip, and we stood up again.

I was tough. But I'd be lucky to overcome Donny. In vampire culture, male-on-female violence wasn't as disapproved of as it was for humans due to less obvious strength differences in male and female vampires. But that didn't equate to *no* differences.

Still, when I wasn't out of control with emotion, I would realise later on that Donny was unlikely to unleash on me completely. Unless he lost his patience, his heart just wasn't in it.

I lunged at him again and bit him a few times until he flung his arm out and sent me flying to the pavement.

Struggling and bolstering myself against the Pizza Hut window, the buzzing fluoro flushed us in a light as ugly as the fight itself.

'Stop. Just stop,' he was saying as I lunged again. 'I'm sorry. I am.' He let himself fall to his knees.

'Why didn't you do something?'

'And get us *all* killed? You're not thinking straight, Sar.'

'Oh, stuff you,' I said in reply. But I sat down on the kerb nearby.

'You know as well as I do what the result of rushing in there would have been.'

'Son of a bitch,' I said, letting my face fall into my hands. 'Give me my keys,' I said, suddenly jumping up.

'I don't think so.' Donny got up and started wiping his face. We both had a few minor wounds, and he wiped his with his t-shirt, smearing the white cotton pink and red.

'We should get going before the cops arrive. There's no way no one noticed two vamps fighting outside the Hut. Hand me the keys,' I ordered.

Donny's poker face gave the game away, though. A split-second semi-glance towards the car told me where the keys were.

Running for the driver's side, we struggled, two bodies trying to win one space. Stuck in a strange, violent hug for a moment, his blood mingled with mine from the cuts and scrapes we were both covered in. But Donny managed to grab the keys. He held them tightly in his fist.

'You owe me, Donny Agosti. *This,* at least,' I hissed at him. That got to him. Of course, he was feeling guilty for what had happened. Donny was a good guy.

We both slowed our struggles, exhausted. 'What, though? What do you plan to do? Rush The Red Line? Guns blazing?'

'I don't even have a gun,' I said stupidly in a voice that said I thought Donny was the idiot.

Donny made a sound, like a rush of air or a grunt, and swivelled around to lean his back against the car.

'What did they do to him, Don? You need to tell me right now.'

'It was bad. I think they drained him. I couldn't do anything. You have to know that.'

I would. I really would. Later.

Donny had been right, of course. Had he jumped in to try to save Will from whatever fate awaited him inside The Red Line, Donny would be dead, Will would still be dead—or whatever had happened to him—and I would be either dead or on the run.

But at that moment, I still didn't care. The anger inside me that Will—*my* Will—had been taken by someone was bubbling up in an unstoppable chemical reaction. It was like someone had added vinegar to a spoonful of bicarbonate of soda. I was running on vampire instincts.

What I needed to do was find Will. Dead or alive.

'His place. Let's check it out. See if we can't find some clue. At the worst, it might be a safe spot to stay for the day. You owe me. Right?' I said. It was unfair, but I said it.

I'd never seen Donny look so crushed. His hand reached for mine, handing over my keys.

Keenly aware that Will was, in all probability, dead already, I still needed to press onwards. Even though it was breaking me in two, I couldn't focus on the worst outcome. I certainly didn't want to believe it. I had to keep going. If the most dire thing had happened, I knew I was headed for revenge. So, I pushed the idea of his death aside. Someone was going to pay dearly for the mistake of hurting him.

CHAPTER
TWENTY-SEVEN

Behind the wheel and with Donny in the passenger seat, I tore away from the Pizza Hut. Its tacky lights faded quickly in the rearview mirror.

'Are we going to his place? What if they're watching it? Or using his place to hide out?' he asked.

Since, in my emotional state, those had to be the stupidest questions I'd heard that evening, I ignored him. Of course, we had to go there. My mind had only one track at that point: Will.

I kept my eyes on the road ahead, slowing for red lights but driving straight through as soon as I could see the streets empty.

'Do you really think this's the best idea?' Donny tried again

I rolled my eyes violently without turning to look at him.

'Sarina, please. The way they dragged him inside and...'

'I have to see. Plus, we need somewhere to stay. My apartment isn't going to be safe. Nor yours.' I gave him a short, hard stare before returning to the road ahead. 'After that, I'm going to The Red Line. I'm gonna burn them to the ground.'

Fighting words, but I wasn't thinking straight. It was

nearly dawn. We would never make it to The Red Line after this, and going to "burn them to the ground" was an ill-chosen plan if ever I'd had one.

I pulled sharply into the parking area at Will's place and didn't wait for Donny.

Approaching Will's door at a run, I slowed when I saw it was ajar. A sliver of light spilled out onto the bare cement porch. Will had never been one for home improvement. That had annoyed me about him, but right then, it was the last thing I cared about. None of my prior irritations meant a thing. Not when *they* had taken him from me.

My mind was still vague about the "they" and the "what", but I was determined to find out. Hell hath no fury like a woman whose love has been stolen.

Donny was close behind me as I pushed the door just a few inches. I took in the sights through the crack—a dark living room that my eyes swiftly adjusted to. The smells—there was blood. And there was silence.

'There's been a fight,' said Donny from behind me, able to smell the blood as well as I could.

There was something odd, disconcerting. I didn't immediately understand because it wasn't a situation with which I was entirely familiar, but it slowed me down. I scanned the living area. Blood had soaked deep into the beige carpet. A few items lay strewn. I saw the blue vase that I had bought for Will in pieces. I'd filled it with fake flowers. It was set on a cabinet that stored his records and photography equipment. A woman's touch that I had imposed on him. The vase lay broken in three sharp pieces on the floor. Some records, usually lined up neatly in the cabinet, were strewn across the coffee table.

A few seconds later, I felt it. Someone was in the bedroom —a live person. I glanced back at Donny. His stance told me he was ready for anything, but his face looked resigned and sad.

'No,' I said to the universe.

Donny looked down at his shoes.

'Oh, God!' I roared into the bedroom to find Will lying there. His body was motionless and marked with the signs of a nasty beating. Purple and blue blotting lined his legs and arms like a wet-in-wet watercolour. I rushed to him, rubbing my hands gently all over his body to check for broken bones. I found several broken ribs, and I suspected a fracture in his jaw. He made little more than a murmur throughout. I lifted his shirt to see more horrifying, flowery impressions on his skin and a deep bite on the top of his thigh.

'Will?' I gently tapped his cheeks, and he faintly grunted.

'Can you hear me?' I said.

I placed my fingers on his carotid artery the way humans do. I didn't need to. I could sense human blood flow, an evident skill for a vampire. But I used my fingers to confirm what I already knew. He'd been drained close to death. A human can lose just 15% of their blood before significant side effects ensue. I estimated that they had drained him nearly halfway based on his current state—a fatal amount.

Whoever had attacked him intended for him to die, or at the very least, didn't care if he lived or died.

A thought flashed across my mind—was Will left here to make some point to me? Was it intended as a warning or punishment for sticking my nose into The Red Line's and Mike's businesses? But I didn't have time for all that.

I heard the click-clack as Donny locked the front door. Then he joined me on the bed, looking stern and resigned. We both knew I had few options.

Even if I transported Will to the hospital in minutes, they may not be able to save him. I had to use my blood to save him. I *had* to.

While vampire blood had beneficial health properties, Will

was so far gone at that point that a small amount of blood wouldn't cut it. So it boiled down to letting him die or ... turning him.

'I have to.'

'I know. But you know the consequences, right?'

'I do.'

'You have to,' Donny said to give me confidence in my decision. 'It's going to open up a world of hell, but there's no other option if you want to save his life.'

I nodded. 'Don, I'm really sorry. About....'

'Look,' he said. 'I'm healed. I gave you some back, too.' I would have chuckled if we weren't in such a harrowing situation.

'Will?' I demanded. I used my authoritative voice when interviewing people to make them feel they had no choice and that I was entirely in charge. 'Will! You'll die if I don't help you.' I leaned in close, holding his cheek and checking his eyes, which began rolling back at that moment.

'Will, I'm turning you.' Of course, there was no reply. Will was moving *beyond*. Beyond being able to decide or speak for himself. Beyond everything that had happened to him that night. If I didn't turn him then and there, he would be dead within the hour.

My teeth descended as I bit deeply into my wrist. Just the two puncture wounds would be enough, given I had adrenaline in my system, which pumped my blood faster than usual. The drops of lukewarm viscous liquid started oozing from the wounds. Vampires are cold creatures compared to human's warmth and heat, but that doesn't mean they are dead cold.

As soon as I got my blood flowing, I placed my wrist over Will's face, letting a few drops fall near his mouth. He was too far gone to do anything about it. I looked at Donny pleadingly.

Donny turned Will over so he lay flat on his back. His head

rested on the bed without a pillow, and his mouth hung open. Donny opened Will's mouth further, and I gently squeezed my wrist. It was all that was needed.

'That's it. Keep it going.' Donny nodded.

Holding my arm above Will, a good flow trickled from my wrist to his mouth. 'This should do it,' I said gently to Donny in place of thanks.

It took several minutes before a bit of colour returned to Will's cheeks. The humans would often use that expression, referring to that rosy undertone they have—a look that vampires didn't lack completely but certainly weren't known for. I enjoyed many aspects of Will's humanity, including that lovely, warm colour.

Eventually, Will's cheeks flushed. A minute later, his fingers wiggled.

He wouldn't rise again, though. Not that night.

TWENTY-EIGHT

Donny and I sat on Will's double bed with Will next to us. I'd lain there with Will only nights before. The sheets, messy and damp with sweat then, were now messy with blood.

My boyfriend wasn't going to "wake up" again. Not as a human. He would be little more than unconscious until after the process of turning had finished. Then he would be dead. Undead that is—a vampire for the rest of his natural life.

Though Donny and I couldn't see the process, Will's humanity disappeared before us. His body was making millions of changes we couldn't see. Scientists were only, just then, researching to understand the process of vampiric turning.

Will looked shockingly beaten after what was done to him, but inside he was changing species.

'I would have made the same decision,' said Donny.

I looked up at him. His eyes were compassionate. I nodded, and he lifted his hand and placed it over mine as it lay on Will's chest. Will still took oxygen, and our hands moved in ragged time with his breath. At some point, probably during the day, while Donny and I were at rest, Will's diaphragm would stop contracting. His lungs would never again take on air. But Will's brain and body would continue to function. Differently, that's all. In my opinion, it was better. But that was subjective. Don't get the wrong idea—vampires love the blood of humans, but —I would give up wanting to eat humans if I could. Not every vampire cared about humans, but I did. Well, some humans. And I knew there were others like me. Donny, for example.

'You never told me how you were made,' Donny asked sharply through the quiet.

I turned to Donny. I knew his origin story. It was uneventful and by-the-book, and he talked about it often. His vampire friend worked for the Department of Corrections. With the vampire population, specifically. They always put vampires with vampires and humans with humans in the prisons. It was a practical issue of safety and security. It would be too easy for a vampire guarding a human to purposely or accidentally use too much force, and a human protecting the vampire population would have to be careful indeed. Vamps so easily overpower humans, so it's a strength-based decision more than anything else...though. There's that pesky little problem of vamps being able to trance humans, too.

Donny was in his mid-twenties at the time. He was gung-ho—and unemployed. But his friend, Paul, saw Donny's valuable qualities. Don was strong and confident and would make a great guard at the Standfort Men's Prison, which was technically just outside of Standfort in a little town that no one cared about unless they were working for corrections.

Paul was with Donny one night at some nightclub on the Boardwalk when he put the idea out there. Had Donny ever considered being made a vampire? Some humans do think of it, and some don't. Some people would give their right arm to be turned, and plenty of vamps would gladly eat that right arm. But vampires can smell rank human desperation from a mile away. Those kinds of humans aren't the ones we generally allow to enter our ranks. Donny had never given it more than a cursory thought before, but when Paul said there would be work in it, well... That interested Donny because he wasn't the type of man who was happy just sitting around. He wanted to make something of himself. Donny was a work-hard, play-hard kind of guy.

Three months later, Paul held a government license that said he could turn Donny Agosti into a vampire. Paul made the turn himself, and there was nothing unusual about that.

Vampires tend to be more open than humans do when it comes to sexuality. There are plenty of gay, lesbian, and bisexual vampires, and you'd be hard-pressed to find one who thought anything of minority sexualities. Humans were becoming more accepting by the late 1990s, but vampires? They were always ahead of the curve in that respect.

However, though the element of intimacy or passion could be introduced, there is nothing inherently sexual about turning a human, and there certainly was nothing sexual in Donny's turning. The way I'd heard the story, at least. It was a practical matter, like a medical treatment. Donny told me, 'Paul just got on with it'. Then, a couple of months later, Donny, the vampire, was buttoning up his uniform for his full-time job at the correctional facility.

I put off sharing my own origin story with a question. I didn't like revisiting it. 'It's Mike, isn't it?' I asked. 'He's gotten wind that we were onto him, and he's done this to Will.'

'It does feel suspect that you found Will on the brink of death. Why didn't they finish him off? Instead, you were left with the decision: let him die or make him illegally? Either way, you get hurt, but of course, you would turn him. It feels like whoever did this wants something over you.'

Donny was right.

'Will's going to be in danger, Don. Everywhere he goes. Everything we all do from now on. What the hell are we going to do?'

'Number one, we have to get him out of here.'

'My parents' house. If it was Mike, he would never imagine I'd take Will there. Not in a million years. Though they know each other, my dad hates Mike.'

'But your dad hates vampires, too. You don't see the conflict there?'

'He won't turn us in. Familial ties have to mean something.'

Once we made the decision, we acted swiftly. Donny moved the car around the back. Will's unit backed into an alley, and the yard had laneway access. We didn't want to be seen moving what would appear to be a dead body.

I cleaned Will up, not wanting my family to see him like that. After a quick wash down, I dressed him in some clean clothing. His body was floppy in my strong arms, and I had to support his neck a few times. I'd heard once that moving someone while they underwent the turn wasn't good practice. But we were trying to save his life. I felt sure that if we stayed at Will's, someone would come looking and find us there before the day was out.

And once the sun rose, Donny and I could not help ourselves, let alone help Will.

CHAPTER
TWENTY-NINE

'You're not bringing your trouble in here, Sarina Massey,' my father said as though I was a ten-year-old girl covered in mud and holding a lizard that I wanted to keep as a pet.

Donny stepped forward. His Hanes t-shirt was mottled with blood but still appearing charming. Or was that only to me, being a vampire and all?

'Mr Massey, sorry to meet you again under these circumstances.' He held out a hand to my father, who took it unenthusiastically. 'You're our only hope right now. If you turn us away, we can't protect Will. We can't protect ourselves. Not after sunrise.'

'Come on, Tom, please, eh?' Susan Massey, my mother, pleaded with her husband. Dad wore the pants, but my mum could be persuasive when she needed to be, and soon, Dad reluctantly opened the door wide enough for us to carry Will in.

'Just today,' he said sternly. 'You leave tonight.'

The commotion woke Marinda, who came down the hall

rubbing her eyes, her Mickey Mouse pyjama set in disarray, the shorts twisted around her lower torso. When she saw the state of Will, who we'd laid down on the couch—on top of some towels Mum brought from the linen closet—she sprung into action. Marinda didn't even wait to ask questions.

'Let's set him up in my room,' Marinda said. Before long, Will lay comfortably on Marinda's bed, and I filled her, Mum and Dad in on the severity of our situation.

'We *all* need to stay here. Donny and I can't go back home tonight. It's too dangerous. I reckon it's Mike, Dad,' I said. I spoke the truth but knew it would also appeal to his dislike of the man.

'Bloody Mike. I knew that vampire was a piece of shit the moment I laid eyes on him. Where are you going to sleep? Won't you burn without special...' Dad was at a loss. He knew next to nothing about vampire needs.

Though pleased that my father seemed to accept our stay, he was right. Where would we sleep?

Marinda came up with the idea. 'The pantry!' She yelled like she was on a game show, and the winner was the first to get a correct answer. 'It'll work. You can easily tape up the cracks once you and Donny are inside.'

'That could work,' said Donny, eyeing Marinda hungrily for a split-second before turning away. He hadn't had time to eat. Neither of us had. Even so, I did not appreciate him looking that way at my sister.

It was decided. Mum's prized walk-in pantry was to be our bedroom for the night.

Mum and Dad stood beside each other. Mum was a couple of inches taller than my dad, while I was at least two inches taller than my mother. They looked like they had no idea what to do next.

'Get anything out of the pantry now that you might need

today. You won't be able to enter for anything. Not only would it let the light through, but it's dangerous to wake a sleeping vamp.'

The look on their faces wasn't one that I relished. If I had been hoping to mend the relationship, that wasn't the best way to go about it.

First, I had to move my car. It couldn't be left outside the Massey home, where someone would recognise it like a beacon screaming to everyone that Donny, Will, and I were inside. So I had to move it quickly. There were only fifteen minutes until dawn.

I drove a few suburbs over and parked near Cooree Beach. Perhaps anyone tracking us would think we had fled underwater or bedded down for the day in one of the many caves along the shoreline. The sun was rising over the horizon and already causing me a bit of an itch. I prepared to run back home to my parent's home, where I was raised and where I had not spent even one night since I was turned.

It was all just too much to contemplate. Heavy and far too hurtful. Will. Of all people. Why hadn't I turned him years ago? We wouldn't be in that mess if I had. I hung my head down, not even seeing the bitumen underneath me, as a deep gargling noise rose from my throat. It curled and curved its way into a 'no'. A big, crazy gargled, 'Nooooo,' that spread gutturally out over the sprawl of the ocean.

'Nooo,' I screamed again and again.

I smashed my fists down onto my thighs. Over and over, I screamed until my screams became sobs, and eventually, I sucked desperately for more air to cry. No tears, of course. It's not the vampire way.

Finally, I pulled myself together. I reckoned I had a good six minutes before the sun did me some damage. I stood up, prepared myself, and ran for my parents' home before anyone arrived, looking for the cause of the unrest.

CHAPTER

THIRTY

Horrified would be an apt description of my feelings when I returned to my family's home to find Donny sucking on Marinda's wrist. I tried to keep my face straight, like it was nothing. But something in my gut turned and churned, and the skin around my eyes felt prickly. Marinda saw it and rushed Donny off.

I didn't know what my problem was. Donny was hungry. Marinda worked the booths. It made sense, and what difference did it make to me? Was it because she was my sister? Their past dalliance? I packed my feelings down deep, vowing not to explore it further.

In Marinda's room, Will lay stock still on the bed. I bent down so the puff of my words reached his cheek and his breath touched mine. Those involuntary lung movements would stop very shortly.

'I'm so sorry. I'm going to make this up to you, Will. It's all going to be okay.' Then I placed an old quilt entirely over Will, head and all. He wouldn't be fully affected by the sunlight that would soon creep in around curtains and under the door. Not until he'd made the complete turn. But it would still be more comfortable for him to be covered entirely.

I caught my parents gaping at us from the doorway. My mother's eyes told me she was frightened.

'He's not dead if that's what you're worried about,' I said.

'Well, he kind of is,' Dad said.

'Okay. Kind of. Yet, as you can see, the undead still do live. Look at me. Look at Donny. Walking around, talking, holding down jobs. Living lives.'

'Spare me the speech, Sarina. I was only making a point.'

I turned away disapprovingly. He was only making a point, sure. But I was dead sick of hearing it.

Passing Marinda, she grabbed my arm and told me quietly, 'I'm sorry if I did the wrong thing. I didn't know that you liked Donny.'

'Are you insane?' I spat at her before I got over the shock of my reaction and regained control of my feelings. 'I don't. So don't worry. There's no problem here. I didn't expect it, that's all.'

Then, since I couldn't deal with the ridiculousness of the idea of my "liking" Donny, I got practical. 'You'll watch over Will, right?'

My sister nodded emphatically, her face serious. I knew I could trust her. She was young, but she had a strong heart.

'You know that Donny and I can't do anything if they come today,' I admitted.

'I know. Who did this to him?'

'Well, technically, I did, but you mean who drained him, right? I don't know for sure, and if I did, I wouldn't be sharing that info with you. You know why.' I stared at her, imploring her to be smart and not to get involved any more than I had involved her already. Substantially. 'I'll be up as soon as the sun goes down. Then we'll have Will to worry about.'

'Sar? He'll be okay, won't he?'

'I hope so. It's not a given. He'd lost a lot of blood before we arrived to find him. You don't have to worry about him rising and attacking you today. If he's going to wake, it will be after sundown, like Donny and I. Most likely a bit after us, which is good.' I'd learned that from hearing my co-workers talk one day.

'I've got this. You don't need to worry. I'll keep my trap shut and do everything I can to protect him, Sar. And you. I love you.'

'You too, li'l sis.'

'Here.' Dad pushed two rolls of gaffa tape and some scissors at me. His forehead creased with worry lines. 'You love this kid?'

'Will? Yep. We'd been together for years. Since before … well, you know. You remember Will. He's a good man. He deserves better than this. Everything I went through … he stuck with me,' I added, knowing it would be hurtful for my father to even think about it. Painful but true.

Dad held his face tight. 'Well, you two sleep well in there.' Dad couldn't deal with the feelings, so he made it sound like we were just any old guests staying in his home. In his pantry! I almost laughed but held it back. Dad and I already had trouble relating. I didn't want to stir that pot.

In the pantry, Donny and I took a roll of gaffa each and began taping up the lines of light around the French doors and up the centre, where a sliver of light would come through. Once we'd done that, we laid out the bedding Mum had left for us. It smelled the same as it did nearly a decade ago when I had lived there. You never forget the smell of home.

We settled down, then. I was relaxing into the dark, listening quietly to the sounds from the house and sensing the day's approach.

I would have preferred to stay with Will or keep him with me in the pantry. But any light reaching him wouldn't be a big issue yet. Plus, if something goes wrong, hopefully, Marinda will notice it and try to help. Whereas, once I was asleep, I would be dead for all intents and purposes. As good as. That's why vampires needed to take such care during the day. Wherever we lay down to slumber had to be secure. We couldn't risk someone untoward gaining access to us during that state.

Lying there, I got to thinking about Steve. Was Mike the cause of his disappearance and turning as well? And if so, why?

Then, from the silence came, 'Your dad's trustworthy. Right?'

'Yeah. He'll be fine.' I believed it was true. Ninety per cent, I believed it. I pushed the other 10 per cent to the dark recesses of my mind. I grimaced lightly and automatically, hoping Donny wasn't looking at me.

'I've been lucky to have accepting parents,' he said.

'Tell me more about it as I drift off,' I said, my eyes closed. I know all about it already, but drifting into a dead sleep while listening to stories was relaxing.

'Well, I discussed it with my parents after Paul suggested turning me. They weren't too happy at first. I was the first from the Italian community here to be turned.' I thought I heard a modicum of pride in his voice. 'But then they came around to the benefits. Good health, the ability to heal, strength, employment and, for the family, having a link with the new vampire community. With the government setting up feeding booths everywhere, they knew I could eat without killing or maiming anyone. That was their main worry solved, I think.'

My eyes were closed, but I knew Donny had rolled to face me. His eyes bore a hole in me from just a foot or two away.

'When I first came home to them after my turn, they were so happy to see me—'

'Wow,' I whispered. I'd heard his story, yet was surprised every time.

'Yeah, it made me love my family even more. I think they were worried something might go wrong. So when I came home a few nights later and looked healthy and happy, they were overjoyed. I think my dad was even a bit proud, to be honest. I've got a big family, of course. When my grandparents arrived from Italy in the 30s, Nonna had already had one child and was pregnant with another. Well, you can imagine that the Agosti family have grown since then. The weekend after I was turned, Dad invited the extended family so they could see how I was and get everyone on the same page. It was a big barbecue in the shed of one of our cane farms. There must have been a hundred people there. All were watching me and asking a hundred questions. Most gave me hugs and kisses and made jokes about how I couldn't eat now. That was hilarious for them, with food being such a big part of our culture.'

I was unwinding there with Donny chatting away. There was something so solid about his personality. He could act the fool, but underneath, there was someone I felt was good and glad to know. The faint traces of his aftershave wafted towards me, sweet and enticing. I turned away from him.

'After the big reveal to my family, they all took it in their stride. They considered me special and were glad to have me on their side. Not the predictable reaction for a human family when one member gets made a vampire. But there you go.'

'Did I tell you about that time Mickey got done for speeding, and he called me up like I could help him? He'd been driving near the river, along Stoney Road, and...'

My mind drifted, thinking how different our situations were. Then I couldn't hold off sleep any more. I entered into blank slumber—a beautiful, semi-permanent death.

CHAPTER
THIRTY-ONE

My eyes shot open the following evening. Donny gave a start but settled when he realised it was me tearing at the gaffa tape that had prevented daylight from reaching us.

Once the pantry doors were open, it took me two seconds to reach Marinda's bedroom. Will remained on the bed, and Marinda had pulled the blanket down to just under his chin, presumably only since darkness fell. I slowed down once I realised I hadn't missed anything.

Hugging Will, I noted his vital signs. His skin felt cool to the touch, and his breathing *had* ceased. Everything looked as fine as a human dying and turning into a vampire was supposed to look, at least, to my knowledge, being a first-time maker.

I felt a wave of relief that let my body physically relax.

When Marinda entered, I was sitting on the edge of the bed. I smiled at her.

'Everything was good with Will today. Before you ask.' She

smiled back and brushed my arm lightly. I even played him Bela Lugosi's Dead by Bauhaus to get him in the mood.'

'Oh, bloody hell,' I said under my breath. 'Can we be serious now? No one staking the place out or calling—nothing weird?'

'Nothing. But you'll have your hands full soon, won't you? From what I know about the process of turning.' Marinda lowered her voice, not wanting our parents to overhear the conversation, 'Some of the vamps I see at Grove Street talk between feeding. Do you know what you're doing?'

Her final question sounded harsh, but I knew she wasn't being nasty. The truth was, I didn't know that much about turning. How could I? I'd experienced it myself but had never turned another person. There was no class to attend. I'd planned to turn Will so I would have schooled up on the process. I would have learned from the vamps I knew and trusted what the process was and planned it out in annoying detail. But whoever was behind this had taken the choice to "be prepared" from me.

My body tensed, and I clenched my hands before realising and consciously unclenching them.

'I don't *really* know what I'm doing and Donny's never turned anyone either. But we got this far between us, and I've got to carry on with it. There's no other choice. I can't call anyone else in on this now. Too dangerous.' I turned to Marinda, who sat on a chair by the window, a tiny crinkle in her brow. With the curtain open, the moonlight highlighted her high cheekbones and left lighter streaks in her hair. Even though she often worked night shifts at the booth, Marinda looked tired after watching over Will all day.

'This didn't occur by accident,' I said. 'It's happened because I'm on to something.' I stopped myself. I mustn't involve Marinda and have her pay the price for it. 'Donny and I, we're going to fix it.'

I glanced back at Will, who lay dead still. 'He'll wake soon, though. Jeez.' I leaned my elbows on my legs and looked down at the carpet. A dust bunny wafted next to an old headband down there. Marinda was never one to keep her room spic and span. Mum and Dad used to insist I keep my room tidy, but they became more relaxed with Marinda, the baby.

I had to ensure Will was cared for after he rose, but I also had to investigate. It was the only way I could keep everyone safe. Will. Donny. My family, now. And myself. How would I manage it?

Donny came through the door stretching. His T-shirt lifted a smidge, flashing a taut stomach. He was fit. I gave him that and looked away quickly. *For crying out loud, Sarina, Will's lying here hovering on the edge of undead!*

'Marinda.' Donny tipped his head like an old-fashioned gentleman. 'Sarina.'

'Donny,' I replied begrudgingly. 'We're in deep trouble. What's our plan?'

There was no time for an answer, though. Will threw the blanket off and jumped up as though we'd been trying to bury him alive.

A strange, gargled sound came from him. The sound of anger mixed with confusion.

I rushed to his side. 'Will, it's okay. You're going to be okay. Do you remember what happened?'

'Wh...what? I don't...'

'You were taken, babe. Someone snatched you, and they drained you. Did you see who it was?'

Marinda and Donny kept back, watching. Now and then, I glanced behind me to make sure they were still there. It was a high-stakes situation, and it helped me to know I wasn't alone in it.

Will's face was pale and tinged grey, like the moon when you look at it through a telescope. It was strangled, too, and it scrunched up as his mind wrestled, trying to recall what had happened the previous night. I rubbed my hand up and down his upper arm a few times. He didn't seem to notice.

'You were at home last night. Then someone came and attacked you. Or maybe you were out somewhere and were snatched? You were taken to a place called The Red Line. Do you remember?'

His eyes opened so widely and quickly that the whites surrounded the deep brown of his irises for a moment.

'He remembers,' said Donny quietly.

'He...he.' Will looked at me, his mouth grimacing, his eyes hurt.

'So it was a male. You got mixed up in something, babe. I'm going to help you.'

'Help me? I remember. It was because of you. That's what he said.'

Hearing those words was like a punch to the face, but I had to remain focused. 'Who, Will?'

Donny got down on his knees and pleaded with Will. 'We can help you, mate.'

Will glanced at Donny, confused for a moment, then began examining his hands, looking at both sides like he couldn't believe it. They looked pale and grey like his face. He would need to feed very soon.

'Do I need a hospital? I need to go to the hospital.'

'No hospitals! We're going to take care of you here. Me, and Marinda and Donny.'

'But he bit me. He...he...'

'I know.' I bowed my head for a moment and took a deep

breath. I had to be strong—no time to fall apart. I didn't have time to baby him, either.

'The thing is,' I continued, 'the hospital can't help you now. Will?' I couldn't be sure he even realised he'd been turned.

He looked up at me like a confused child.

'You were nearly dead when Donny and I found you at your unit last night. You wouldn't have survived.'

'But I *did* survive.'

'Yes.' I moved my position awkwardly as I tried to think of what to say next. 'You only survived because...'

'I'm okay now. I made it.'

'Well, you...you were this close to death, Will.' I placed my index finger and my thumb together.

'You,' Will said finally, the word like a sharp slap. 'You!' he boomed.

'You would have died, Will. I had a choice to let you die or to make you a vampire. Can you understand that?' I pleaded with him using my eyes, but the whites of his eyes flashed again.

Will screamed. 'You let him eat me, and then you made me a vampire!'

CHAPTER
THIRTY-TWO

Footsteps rushed toward Marinda's bedroom. It was Mum and Dad.

Great. It was the very worst moment of my life, and it was so great that everyone was getting involved.

Will's anger had bubbled over, and I *had* to make him understand.

'Please go,' I said to my mum and dad. 'I'm sorry for the disturbance, but I've got this.'

'Doesn't sound like it...' I heard Dad mumble, but I could tell he was walking back up the hall because his grumbling faded.

'Okay,' I said, keeping eye contact with Will. 'I need you to listen to me. You may be angry with me—though I did not "let" anyone eat you. None of that's important right now. Maybe you hate me.' I shrugged. 'You're in a precarious position. We all are. They could come for us all. I need you to put your feelings aside now. Was it Mike who took you? My boss from After Dark. Did he drain you?'

Will settled down a little. The turn was emotional for most

vampires. I hoped Will's feelings would level out at sooner rather than later.

'Mike? I remember him,' Will said.

'From last night?'

'I don't know.' Will was looking distracted now and kept looking over at Marinda. I knew what that meant, and I knew I had to do something, or the whole situation would bubble right over. If it came to that, I might be unable to rein him in. New vamps were temperamental and unpredictable. I knew that much.

'We have to get him somewhere he can feed,' I told Marinda and Donny, who remained blocking the door.

A guttural growl came from his lips. It was unnerving— and I was used to vampires. Of course, I wasn't "used to" my boyfriend of so many years becoming a vamp and growling because he wanted to eat my sister. That part was new. And I wasn't a fan of it.

'We can't take him to a booth. He'll get caught. We all will,' I said to anyone who was listening.

'I can do it,' Marinda replied.

I looked at her and shook my head. At that point, I was beyond jealousy, but my sister, with her beautiful soul, shouldn't have been placed in that position. I did know that the first feed could be rough on the human. New vampires were hungry to the core, and you had to be careful with them. They could tear a person apart without the intent to hurt them.

'What other options are there?' Donny asked.

'Well ... we could ... you must know someone we could call in?'

'Why me? If you don't know anyone.' Donny scoffed at me.

Marinda began, 'I can do thi—'

But in one second, Will skipped over to the opposite side of the bed. He circumvented it—as well as Donny and I—and attached himself to Marinda's neck.

By the time Donny and I turned around, all we could do was hold on to Will to ensure he didn't drag Marinda down onto the floor and take every drop of life-blood she had.

Will's body shook with each gulp. Dribbles of rich red droplets plopped to the surrounding floor. Mum and Dad would be double pissed off that I'd allowed Marinda to be a meal and ruined the carpet.

'I'm okay,' Marinda whispered. 'Just don't leave me.'

I nodded and held her eye contact, occasionally checking Will. After a few minutes, I noticed his skin taking on a delicate pink hue. Meanwhile, Marinda's cheeks were losing their colour. It was time for Will to stop.

'Will, you need to disengage now. Will!'

Donny gave me a nod. We both knew what to do. We previously removed a vampire or two from humans in our work. We'd removed humans from vampires, too. It happened less often and usually involved a vampire who'd been silvered. Silver is vampire kryptonite. Occasionally, rather than acting in self-defence, a human might be so desperate to become a vampire that they try to turn themselves. A strange situation indeed.

We moved forward and took hold of Will's head and hair, with one hand each while using the other to wrench his mouth from Marinda's neck by wedging our fingers into the sides of it.

Pulling him back sharply, we threw Will to the bed and stood firm between him and Marinda. Will would never wish harm on Marinda. But instincts kicking in during the turn could override moral character, like being an adolescent again —immature brains. We just needed to keep him *and* Marinda safe ...

Shit, I thought. We needed to keep us all safe. But how?

Will jumped to the bed and crouched, wobbling slightly as he balanced there on the innerspring mattress. He looked ferocious, and though he might come at us at any moment, I felt an attraction to him like I'd never felt before. I could see the pulse of his carotid artery from where I stood. With Marinda's blood, he looked strong and healthy—clearly, he felt it. His blood pressure was perfect. Will's mind would take longer to catch up, however.

'Is everything okay in there?' Dad yelled from the kitchen, and I appreciated that he and Mum hadn't come running in to see what the new commotion was about. It wouldn't have helped the situation.

'We're fine, Dad. Stay where you are.'

'Well, it doesn't sound fine,' Mum called then.

'Well, obviously, it's a difficult situation. But we're handling it. Okay?'

'What about Marinda? Is she okay?'

'Yes, Dad,' Marinda yelled. 'I'm fine.'

Oops. I'd forgotten about poor Marinda. I told Will, 'Calm down and don't touch Marinda again.' Then I turned to help Marinda.

'Did I hurt her?' Will spoke suddenly with such a restrained tone that I immediately glanced back at him.

'She'll be fine,' I said. 'She let you eat from her.' Well, she would have if he had waited long enough. It was hardly the time to have that discussion, so I told him, 'Which you needed, but now is the time to leave her alone and let her restore her strength.'

'Of course,' he said, as though he were regular Will again. I couldn't trust it, though. Not at all.

I began cleaning Marinda up by squeezing blood from my finger to close her neck wounds. The skin on my finger was already punctured from removing Will a minute earlier. It took only a little encouragement to get my blood flowing again.

After I healed Marinda, I also used my blood on Donny's fingers, and he closed the wound on my finger. The rub with healing vampires was that it couldn't be *your* blood. It was irritating at times, but sociologists were already designing studies based on theories of it being an evolutionary process to promote contact between vampires. To encourage them to live in groups rather than as lonely, solitary creatures on the fringes of society.

Marinda looked drawn and needed recovery, so I sent her to rest on the couch. She would be the human in the house most capable of knowing how to care for herself after allowing a vamp to feed on her, despite there being nothing quite like the hunger of a "new" vamp.

We had to make a plan—just Donny, Will, and me.

'Don, my gut feeling is it's Mike. I've got to go after him. If I don't, he's going to come for us. Our families. You feel it, too, right?'

Donny moved a bit closer to me and leaned in. 'What are we gonna do with Baby?' He made irritating air quotes around "baby".

I wasn't sure if he was referring to Will being a baby vamp —which would make sense—or teasing me about my pet name for Will—which seemed more likely for Don. But I didn't incline to retort.

'I don't know,' I said, panic rising.

'I do. Let me call Lindsay. She might be able to help. After all, she's got Steve somewhere around and survived it.'

'You would do that? With your precious Lindsay?' I immediately regretted voicing that, but it was too late.

Donny gave me a strange look. 'I'll go and call them.'

Will sat on the bed, bedraggled. Should I put him in the

shower? I stretched over to touch his shoulder, but he turned and snarled at me as I reached. His fangs gleamed. Though I recoiled fast enough to miss the two points, they were gorgeous, sharp as needles near the tips.

I was both horrified and in awe of Will's out-of-control instincts. Vampirism has its downsides, but it can be breathtaking. The vigour, the power—those teeth that could sheath on will. Well, most of the time. There were other aspects, too. Will's skin was taking on a much smoother appearance, and he was already faster than any human being that had ever lived.

Will calmed again, and I sat down beside him on the bed. I gently took his hand. He neither participated nor prevented me.

'Will, I'm sorry that I had to do this. I mean, I know we decided on it. But I'm sorry it happened this way. It's not what I wanted. I should have decided earlier so we could control the event and make it...pleasant.'

He stared at a wicker basket on the floor. I heard a light grunt.

'Right now, I need you to rally, babe.' With my fingers on his chin, I turned his face toward me. 'Whatever feelings you might have about what happened—and about your new state —I need you to put them aside for me. Can you do that?'

Complete silence was the answer. Perturbing.

I had to press the other issue as well. I needed to know. 'Mike drained you, right?'

'Mike,' Will replied, but his face looked shocked, as though just hearing the name was insulting. I left it at that, not wanting to upset or stir him further.

Night had fallen. Anything could happen. A posse of vampires could arrive at my parents' home. For all we knew, they were kitted up and piling into a truck as we sat there. This decision of mine not to let the investigation go was now endangering everyone I cared about.

'I know you'll do the right thing, Will.' I stood up and made a barrier across the door with my hand. Just in case Will, my baby vamp, wanted to get out and explore the world that night. The last thing we needed.

'Don?' I waited. 'Donny! Anything?' I asked, peering out and down the hallway.

CHAPTER

THIRTY-THREE

onny put his head around the corner from the kitchen to look up the hall at me, my head poking out of Marinda's bedroom door. He had Mum and Dad's mustard-coloured wall phone to his ear, and he put a finger to his lip to tell me to hush down. He was still trying to work it all out.

At that point, Will began to arc up, shaking out his limbs like a professional swimmer warming up.

I did *not* like that at all. It had all the hallmarks of deep and worrying trouble with a capital T.

'Will?' I said, drawing out his name to give it more meaning. 'Please stay calm.'

He stood up, full of beans, and looked hard at me. God damn, he looked terrific. It wasn't helpful to think about how damn hot he looked. But it *was* honest.

'I need to go outside.'

'Nope,' I said. 'Wrong. You don't, and you mustn't. It's too risky for you to run off right now. What about Marinda and my parents? Do you think whoever did this will just let them go? Donny. Me, Will?'

He started jumping up and down like he was in a mosh pit at a rock concert. I knew what was happening. Vampire blood was pumping hard around his body, and he was full of nervous, if pleasurable, energy. He was enjoying the feel of his new body. His new life.

'Donny! I'm going to need help here,' I called. But it was Marinda I heard coming down the hall.

Still at the door, I put my hand out towards her. 'No. Not you.'

'Coming,' called Donny. He reached Marinda's door before I'd finished processing his reply. When I said vampires are fast, I wasn't mucking around.

'Hold the door.' Leaving Donny as sentry, I found Marinda's timber jewellery box with its bright blue velvet lining. I scrabbled around inside it until I felt a pain in my hand and pulled away. Scanning the room, I saw what I needed—a scarf draped on a chair alongside dirty clothes that perhaps Marinda had worn the day before. I wrapped the scarf around my hand and took a necklace from the jewellery box. The chain was thick and silver and had a pendant with embedded turquoise hanging from it.

Donny watched me and nodded as I called out to Marinda, 'Okay, now we need you.'

Will continued with his warm-up. The spectacle was amusing—or it would have been if I'd had time to stop and enjoy the experience with him. We should have been out in the rainforest or some other place where we were alone, where Will could run free with little chance of running into humans that he could harm.

I also felt dreadful about what I was about to do. I *really* did.

Donny was still in the doorway, watching. He knew the plan without me telling him and was ready to go.

'Is Lindsay coming?'

'Yep. And Steve,' said Donny.

'Steve, hey? Good.' I bent under Donny's arm to whisper to Marinda, who had been waiting there, looking confused. Ten seconds later, we put my plan into action.

Donny and I ran at Will, flipping him onto the bed. His teeth made a show as he turned his head this way and that, trying to bite us.

'I'm sorry, babe. So sorry. You'll understand later.' Then I yelled, 'Okay.'

Marinda raced in from the doorway with the necklace in hand. Reaching over the struggling Will, she tried to wrap the chain around his neck. It was hard going with how he thrashed, but eventually she managed it. Will groaned, and his body slowed right down.

'More!' I tipped my head towards my sister, who raced for the jewellery box. There was light clinking of metals before she came back with three rings. Will lay still then, and it was easy enough for Marinda to put the rings on his fingers.

I felt despicable, but we created a zonked-out creature we could control by doing that to him. It was in all our best interests, even Will's. We did what we had to. Donny and I turned Will on his back to ensure we controlled the situation. We tied his hands stretched out onto the bed head using Marinda's scarves. He was unlikely to remove the rings, let alone the necklace, while silvered and tied like that.

Silver caused pain at the site it touched and made vampires feel ill. It's a bit like having a horrendous stomach ache. Will certainly wouldn't be able to fight Donny and me with those four silver items touching him. One human, maybe. But vampires, no.

Sales of quality silver jewellery had gone through the roof once its effects on vampires became public knowledge. Everyone, even the gold set, started wearing at least one or two pieces of silver, hoping it would keep them safe. The government had to legislate against people using silver to attack vampires, too, unless it was in self-defence.

I kneeled on the bed to see Will's face. 'I'm so sorry,' I told him, but his eyes burned a hole through me. He was beyond angry, and it gave me, a cold-blooded creature, a chill.

I had to admit I would be pissed off, too. I'd been silvered twice. Once on the job by some little pipsqueak that hated vamps. That one had underestimated my strength. But after fighting him off that night, I did the right thing and reported the incident to the police.

The other time was during one of my extracurriculars. Once the bloke realised I was a vampire, he turned on me, and I was unlucky that he was wealthy. The candlestick he reached for and whacked me in the face with was silver, or at least silver-plated. It burnt my face and nearly caused a complete loss for me. Ultimately, I overcame him, but the experience taught me not to be complacent.

A car pulled up outside. With a short commotion at the front door, Lindsay and Steve soon appeared at Marinda's bedroom door. Lindsay's little Rachel cut bounced about, and I finally got my first look at Steve. The centre of all the trouble. I'd imagined him from his photograph and descriptions as more slight than what he was. Well-built was a more apt description. He should be able to look after Will, I thought.

Marinda backed out of the room and disappeared. Smart cookie.

The introductions were brief. We weren't in a position for a big "get to know each other" session. I let Donny speak to Lindsay and Steve while I tried to update Will on the plan.

'Will. I need you to listen and listen well. You're going with Donny's friend Lindsay and the boy who's a vampire now. His name's Steve. They're going to look after you while you settle into the change. Do you understand me?'

'Take it off,' Will said, his face a tragic mix of anger and nausea.

'You know I can't remove the silver. We've put that on for everyone's safety. Yours included.'

His state of mind continued to err on the side of "the world is against me" and, if I was to give my opinion, carried a solid smattering of "just let me kill someone".

I leaned in quickly and touched my lips to his. I was trying something out and sensed an immediate change in him. His focus turned to me. I had stirred his passion, just as I'd thought I would. I remembered what that was like early on. All instincts, desires and stamina, with little sense. It was a ploy, and while I was ashamed to have used it, it had the desired effect. Will's battle expression died down, and fortunately, as I stepped away from him with my hand up to tell him to wait, he sank into quiet.

Steve and Lindsay stood talking with Donny. I could see them as a couple. Steve was around 5'6", handsome, solid, and cheeky. In opposition, yet fitting perfectly, Lindsay was in a pint-sized, cute and friendly package.

When I was human, and before Will, I'd dated a few people. That was back when vampires lived only in book series by Anne Rice and movies like Nosferatu and Dracula—all of which I ate up.

My boyfriends had run the gamut from sports jock to funny man. I had been searching for "my type", or I didn't have one. But then I met Will. When I saw him, I knew he was it. Before I was turned, anyway. Back then, I saw our fantastic life ahead of us as two humans. Having fun in our youth then, I assumed, an engagement, marriage, and eventually children. There was an understanding between us when we met. Like we naturally got each other. Is that love? It was to me.

I turned my gaze to Donny, the only other man I had that much to do with besides Will. And Mike, as my boss. Donny and I had never dated. I'd always been with Will. But as the thought of Donny as a possible romantic partner snuck into my head, I sniggered suddenly, causing Don, Lindsay, and Steve to turn and look at me.

'Sorry,' I said stupidly. 'It's just the situation, you know? What a mess!' I hoped they would join me in scoffing at the dreadful set of circumstances that we'd all found ourselves in. Fortunately, they did just that. Donny offered a chuckle.

Good save.

Yet there was a little stabbing feeling like I'd been unkind and wished to take it all back.

I sat down again on the bed beside Will and studied the boy more. Steve Gorman. No doubt it was a sign of my age— human, with my few vamp years added on—that I continued to think of him as a boy. He was a grown man and much more of a man than I'd expected. But he was still young. In university and finding his feet as an adult. At least he had been. Now, he would have to find his feet as a vampire, just as Will would. Yet Steve looked calm and entirely in control of his situation. That surprised me, given the short time he'd had between his abduction and turning.

Perhaps Lindsay's support was what had helped him. That gave me even more optimism that they could do their best looking after Will.

I turned to Will. 'You must not try to eat from Lindsay. Do you understand?'

He looked vaguely at me. I shook his arm, imploring him.

'You mustn't. You'll get life-blood, but it has to be from the right person at the right time. Understand?'

He nodded, and I hoped that Lindsay and Steve's support would be precisely what he needed. The thought of him having them to guide him made me feel less panicky and regretful that it wouldn't be me there—as it should have been. But I had to take care of things that couldn't wait.

THIRTY-FOUR

I was placing a ton of trust in Lindsay and Steve. 'You're sure they're reliable, right?' I needled Donny after the pair had left with the love of my life in tow.

'I'd bet my teeth on it,' said Donny, flashing me a quick grin before turning back to watch the road. 'Well, Lindsay, anyway.'

Great.

'I'm surprised you want to have anything to do with Steve since he's, you know, with Lindsay.'

Donny stopped still and looked me in the eye. 'What do you think's going on here, Sarina Massey? I care about Lindsay, but that ship sailed a long time ago. I'm not trying to get back with her, and I'm not trying to prevent her from living her life.'

My mind worked quickly, trying to play catch-up before I nodded. Then my next question came, 'Why do you think Will won't tell me who drained him?'

'Eh, Will,' Donny mumbled. 'You know what it's like, Sar. Most vampires made by force have that weird love-hate thing going on with their makers.'

Well, he was right about that.

'Even though technically *you* did the turning, someone else was responsible for setting it off, and he doesn't want to dob in the vamp that did it for whatever reason.'

'Yeah, but what reason?'

'I dunno, but it can happen like this occasionally. Maybe something innate, like a chemical in his brain. Plus, the bloke's probably traumatised.'

'But I made him.'

'I know, love. I know. And usually, that's where the key's found. But in this case, a lot is going on. He wanted to be turned but that doesn't mean he'll just accept having been abducted and attacked. Feelings are complex, Sar. You know that.'

His comment made my eyes sting.

Stupid Donny, talking sense. There *were* complications in this case, even though I didn't want there to be.

After picking up his car from home, Donny drove us to the police station near The Red Line. I had contacted Raquel Gorman as soon as Steve and Lindsay left with Will. I was placing a lot of trust in her, but nothing she said during our phone call gave me cause for suspicion. We were told to meet at the station because a raid was organised for The Red Line. Our attendance would be welcomed, Gorman told me. When I asked about Mike, she assured me the operation was secret and that he would be picked up when her forces kicked off at The Red Line.

Despite that, Donny and I remained suitably nervous. So much was at stake. I noted Donny's sideways glances whenever a car pulled up next to us. Plus, he was checking the rearview mirror constantly. There were many ways this manoeuvre could go sideways, and our being ambushed and taken out was just one of them.

I yawned. Yes, vampires yawn. It hadn't been an ideal sleep

with Donny and me cramped together in Mum and Dad's pantry. I had woken a dozen times, which is unusual for vampires. Overall, we tend to have fewer sleep problems than humans. Our sleep is naturally solid. Yet that night, each time I woke, it took me a few minutes to get back to sleep. At one point, I reached out to Donny just to feel someone there. He was sleeping like the dead, his thick chest solid underneath my palm. I pulled my hand back quickly. Who was I to touch him like that while he slept? Then I drifted back to sleep.

After Will had driven away with his new minders, Donny and I cleaned up at Mum and Dad's. As best we could. The carpet would never be the same, and I would replace it for them after the drama settled. But we removed all the tape from the pantry, packed the bedding, then took to Marinda's deodorant sprays and used her comb and brush. I looked through her makeup for some dark red lipstick, my shade. But Marinda preferred subtle shades. I eventually settled on a neutral, matte colour. I was grasping for anything that might make me feel normal.

When Donny pulled into a parking spot around the corner from the police station, he switched off the ignition and looked at me.

'What?' I said.

'This is big, Sarina.'

'I know, Don. I know. Look—'

'Stop. You don't have to.'

'No, I do,' I said. 'I can't thank you enough for getting on board with this. You didn't have to.'

'Well, it is my job.'

We both chuckled. It *was* his job. And mine.

'You still didn't have to,' I said, finally. 'We both know it's dangerous and to chicken out would have been easy. You're a good friend.'

'I really am.' He grinned stupidly at me.

'Seriously. I appreciate it, Don. I need you to know that.'

'Why're you getting all serious, Sarina? We're gonna be fine. Quit acting like this is the end, woman.'

I opened my arms out towards him. It took him a second to work out what I was doing. It wasn't like we hugged each other regularly. I wasn't sure we'd ever displayed that type of affection in all the years we'd worked together. But a bad feeling was brewing inside me about the night ahead, and I wanted to get things right with him before we proceeded.

Holding each other tightly for a few seconds, I smelled Marinda's deodorant underneath the odour of a vampire male —Donny smell. His dark hair scratched my face. I went to pull back, but he held on for half a second more before loosening his grip.

'I'm beginning to think you've got a crush on me, Sarina Massey.' Well, that did the trick. I pushed him away swiftly.

'As if.'

But had I wanted to continue that hug? Or had I ended it because I thought I should?

Donny didn't even smile like he usually would. 'You're not coming with me to The Red Line, are you?' he said solemnly.

'No.'

We let a long silence hang between us. It was ripe with worry, fear, and just a thin thread of hope.

'It's Mike. Isn't it? We can work quickly together. I'll go with you. We can get in before Mayor Gorman's forces get there. You and me. The dynamic duo. As always.'

'Uh-uh. I've got this. I don't want to drag you down with me. I've got to quickly, though.'

It would only take the Mayor's trusted force members an hour or two to get organised and on their way. I had to get Mike first.

'I get why you wanna do this, Sarina, but you need backup. If he's the one who did this to Will, imagine what he'll do to you if he gets the chance.'

'You think I don't know?' I snapped. 'I know more than anyone—and if? Who else is responsible? We saw Mike drag Will into that hellhole.' I felt a little twinge around my incisors, like they wanted to pop out and have their say about the situation. I stifled it. There would be a time for that.

Donny put his hands up. He was giving up on it. I won. Then he leaned over and kissed me on the forehead. It was gentle and sweet and made me think of another way Donny and I might relate to each other. But that wasn't how things were. That's not who Donny was to me. I had Will, and my life was planned out before me, especially with Will becoming vampire.

'I want to see you alive and kicking later tonight.'

'You got it,' I said, giving him a nod. Then I got out of the car and gunned it on foot towards Mike's.

On the way there, my muscle fibres worked double-time, my blood pumping intensely as my mind wrestled itself.

I'm going to capture him. Please do not take him out. Donny'll know if you do that. They'll all work it out. You've got to be smart about this.

But he needs to die. He took Will's life away. But I've got to stay in control. I can do it. Focus. FOCUS.

But inside, I had that twitchy feeling bubbling. The feeling I get when I've got someone evil in my sights. When I've done my digging around and watched them. The surety that it will happen. It builds up, like pressure.

I had two very different ways I could go, and as I approached his house, dark with the waning moon hanging above, I already knew how it would go.

THIRTY-FIVE

In the shadowy interior of Mike's living room, I waited. The house was empty when I arrived, raising concern that perhaps Mike had realised the danger. Had he moved to a safe place with his human wife, Jenny, and their two adopted children? Mike was one of the first vampires in Australia to be granted adoption rights. You had to be with a human partner and jump through some hoops, but he'd managed it.

I was pleased Jenny and the kids weren't there, of course. It could have gotten complicated otherwise. I certainly didn't want her or those children harmed or embroiled in this. I'd met Jenny many times at After Dark Christmas parties, and I had no beef with her besides her taste in men.

Though I had refused for several years to take the plunge and make Will a vampire, it was uncommon for relationships between humans and vampires to drag on long without the issue of "turning" raising its head. Without it, relationships would usually fizzle under the pressure of human ageing. Not pleasant, but it was what it was. Still, Mike and his human seemed to have succeeded in it. I decided I should question him about that to learn what I could. Before I did, well … whatever to him. Obliterating him in revenge, perhaps?

How do you make it work? Is it a struggle? Why doesn't Jenny want to be turned? Or does she? How do you refrain from eating her and the kids when you get superhungry? I had so many questions.

In the quiet of their home, there was time to poke around. It felt as though Mike was suffering from nostalgia. Vestiges of humanity lay everywhere—photo albums from the 70s and 80s, framed family pictures, a sunhat hanging by the door. But when I looked closer, I saw that the connections were more from Jenny's side. After all, Mike was nearly a century old, and his immediate family, from before the turn, would be long passed.

I wondered if my apartment would have looked similar if I had moved Will in with me without turning him. Reaching up, I carefully took a plaque off the wall for closer inspection—an award from the Standfordt Business Association. My conversation with my father came to mind. What was it with Mike and his ridiculous involvement in that association? He must *really* have wanted to blend in with the humans for some reason. Did it help Mike to appear "innocent" and "normal" by involving himself in human activities? Or was he up to something else?

After half an hour, voices carried from down the street. Two voices. It didn't bode well that Mike wasn't alone. I was already up for a vampire-on-vampire fight—and against a male, no less. There was no guarantee I would come out the victor. But I had to try. I owed it to Will.

My skin prickled with the possibility that refusing Donny's help was a mistake.

Despite a light rain falling, it only took me a moment to smell that the second person was human. That was better. I wouldn't take long to remove a human from the fray. However, it wouldn't be ideal for the human.

Crouching still behind the couch, I couldn't be seen when the front door opened. I listened.

The human was talking with Mike with such a familiar baritone rasp and, once I thought about it, a familiar smell. My blood pressure rose sharply, and I felt off balance. It was a voice I'd heard my entire life.

It can't be.

'You have to let her go. You can't do this to me. After everything I've done for you! I've been loyal. I did everything you asked of me,' opined the human. 'I helped you get in with the Association, didn't I? Helped you put all yer tentacles through everything. Just like you wanted.'

'This isn't personal, and you know it. Grow up, Tom,' came Mike's reply.

'But there has to be another way. Enough damage has been done already,' I heard my father tell Mike—my own father. 'You said if I did what you told me, Sarina would be okay! Ya, power-hungry bastard!'

That answered my question about why Mike was so involved in the Standfort Business Association. Mike was more ambitious than I'd imagined.

'Shut it!' Mike said abruptly.

He sensed me there. God damn, I mouthed.

Could the situation be any worse?

I rushed for the hall and pushed myself flat against the side of a bookshelf as Mike entered the living room while my father remained on the small porch, peering inside. Observing them, I felt a hideous, sick feeling well in my gut that my father should be involved in it all.

What has he gone and done?

Mike's eyes searched the room, and he smelled the air as he

went. There was no need to turn the light to see. His vampire sight was excellent. Meanwhile, I hoped that having used Marinda's deodorant might help hide my identity for the time being, though deep down, I knew I was kidding myself.

My father, still by the front door, flapped his hand against the inside wall, searching for the light switch. He was blind in the dark, but I could see him. The whites of his eyes shone like beacons, letting us all know he was scared witless.

'Sarina!' Mike called out.

Dammit!

Mike knew, of course. He would have smelled me early. But that was the exact moment Dad realised, and his face changed in the dim light just before he found the switch.

Humans could be so hopeless. From my spot beside the bookshelf, I saw Dad's face scrunch up like he'd just heard the worst news of his life. Crinkling under the weight of the realisation that his daughter had listened to his conversation with Mike and now knew he was involved. His flesh and blood was now in terrible danger, and he had helped create the situation in some way I had yet to ascertain. Now, he was powerless to prevent it.

'Sar-in-ahh!' Mike called.

I stepped out of the shadow of the hall bookcase toward the lounge, but my dad still couldn't see me. He was standing at the door, blinking his eyes in response to the sudden flush of light.

'What in hell have you done, Dad?' I should have gone straight for Mike, but my emotions got better. I felt gutted.

'I'm sorry, Sarina. I didn't know.'

'You stupid little girl.' Mike looked smugly at me. Sprinkles of rain dotted his face his and hair. He used his hand to push back a lock of hair that flopped in his forehead's centre, perhaps heavy with moisture. 'Come on. I'm ready.'

'You. You!' My voice roared at him.

We were standing in a triangle with a few metres between us.

Dad started, 'You don't know how sorry I a—'

'For what, though? Just how deep are you in this?'

'It's bad, sweetie. It's so bad. But I did it for you.' His eyes were red.

'You have no idea.' Mike laughed.

Addressing my father, I asked, 'What do you mean you did it for me?'

'Mike said he was going to ruin your career, Sarina. Or worse! He said if I didn't do what he told me—'

'What did he tell you to do?' I stared my father down.

'To stay quiet. When I found out he was connected to that place. The Red Line. Plus, he was getting others in the Association to do his bidding. I couldn't abide by that, Sarina. I couldn't! But then he said you were done if I put a step wrong. I didn't know what you do at work, but I know it's your career. It keeps you with a roof over your head. I didn't want you to be destitute or for Mike to harm you.'

I thought I saw Dad's spirit crumble entirely then, but my dad still had the smarts to stay by the door. Would he run for it and leave me to deal with Mike?

'Go on. Ask him,' Mike said, gesturing his head towards my father. 'I know you're thinking about it.'

'You shut the hell up. Stay back over there.' I pointed at Mike as the muscles in my legs quivered in readiness. I was thinking about it, though. Was the love of my life now a vampire because of something my father had done?'

Wrinkles formed along Mike's chin and next to his eyes as he laughed at me.

For a moment, I couldn't decide what to do. I looked back

and forth between the two of them. My head told me to get on Mike immediately, but my heart focused on Dad.

Finally, I cracked. 'Did you have anything to do with Will's turning?' My eyes bore into my father's.

He looked desperate and told me, 'Not knowingly, Sar. I didn't know this was going to happen. I only found out after you brought him—'

'For fuck's sake, Dad. Shut up. Just shut up!' Dad couldn't get anything right. Hadn't he done enough without telling Mike where I'd taken Will after I saved him from dying? Not only was my dad involved with the shadiest of vampires, but he was terminally naïve at best and, more likely, a complete and utter idiot.

'He's gone, Mike. You won't find him now,' I hissed in Mike's direction. I was getting frantic.

Mike scoffed at me.

My muscles continued tensing in preparation for an inevitable fight. 'I will kill you myself if you had anything directly to do with what happened to Will!' I screamed at Dad.

'I swear I didn't know. I swear it.'

'Oh, bullshit,' came Mike's smarmy voice again. 'He knew enough, trust me.'

It was my turn to scoff in Mike's direction. Heartily. As if I would trust him! That ship had sailed.

Dad started up again. 'That's not true. I would never, Sarina.'

'Two grown liars bleating at me.' I looked back and forth between the two of them, my rage about to spill over. Then, without warning, I turned and launched myself at Mike.

CHAPTER

THIRTY-SIX

Mike grabbed me by the neck as I flew at him, my hands grasping at him and my teeth bared. It took only a second to remove the grip of one of his hands. Then, I could punch him squarely in the face. That dislodged his second hand. He stumbled back a couple of feet while I re-launched my fist, but he was too quick and grabbed my wrist mid-punch.

I stepped back and swung, pulling him down over me as we tumbled to the floor. Wrestling, I took a bite of his shoulder, tearing through his cream button-up and removing some flesh. He was using both hands on one of my arms, trying to break it. Unsuccessful, we finally parted for a second. I used the moment to jump into a standing position.

Mike lunged for me again, throwing me against the wall with greater strength. It shook down a picture hanging there and set the hall bookcase to a wobble. A few seconds later, the shelf crashed across the hall diagonally, leaving a triangular tunnel underneath.

As I rested against the wall, Mike grabbed my leg and

yanked me towards him. I kicked out, toppling him backwards and took the opportunity to get defensive by crawling underneath the overturned bookshelf. I hoped I could see the situation more clearly from the other side.

But I wasn't quick enough. Mike used his body as a weapon by making himself a ball and coming down hard on me. I didn't breathe, so winding wasn't the problem, but I was left incapacitated for a few seconds. It gave Mike time to drag me out towards him again.

As I tried to recover from the pounding, he sank his teeth into my arm, chest, and neck. Blood gushed, particularly from the neck wound. Out of instinct, I reached for it and applied pressure, the blood slippery and continuing to ooze from the ragged punctures. My hand kept slipping, and Mike kept biting.

Rubbing the wetness from my hands quickly onto my pants, I gave Mike some back. Biting him again, I turned my head sharply to tear at his flesh. It worked. He moved up and off me in a flash.

I stood up again, setting my feet in boxer position, shoulder width apart, feet flat, and raising my fisted hands. I was ready.

Mike was up, too. We squared off, stepping around each other a few times before I caught him by surprise with an agile kick to his head. A thwack followed the solid thump as his head bent back and hit the wall. His face flushed with crimson. Teeth bared at me through a raging grimace as his hand reached me.

But I moved quickly, spinning my other leg at him, aiming high again.

That time, Mike anticipated the move and transferred his weight to his other foot, causing me to miss him altogether. He gripped my shirt and pulled it, so we both fell over the back of the couch and onto its cushions, coming to a standstill on the floor.

Mike was underneath, which couldn't have worked out better for me. I squashed my hands into his face, twisting and twisting until his face turned toward the floor. I straddled him and moved my legs down to grip his. Again, I bent his head further and further.

Twisting, twisting, until ... snap.

Mike's body was motionless on the faded living room rug. Aside from his eyes flicking from side to side, looking for a way out. If I didn't finish the job, he would soon recover enough to get up and come for me again. I rushed to the kitchen, passing Dad at the front door and scowling at him as he stood wide-eyed and white as a ghost.

Taking a large knife from a timber kitchen block, I returned and straddled Mike again. I turned his face towards me since he was unable to do it. I wanted him to see me.

'You do—don't think...' He stopped his slurred sentence to look at me long before continuing. 'That this is it. Do you?'

'Oh, this *is* it, you whingeing little speck of dust vampire. This is the end of the line for you. Whatever you've been up to, dodgy dealings and threatening Standfort citizens. Well, you picked on the wrong man when you targeted Will. Hell, you picked on the wrong man in turning Steve Gorman.' I cackled with laughter.

It was deeply satisfying to know that Mike had given Donny and I, his best detectives, the case to find Steve, but we'd turned it around and found out about him instead. Of course, we would take this to the very end and solve it. We always did. If Mike had ever entertained the thought that I wouldn't take this investigation to its endpoint, then his underestimation of me was the icing on my hate cake.

Mike tried to laugh, but it was a broken-up choke as he lay

on the red carpet, his skin pale against it, his—and my own—blood blending with it.

'If I had one ... just one w-wish,' he said, swallowing hard. 'It'd be to see your face when you find out the truth. You really think this e ... ends with me?'

It was an odd wish, considering he lay almost dead on the floor. But it rang a small alarm bell for me. I didn't doubt that was his point, but was there anything in it? Or was he toying with me?

He had no power at that moment. I'd broken his neck, and that would take time to heal—though it *would* heal. It was only a matter of time. And there I was, on top of him, a knife sitting beside me on the coffee table, ready. Mike only had words. He could only sow the seeds of doubt to mess with me, which was the most likely explanation.

But what if it's something more?

I checked for my father, but he wasn't by the door. I scanned the room and couldn't see him, though I sensed he wasn't far. There was a scrape outside. He was hiding on the entrance porch, probably. I was confident he wouldn't try to save Mike or harm me.

I turned back to Mike. Sad little Mike.

'Seems like I'm the boss now,' I said. 'Whatever you did, you cheap waste of space. I own you now, and you're about to lose your immortality.'

Mike pursed his lips, and though he couldn't nod, a flutter in his chin suggested acceptance.

Letting go of his head, it flopped. I took the knife in both hands, held it over his chest and bore it down with all the force I had.

CHAPTER
THIRTY-SEVEN

A gulp of horror and a scrambling sound from the porch brought me back to reality. I'm sure my father would remember this for the rest of his life.

The first time I killed a vampire, it changed me. It's so powerful to take away such a commanding creature who would otherwise live forever. But finding and taking out vamps was my job, and I had grown well-accustomed to the feeling of it. I'd made my peace with it.

Mike, though? Well, good riddance after what he'd done to Will.

In a second, I reached my dad and grabbed him by his shirt collar to drag him back inside. My father had stayed out of the fray. Smart. He was rightly afraid of what I would do to him, and it was time to find out.

A sudden rush of air made me swivel, though. Someone was there. I turned to see Donny standing in front of me.

'Thank God you're alive,' he said earnestly, his family being catholic. 'Looks like I missed all the fun, though. Also, you're bleeding,' he added, grinning at me there, holding my quivering father by the collar.

'What are you doing h... No. Never mind.' Without thought, I rushed at Donny and grabbed him around the neck with both arms. He wrapped his arms around me and squeezed me in return. 'I got it done,' I whispered into the curve of his neck.

'You did well, Little Sarina. You're a tough cookie.'

'You know not to mention cookies around me, Don. You're very annoying,' I said without letting go of him.

For some reason, cookies, or biccies as we called them in Australia, were one of the most stomach-churning human foods for me since the turn—something about their sweet smell.

Our thoughts returned to the situation we'd been dumped in, and we pushed away from each other. I felt the sting of appearing soft and needy around him. Plus, it had been such an emotional reaction to hug him like that. Embarrassing.

'So, what's going on here, then? Gidday, Mr Massey.' Donny waved his hand at Dad, who'd had the wherewithal to remain silent throughout our physical display of ... relief.

'You're not going anywhere, are you, Mr Massey?' Donny added in a voice that meant he was looking down on you. Not waiting for an answer, he said, 'You wouldn't get two metres away before we'd catch you.' He chuckled and added, 'Plus, we'd be super-pissed at you, Mr Massey. I know you don't want that.'

I let go of Dad, who was trembling, and he shook himself off.

I had so many questions to ask Dad and Donny. But also so much to tell Don. Where to start? My head was spinning.

'Whoa,' said Donny gently, sensing my mental confusion. 'Come. Sit.' He made for the couch but found Mike's disintegrated corpse on the carpet in front of it. A floppy mess of skin and bone, and blood that would leave a mega-stain. 'The dining room, perhaps?' said Donny wryly.

When the three of us were seated around the dining table, Donny healed me, gently applying his blood where I needed it. I started to feel much better and began voicing my concerns. As far as I knew, they were the only *pressing* issues. I hoped Dad would be forthcoming with information, especially now that Mike was dispatched. Of course, if my dad didn't know more, I became acutely aware that I may have just killed the one person who could have enlightened us.

'Mike suggested there was a bigger story. Perhaps someone else was involved in all this. But he was probably just trying to stop me from killing him.'

'Yet you killed him,' said Donny.

'Yeah, I might have gotten caught up in the moment. What with my anger over Will.' I shrugged. I couldn't change it now.

Donny turned to my dad. 'You. What can *you* tell us?'

'Nothing. I swear it. You have to believe m—'

'We don't have to believe anyone!' I snapped. 'And certainly not you! Spill.'

'I don't know anything,' he said quietly and stared at the tray in the centre of the table that contained serviettes, toothpicks and salt and pepper shakers. I thought of Jenny and how I'd ruined her carpet. Then I remembered I'd killed her husband. That might be the more considerable heartbreak for her ... Then again, I didn't know her well.

I decided to let Dad simmer and squinted at Donny. 'Why aren't you off storming The Red Line?'

'I was worried about you. Anything could have happened, from Mike getting the best of you to the Brisbane force arriving before you had time to get the job done and get away. But it seems I need not have worried.'

'You should have known that,' I quipped back. Deep down,

I felt satisfied that Donny cared enough about me to be worried. Enough that he would give up the excitement of a large police operation to check on my safety. It meant something because Donny lived for that high-octane work.

Dad sat quietly like a sorry child on a "naughty step". Then he made a grunting noise and adjusted his butt on the dining chair to our attention. As soon as I saw his face, I knew.

'Good. You're ready to tell us, then?' I said roughly.

'Well, I don't know *who*, but... You won't hurt me, right, Sarina? I mean, I'm your dad, and that must count for something?'

'Of course, I won't kill you, Dad. But hurt's subjective.'

His eyes bulged, but I stared him down until he spilled.

'Mike was telling you the truth, Sarina. He's not the top dog. He wanted to be, for sure.' Dad leaned in towards us, raising his thick eyebrows as he spoke to us as though in confidence. 'There *is* someone else. I'm telling you. But I don't know who.'

That news went straight to my gut, which churned at the thought. That someone out there was more powerful and dangerous than Mike was deeply disturbing. And in my rage, had I killed the one person who might shed more light on the situation?

'You need to tell us who that is right now,' I ordered, even though it was futile.

'I can't. I don't kno—'

I crossed the table and wrapped my fingers around my father's neck. I was gentle enough, given I'd just found out he'd been involved in Mike's dirty dealings, and I still couldn't say with certainty that he didn't know what was happening to Will.

'They kept me out of it,' Dad said quickly. 'Sarina, Mike was threatening you. Me. Our whole family. I wasn't lying about that.'

He wasn't spilling the beans on vampires!

Giving up on Dad, I told Donny, 'We have to find out who it is. And quick. Humans and vamps aren't safe while that person is out there.'

THIRTY-EIGHT

Despite my anger at Dad's involvement in Mike's mess, I advised him to pack and get Mum and Marinda to a motel in Cairns asap. I couldn't be sure how bad the situation would get, and I didn't want them caught in the cross-fire. I could deal with my father's double-crossing later.

Dropping him off, he ran up the drive towards home as Marinda rushed towards us.

'How do you know Steve?' she asked, left of field.

'Wait. How do *you* know Steve?' I shot back.

'From Uni. Everyone knows him. He's such an up-himself dick. Dude thinks he's sooo special cos his mum's the mayor or something. Like, whatever, dude. We don't care!' Then she leaned in closer. 'Plus, he deals on campus. Before he disap-peared, I mean. Do you think that's why he disappeared? Maybe he stole drugs or mon—'

'Wait, a drug dealer?'

'What do you think? Yes, drugs. Although other stuff, too, I guess. He was always up to something. Always scheming. He looks fine, though. I'll give him that,' said Marinda, pausing momentarily to open her eyes up wide as she thought about just how fine Steve looked.

Talk about bad taste.

Then Marinda came back to earth. 'But his personality's so freaking bogus.'

'What other things did he get up to?'

'Womanising...and stuff. I dunno. I'm a good girl.' She winked at me. 'But seriously, I don't know any more than I've told you, sis. I never had much to do with him outside of one class we had together.'

I looked through the windshield silently, mulling over the new information. In all the time since Donny and I had received Steve's case file, we'd framed him as naïve, possibly even a strait-laced kid. A *good* kid. That was our impression. But Marinda was suggesting a different scenario. If she was right, how did we miss that?

'Donny. Why didn't we know that?' I asked, with a hint of blame.

'Don't ask me, Sar.' He slapped the steering wheel with his palm, a new reality dawning on him. 'Perhaps we're shit detectives, after all.'

'That's why it surprised me you gave Will to him last night. I wouldn't trust the guy,' said Marinda.

Her words gave me a strange and unwanted feeling in my stomach again.

Suddenly, Marinda's demeanour changed, and she asked me excitedly, 'Is that the case you're on, Sar? If it's Steve's case, you can tell me. I promise I won't tell anyone. Pinky swear,' she whisper-yelled at me, crossing her fingers together and waving them in my face.

'I have to go, sweetie. Sorry.'

'It's your case, isn't it?' Marinda asked. But she knew already. 'And what's the deal with The Red Line place?'

Ignoring her questions, I gave her a quick kiss through the window. 'Keep your mouth shut,' I told her. 'Your lives could depend on it. For real.'

Marinda mouthed, 'Over and out!' in the light from our headlights as Donny reversed onto the street.

I just had time to yell at her, 'Get inside,' as we tore out of the drive. 'Over and out,' I whispered.

While I trusted Marinda, I couldn't be sure her judgement of Steve was based on genuine knowledge of him or tinged with gossip. But she had put the ever-loving fear in me about Will being left with Steve, even if Lindsay was there. They said they were taking Will to Lindsay's house, which I was too preoccupied to think much of at the time. Suddenly, it seemed an odd choice. Why hadn't they gone somewhere unknown, where they'd be less likely found?

I gnashed my jaw on the drive to Lindsay's, and on arrival, I was out of Donny's Commodore before it was even stationary. I ran for the door with my still blood-stained black and white striped top, and my face and neck healed but still a mess of dried blood. Finding it unlocked, in half a second, I was down the hall.

Will stood in the lounge. His faded black jeans hugged his thighs, and his Red Hot Chilli Peppers t-shirt was thick with blood around the neck area. Weren't we a pair? He looked well … and handsome. My body relaxed. Never had I felt so relieved to see him.

Feeling rather than thinking, I rushed at him and was shocked when his hand came up to stop me in my tracks. It was so unexpected that I was flung back into the wall, snapping a few tongue-in-groove boards. But hitting the wall was nothing compared to the burning pain as my heart broke in two.

'Sarina!' Donny reached out to help me out of the wall. Lost in hurt feelings, I took his hand unconsciously.

What was the situation I had walked into?

I looked around the room. It looked the same as when Donny and I had questioned Lindsay, except, this time, Steve was surveying the situation from the corner, sitting on a new, single lounge chair. He didn't seem concerned by the altercation between Will and I.

Meanwhile, Lindsay stood at the entrance to the hall, confused like me. Or was she worried? She seemed jumpy, and maybe that was my fault. It must be scary for a human to have a vampire they don't know well rush into their house as I had just done. Yet she gave me a strained look of compassion when I glanced at her.

'Will?' I said.

He heard me, of course, but looked at the floor. I studied him. A beautiful luminosity had settled over his complexion. He looked so good and strong. So strong. I noted his muscles barely hidden beneath the sleeves of that old tee. But when my eyes came to rest on his face, my stomach roiled.

'What is it? What's happened?' I reached my hand towards him again but stopped short of touching him.

Will took the quickest glance towards Steve before turning back to face me. 'You can't expect me just to forgive you.'

'I never meant for this to happen, Will. It's my job,' I argued. 'I didn't know they'd come for you.'

'I would have let you eat from me. All those years, I asked you to let me in! Allow me into your life. I even begged you once!'

'I know, I know. And I wanted to. I would have. I was about t—'

'Would you? Were you, though?'

He hated me. I could see it in his eyes. My thoughts felt like they were doing spirals inside my mind. Shouldn't he be more forgiving, considering I made him? Making a vampire involves a blood bond, but he was being so ... so ... obnoxious. I couldn't stand it. I turned my gaze away.

The silence between us was painful and raw, and the darkness in the lounge seemed to swallow me up for a while.

It was true that my job had drawn Will into this mess, and if I had decided to turn him earlier, it wouldn't have happened that way—violent and nasty. I scanned the room. Everyone was silent. The only noise came from insects outside, the crashing of waves in the distance, and the occasional swooshing sound of blood inside my body.

Lindsay looked like she'd just received news of her dog dying, and she quickly twisted away from me. Humans have so many feelings. Deep, fleeting, and barely understandable for much of the time. Steve bore through me with a cold yet interested stare. Donny had his hand on my shoulder. I shrugged violently and dislodged it.

I felt almost like I could cry. How very bloody human of me! But I would never allow myself to be overcome in that situation. I held on to those feelings, stuffing them inside myself, hardening my exterior. I made myself solid like stone.

'So that's it?' I said to Will.

'Yes,' came the reply I didn't want to hear.

I heard a scoff from the corner. I turned to scowl at Steve. *Little shit. What the hell is his problem?*

'I'll be staying with Steve and Lindsay,' said Will with finality, breaking my thoughts on Steve. There may have been a split-second change in my facial expression before I became stone again. Time to move forward, I told myself.

'There are legal checks and balances to be made,' I said stiffly.

With The Red Line's raid well underway, I assumed it was a safe time to return Steve to Mrs Gorman's home, plus Will also needed to be processed. It pained me, but under the law, Will was considered illegal.

On the positive side, even if those responsible for Steve's turn and Will's draining weren't picked up at the brothel during the raid, it was doubtful any of the culprits would prioritise finding the two of them. *Surely?* Not while the police were actively searching for those involved. My educated guess told me anyone not caught up in the raid would be too focused on getting out of Standfort, like rats deserting their sinking ship.

I requested the use of Lindsay's telephone to set up bringing in Steve and Will. My fingers pressed the numbers on the handset as I read Mayor Gorman's phone number from the notebook I carried in my back pocket. The Mayor answered in seconds. I told her I'd be delivering them to her home, warning her I'd also have Steve's human girlfriend and another illegally made vampire with me.

I placed the handset gently down on its receiver, ending the call. My hand remained resting on the phone as I thought. There was a feeling of something amiss. I mean, apart from the love of my life cutting me off.

Having racked my brain with no return on it, I swung around to address the new vamps. 'You understand that both of you are in danger because you were turned illegally? By law.'

'Yes,' Will said pointedly. Was that a snarl?

'Well, let's go,' I said, glancing at Steve. There was a slight upturn in the corners of his mouth. If Marinda hadn't told me what she knew of Steve, I'd have assumed the little boy was looking forward to seeing his mummy. But now ... who knew? He was starting to get on my nerves. That, I could say for sure.

I began down the hall, passing Donny, who wore a look of compassion that did little but stoke my temper. I focused on the floor.

As we bundled into Donny's sedan, I told them, 'I can't guarantee anything regarding the law. But I think they'll look sympathetically at your situation, with both of you created against your will.'

Steve chuckled, his naivety and gumption impressing and exasperating me. 'Like you, Sarina,' he said.

I folded down the passenger seat sun visor and used it to look at Steve via the mirror. His messy fringe framed his face.

'So you know my backstory, then?'

'I do.' His eyes glistened, and my arms felt cold, even for a vampire.

I glanced at Will, assuming he had to be the blabbermouth. But I didn't let my eyes rest there.

THIRTY-NINE

W alking up the front steps of the mayor's home, I quickly counted in my head. Inside, I sensed two humans and five vampires. It wasn't ideal, but this was the mayor's biological son I was returning. Surely, it wouldn't be a trap for Donny and me. Or Will?

At the top of the stairs, the hall led us into the living area, the room we'd been in just the night before. I went first. Donny was behind me, giving me a sense of security. Then came Steve, Will and Lindsay.

The living room harboured an air of officiousness it had lacked the last time I was there. I immediately knew that the vampires, force members, were present to care for the illegals. It made sense, but Will being one of them broke my heart again.

Immediately, Mrs Gorman rushed for Steve as several of the vamps quickly moved into position, flanking her. They were dressed in combat gear as though perhaps they'd been on their way to The Red Line but had been peeled off at the last minute to take care of this situation instead.

Like any mother would be, Mrs Gorman was awash with emotion. Holding her son tightly, tears of joy rolled down her cheeks, and in between were some messages of thanks aimed at Donny and me for bringing Steve home. We were glad we'd been able to help, of course.

Steve hugged his mother back and looked pleased—very pleased. What did that boy find so damn amusing? I was beginning to think something was wrong with his brain.

Meanwhile, Donny chatted with a force member. The five force members were kitted in black with bulletproof vests. I sidled up to Donny for an update.

'So, have you heard how The Red Line raid went?' I said in a whispered voice near him.

'They hit the jackpot. I reckon it was that madam there...' He paused and shut his eyes tightly as though it would help him remember.

'Madame Shey,' I said. My mouth puckered to voice her name. The yellow-blonde hair, the skin that looked like she'd smoked for fifty years. But perfect makeup and expensive clothing. I could see it all in my mind's eye.

'Yes, her. She's the one at the top. Well, I reckon, anyway.'

'They're not sure of it?'

He shrugged. 'Well, that's what it looks like. Shey was in charge of the place, the books, and the captives. She had a fair bit of power in town.'

'Well, it's great news then. A human, hey? I'm surprised. If they have the top dog, Will's safety is likely, which is a positive. Unless the law chooses to end him. But we are safe.'

'We are.' Donny's enthusiasm seemed dented, but he continued. 'They got a lot in the raid. A couple of big Standfort names were in there at the time. That's gonna be funny when it hits the papers. But better than that, they found those captive humans from the farmhouse.' He leaned in a little closer, his words tickling my ear and causing me to reach up and tuck a few strands of hair behind it. 'The ones you saw being bussed in and out. I reckon you'll get a promotion out of this, Sar.'

Was he joking? 'I didn't save them,' I said quickly.

'You found them. When I was still making excuses, you went on your own to investigate.' He put his arm around my shoulder and squeezed me. I glanced towards Will, but he wasn't looking back.

'The way the vamp told it...' Donny pointed to a force member. 'The way those humans were living, love. No human or vampire should ever have been made to live like that.'

There it was. That salt of the earth, yet confusing, nature of Donny. A womaniser who genuinely loved and cared for people? Whatever he was, for him, love was an action, and I did appreciate that.

Lowering his voice even further, Donny asked, 'So, what about your Babe? What are you going to do?'

That got Will's attention. I saw Will start to turn, but then he stopped himself and looked ahead, resentful.

'Let's not talk about it now, Don,' I said, and he nodded.

Eventually, Mayor Gorman expelled her pent-up motherly love and relief. She straightened herself out, pushed back her shoulders and wiped away her tears with a scrunched-up tissue from her blouse. Taking on a serious, professional air, she had entered mayor mode.

'I want to thank you, Sarina Massey and Donny Agosti, for your care. It's through your honest and faithful policing that my son has been returned to me. I can't tell you how much I appreciate that.' Her eyes looked watery again, but she pushed through it. 'There are still hoops that we have to get through. Even though my son was made a vampire by a crime committed against him, there are still laws and procedures we have to follow. The same goes for William here.'

Will stood stock still and took no notice of me.

'Everything has to be done per the law. I take my job as mayor very seriously, and my ultimate responsibility is to the Standfort community.'

Jeez, I thought. *She thinks she's running for election again.*

I noticed Mayor Gorman turned a little towards Steve, as though this part of the message was meant more for him. 'Even though it's difficult, we must follow the law to the letter. I don't want anything we do to work against us in court against Steve. Or Will,' she added quickly as an afterthought. 'So it's vital you boys are on your best behaviour. Do you understand what I'm saying?'

At that moment, she gave her son a look, and it all became clear to me. Mrs Gorman *knew* what sort of person her son was. He wasn't the naïve, upstanding young university student we'd initially been told of. He was trouble, and his mother knew it. She was worried that Steve wouldn't be able to hold it together even for a short time—not even to save his own life!

My eyes had already rolled before I realised what I was doing. Fortunately, a scan revealed only Donny had seen, and he flashed me a smile. Lovely white teeth, no pointy canines in sight. His upper body jiggled with a few silent chuckles before he resolved it and began following the conversation again.

'Of course, Mother,' came Steve's voice. Mother? Everyone looked at him standing there, his arms stretched out like he thought he was Jesus Christ. A strange boy indeed.

'These force members are here to take you in, but full justice will be sought.' Mayor Gorman looked back and forth between Steve and Will. They were now captives.

Will stood still, but he was tense. I could feel it. It's a vampire thing, like an extra sense. I took a few steps forward to get a better look at Will. The stolidness from earlier was giving way to anxiety. Was that a tremor I saw in his hands? Just then,

Will stole a glance in my direction. It was so fast any human would have missed it. But it disturbed me. Will was worried. Was he concerned he couldn't trust the Mayor? The police? The law *could* be an ass ...

I scanned the room. Donny was listening to the mayor. Steve stood still, his broad face masculine and smug, his usually slicked hair a little wayward, probably from his mother's hugs. He was the mayor's son and undoubtedly felt more confident making his way through the coming legal processes than Will would.

Then I remembered something Ruby Treemer had told me and Donny back at Mack's Restaurant before her death. *What was it she said? Something about a changeover in vampire management. Not the government's control of vamps, but the criminal element.*

Then my mind went to my sister's words. Marinda said Donny and I had seen a very different version of Steve than she and their university cohort knew. Was she right? Then, my dad. He backed up Mike's version that there was someone new...

An up-and-comer!

That's what Ruby had said. There was an up-and-comer. I'd thought she meant a big name from down south or who'd arrived in Australia from overseas. But what if the person was literal *young* blood ... from right there in Standfort?

What if it was Steve?

But what would Steve have to offer anyone? Young in two ways, human and vampire age—he was nothing in the scheme of things. A nobody. Except that he wasn't exactly a nobody, was he? He was the mayor's son and a character who thought highly of himself.

Once I reviewed everything Ruby, Marinda, and my father had said and looked at Steve standing there before us, it all clicked into place. Lindsay caught my eye. Fear-tinged, plate-shaped eyes burned into mine.

I turned just in time to see a crazed look flicker across Steve's face. Madame Shey wasn't the boss of the Standfort underworld. It was Steve!

He was a storm of youth, overconfidence and contacts.

'Donny! It's Steve,' I yelled.

CHAPTER

FORTY

I threw myself into action, pushing the humans out of the way. Once I knew Steve was our target—the new criminal head of Standfort's underworld vampire community —I wasted no time. A vampire officer reached for his gun and raised it in *my* direction. I had only a millisecond to question what was happening before I realised some of the force members in attendance had already been compromised.

Will pitched himself towards the traitorous vamp and began struggling with him, preventing him from firing his weapon at me. Donny took a second to catch up, then went straight for Steve.

But Steve Gorman was fast, and the whole scene was mayhem. Lindsay's screams pierced the air as though she was in a slasher film, complete with her arms bent at the elbow, framing her mouth as though she wanted to make the noise as loud as possible. A swish of vampire movement crisscrossed the lounge room.

Donny reached Steve just as Steve aimed a wooden stake towards one of the attending force members. At least it told us that not all of them worked for the wrong side. But ultimately, it complicated the scene.

Leaving them to fight it out, I shuffled Raquel and Lindsay towards the hall.

'Go to the bathroom and lock the door. Stay quiet,' I ordered. Both were trembling. Lindsay's face was tear-stained, and the Mayor looked white as a sheet. She knew Steve was wayward, but I doubted she'd known the extent of his sociopathy. Or power.

Back in the lounge's chaos, a second Force member turned on Will while he grappled with the first one.

Out of five of them, just how many were already on Steve's payroll?

I flew across the room to back Will up. One quickly turned his attention to me and flung me across the room under the weight of his backhand. I hit the TV unit and sent the heavy cube to the floor, but it would take more than that to stop me. I picked myself up, grabbed a solid glass vase from a side table and aimed it at his head. The vampire fell to the ground, rubbing his face, his eyes blinking repeatedly. He wouldn't remain stunned for long, so I kept up the pressure, smashing the vase across his face a few more times.

A vampire couldn't go down permanently by vase alone, so I scanned the room until my eyes settled on a timber side table with legs two and a half feet long. Perfect. Breaking off a leg in the middle, leaving sharp timber shards on one end, I readied myself.

The Force member was unsteady but on his feet by then. He wiped blood from around his eyes as he searched for me. I had no time to mess around with Donny, Will, and two Force members fighting off Steve and his "on the payroll" vamps already.

Then the worst happened. Steve's attention moved away

from Donny. He took a flying leap across the room, taking out a Force member with a knife forced into her side that reached her heart. I felt confused about when and how a knife had entered the play, but then Steve landed on his feet beside another force member and dispatched him, as well.

At that point, it was Donny and me against three combat-ready vampire henchmen and Steve, who was proving himself to be much more competent than I could ever have imagined.

Great.

Donny's eyes and feet followed Steve, continuing to attack him. But Steve was substantial in his skills. What was he? Some new type of SuperVamp? Who the hell made him?

With the question of how many of the vampire force members were on Steve's payroll answered by that point, I launched at one of the three remaining—slamming my home-made stake down into the left side of his chest through a gap in the armour. His body instantly began to sag until he fell on the carpet in a mess.

That's the end for the immortal. Pathetic.

Will grappled with another force member on the floor, the vampire above him and gaining. I eased the stake effortlessly from the dead vampire and impaled the second one with substantial force to save Will. As the body fell limply on top of my boyfriend—or ex-boyfriend—I pushed on. Will could get himself up off the floor. If he couldn't do that, he needed to vamp up!

Donny was in the opposite corner, fighting the last force member who was part of Steve's team of criminals. At the same time, Steve looked ready to jump in and take out Donny himself. He was a force to be reckoned with. No wonder he'd managed to gain so much power.

I threw my stake to Donny, who caught it a foot above his head and drove it diagonally into the vamp. Then I rushed to break off a second table leg and gave it to Will, so we were all armed. Steve gave Donny a double kick with his legs, sending him across the room and smashing a hole in the drywall near the stairs. Thankfully, it wasn't brick. Donny struggled, his trunk stuck inside the wall. But then he managed to break free, a look of utter determination on his face. He crossed the room like the Terminator as Steve stood ready.

Assuming this would be the most brutal fight yet, given Steve's super-strength, I raised my stake. But Steve turned away suddenly instead of coming at me or Donny. Or Will. Steve leapt right through the open living room window, a loud metal clang ringing out as he landed hard on the garage roof below. I dove toward the window after him but only saw a flicker of movement as he ran off through some trees two doors down.

I knew immediately we'd be hard-pressed to catch him. He had escaped.

Stunned that Steve had done a runner, Donny stood there, skin patchy red from the fight and a trickle of blood running down his face.

We surveyed the damage and found the five Task Force members gooey on the carpet. Two that Steve had killed, one decapitated before Steve had punctured her heart, probably with the knife. Then there were the three who had been working for him.

I rushed to help Will. He was still flinging sticky vampire bits off himself and looking disgusted. New vamps and their sensitivities! Glistening with bright blood from the dead vampire, as I reached him, he moved away.

Of course. I had forgotten where our relationship was at. I had no right to go against Will's wishes. Yet, though I would never have voiced it to anyone, I desperately wanted to take him in my arms and help him through. And for him to help me. 'You okay?' I asked.

'Nothing that won't heal. Right? I'm a vampire now, so...' He shrugged. His face gave away little emotion.

'If you have any open wounds, you need to...' I mimed placing my finger on my canine and pressing. 'But it has to be from another vampire. I can do it if you want. You rub some blood onto the wound to close it up.'

'Do you think I don't know that?' he replied, sounding juvenile. 'I still learned things while you held me at arm's length!'

The words cut me like a knife, but I deserved it. Will wasn't screaming at me or attacking me. That was something. But I sure wish this turning thing had gone the way it usually does, with the newly turned vampire having a strong and, usually, loving connection to the one who turned them. Not that maker and progeny relationships weren't tumultuous. That was just as likely in vamp relationships as in human ones.

How very typical that the rare "anomaly" of progeny not respecting their maker would occur in Will and my case, I thought, feeling sorry for myself.

I remembered my "work husband", a welcome distraction. 'Donny?' I called.

He was already punching in numbers on Raquel Gorman's kitchen phone with one hand while holding his ribs with the other. 'I'm calling the Brisbane Task Force. Ours is compromised. Obviously.'

I moved closer and lifted his shirt over his ribs as the call connected. There was a tiny puncture wound where I assumed Steve had tried to stake him with something. The entire event had been a close call for all of us, but everyone I cared for had made it through.

I placed my wrist to my mouth and lowered my teeth,

which had only snapped away moments after the fight. I broke through my skin with an almost imperceptible pop. While Donny spoke to a Brisbane team, alerting them we needed help in Standfort, I applied the blood from my wrist to his wound. I watched his stomach undulate gently as he spoke, and I saw his wound heal moment by moment. I caught odd words, 'Steve is on the run,' 'The Red Line raided,' 'The Gorman house.'

Then Donny was a machine gun of, 'Right. Right. Yep. Done. Right,' until he placed the receiver back on the hook. He turned towards me but looked past. Turning, I saw Will standing behind us with an inscrutable look that soon turned to anger. He stalked away.

'Will!' I called. 'You know you have to be taken in.'

'I know. I didn't think it would be by you two.' His face was red and strangled.

'It's nothing personal, mate,' Donny offered.

'Isn't it?'

Will stared Donny down until I told Donny to go and check on Mayor Gorman and Lindsay in the bathroom.

I went to Will. 'Will, this isn't the time or place for petty jealousies. We've got enough on our plates. Donny can heal you when he comes back. Don't argue unless you'd prefer I do it. But I need to know something. You were with Steve all that time before I came to pick you up. Did you know what he was up to?'

Will slumped on the couch and stared at the bloody war zone of a floor.

'When the Brisbane Force arrives, they're going to ask you, and they'll get their answer, too. Trust me on that.'

He scoffed then but must have known I was right. 'I knew. He was big-noting himself the whole bloody time. I didn't realise how serious he was, though, and I certainly didn't know how capable he was. Or how mental.'

'So you weren't in on it?'

'God, no! I swear to you. Why would I want to kill those peop—I mean, vamps? I've had no beef with them.'

I nodded, then looked at him more seriously than ever before. 'Play this right, Will. Your life depends on it.'

Mayor Gorman and Lindsay's stress was palpable as they returned to the lounge. Between claggy mounds of dead vampires, broken furniture and walls, and then the realisation that Steve had been the driving force of it all, Mayor Gorman soon held her head in her hands. I couldn't tell if the Mayor was crying, but Lindsay was sobbing.

It felt like my only chance to do anything I could for Will, though.

'Mayor Gorman, I must explain what happened with William Foster.' I pointed at Will. 'First, let me say that I'm so very sorry about Steve. I know it must be hard for you as a mum, and feel for you. But please understand I would never make a vampire illegally, except … except Mike had taken Will. My boyfriend was dying, and I had to make a split-second decision. To let him die, or … I love Will, you see. He's a good man, too. He would never have agreed to an illegal turning. We had planned to fill in the paperwork soon to turn him legally.'

Mayer Gorman was still covering her face with her hands when I began talking, but soon, she removed them, wiped her face, and nodded as I explained. I appreciated that. During possibly the worst moment of her life, she was compassionate and professional enough to show Will and me that courtesy.

'When I found him, he was…' My voice tripped up at that moment. 'He'd lost so much blood. He was drained and so close to death that even a hospital wouldn't have been able to save him. The *only* thing I could do was to give Will my blood. He's the love of my life...I couldn't just watch him die.'

Will stayed back, remaining quiet, but I felt his gaze bore holes through me.

'It's not up to me. You know that,' Mayor Gorman said finally. 'I can't make any guarantees, but I'll put in a positive word for you when I give my statement.'

'Thank you. Thank you so much.' I was gushing like a teenager being offered a chance at their dream job. But the thought of Will being put down because of my choice was so painful.

When I looked back at Will, he'd moved away. He was standing by the same window Steve had escaped from. Was he contemplating running after him? It would be the biggest mistake of his now undead life. But soon, he sighed and turned back towards us all.

FORTY-ONE

By midnight, two dozen vampires from the Brisbane Task Force had set down by helicopter in the middle of Standfort State High School's oval. It wasn't about hate or fear-mongering. Humans couldn't ignore the criminal activity of vampires. We were more powerful and could easily overcome humans. That was reality.

Will had been taken into custody willingly and politely, as I'd advised him to. He would be held, though. I offered to water his plants, but my offer wasn't well received. I expected no more.

By early the following morning, Donny and I had been questioned. On our way out, we got a warning that, as we might be called on again at any time, we shouldn't travel.

Damn. There goes that week I planned on Vanuatu's stunning beaches, catching a tan.

As we left the Standfort Police Station, Donny was torn emotionally. I sensed his worry about Lindsay.

'She'll be okay,' I said. 'She left for Cairns, right?'

'Lindsay? Yep.'

'He's not going to find her there. I'm sure of it.'

'He's a whack job, Sarina. How do we know what he will and won't do? Plus, he's got connections. People and vamps were working with him. And what's with his stren—'

'Seriously strong,' I butted in. 'I know. What is with that?'

'Caught me by surprise, I tell you. How can a new vamp be that together ... that organised and...'

'It's going to make capturing him more difficult, that's for sure. We underestimated him. That won't happen a second time.'

The Task Force was there, and they would go all out to find Steve. But Donny and I were deeply engaged in the case by then. Though we were supposed to investigate the Wine and Cheese murder, I had more than one reason for preferring to put that case aside to keep following the Steve Gorman one. We wanted Steve done—needed him done. And ASAP.

'Well?' I said.

'Let's do it,' came Donny's reply. 'Let's bring that little miscreant in.'

I saw that dog-with-a-bone look that set Donny apart from other detectives at After Dark and made him my perfect partner. I slapped him on the shoulder, and we jumped into Don's car.

'Where do we start?' I asked.

'Well, Steve's not stupid enough to hide out at The Red Line straight after a raid,' said Donny.

'Or Lindsay's place.' Emotion flickered across Donny's face for a split second, but Lindsay would have been safely hidden by then. I had to believe that. 'Or Mayor Gorman's place—even though the police would have left by now,' I added.

'He's not going to go anywhere public for a while.'

'John Martin and Damion Lau. They're in this,' I thought aloud.

'Right. We could try the booths & Mack's. Plus, I know where Martin lives.'

'How do you know that?' I asked.

'Eh,' he said. 'You hear things. He's got a wife at home.'

'Eww.' I hadn't known that. Sometimes they would turn their partner at some point, assuming they relished spending eternity together. I supposed it was one way to determine whether your partner really loved you. It was hard to imagine *anyone* loving John Martin that much. But by 1997, there were even cases of adult children being turned. People magazine had done a spread on whole families who had become vampires. The public loved reading about these unusual situations. My mind turned back to Will, of course. But I pushed those thoughts and feelings away again.

'I can't believe Standfort's biggest sleaze has a wife,' I said. 'Imagine being her!? I'd rather be yours,' I said pointedly, yet jokingly, immediately wishing I hadn't.

'So you've thought about it, then,' Donny said seriously.

'Get lost,' I replied, paring a ladylike voice with my rudeness. 'Okay. There are four booths. Drop me at the Blood Bank, and I can walk to Grove Street from there. You take the car and stop at the other two. Yes?'

'Good plan.' The Blood Bank was no bank, just a cleverly named booth business. Donny looked at his watch. 'We'll be done in forty-five minutes.'

We had two hours until sunrise, so doing the booths first would mean we would still have an hour to try any other ideas we came up with.

THE BLOOD BANK WAS A NEWER, upmarket booth establishment that Donny preferred. But in terms of intel, the receptionist and the books handed over to me to scan when I showed my After Dark badge offered nothing of use.

Twenty minutes later, I arrived at Grove Street. It *was* decrepit in comparison. I made a mental note: suggest Marinda apply at The Blood Bank. My sister deserved the best.

'Sam! Glad you're on tonight. I'm here on business.' I flashed my badge even though he'd seen it before. As I've said, rules for vampires and their behaviour are necessarily as strict as any significant laws for humans. 'Has John Martin come through recently?'

'No. Haven't seen him for ages,' Sam said. There was an unusual intonation in his voice. My eyes zeroed in on him. His black hair, dyed to almost blue, hung across his eyes—and his eyes focused on the countertop. My gaze shifted to his hands. You didn't need to be a vampire to notice their tremor. He could barely hold a pencil.

'What about Damion Lau?' I said to test him.

'Not him either.'

Sam's lying mouth caught my eye that time before he quickly stared at the counter. The register lay in front of him with its thick-lined pages and red cover. An open can of Pepsi and a cup holding an array of pens and pencils sat next to it.

'Push your fringe back behind your ear,' I told him. He jumped a little but did as requested, allowing me to see his eyes. 'Sam, I'm a government official. You know you can get in trouble for lying to me.'

'I know.' His voice was a whimper. 'I know nothing. I swear.' His face tightened as he began rubbing his forearm with a shaky hand.

'Look at me.' I zeroed in on Sam's almond-shaped eyes as soon as he raised his face to me again, holding his gaze. It was as though an invisible string attached us. I began pooling my energy, focusing it on the connection. The baby on Sam's

Nirvana, Nevermind, t-shirt rose and fell with his breath, but he was otherwise still.

I felt keen awareness of how the process had drained me, but finally, I knew I had him captured. His mind was in a trance, and I maintained total control over him.

'Is Damion here now?' I said, placing my feet wider and glancing at the door to the booths.

'No,' said Sam, never taking his eyes off mine. Except to blink, of course.

'Give me the book.' During a trance state, I could do away with niceties like 'please'. What did it matter? 'Now. Tell me what you know,' I said.

Sam pushed the ledger toward me. Then his finger moved back through the twenty-centimetre gap between the glass screen and the counter to point. His shabby black-polished finger touched on a name. Derek Loman. I didn't recognise it.

He leaned closer to the glass, which had holes bored through it at head height, like the ones on a rotary phone handset. In a low voice, he said, 'He gave that weird name and had genuine-looking identification. But he'd been in here before. As Damion Lau.'

My lips pursed, and I leaned back as I took it all in. Looking at the ledger again, I raised my eyes to look at Sam. He'd done the wrong thing. I still remembered what it was like to be human, though. Sam was only trying to stay alive. I knew it. I let out a deep sigh, but then I saw it.

Halfway down the ledger and directly above the name Derek Loman. My index finger tapped twice on it, my undead heart skipping a beat. I looked seriously at Sam.

Will.

'Will Foster? Tell me about him.'

'He was new. A bit out of control. You know how they get.'

Without being tranced, you can bet he would have chosen

his words more carefully out of fear. But, honestly, I often felt relief when humans spoke candidly. I knew very well "how vamps get" when they've just been turned. That didn't upset me to hear, nor was it my issue. The issue was Will. My Will. They're at the booth drinking from God knows who. My eyes felt scratchy. Anything to do with Will made my heart ache at that point.

'Will didn't come in by himself, though, right? Damion brought him in.'

Sam nodded. His eyes had that shiny look as though zilch was going on behind them. They were glazed but still looking right at me.

Will had been palmed off onto Damion. So what was Steve up to?

I snapped my fingers suddenly and loudly at Sam's head height. He shook his head slowly, a furrow creeping into his forehead and between his eyes.

'Don't be confused, Sam. I tranced you to find out what you knew. You'll be fine.'

'Am I in trouble?'

'Not with me. But you let a known vampire through using a fake ID. You know you broke the rules.'

'I knew I was doing the wrong thing, but I was so scared, Sarina. You've seen him. He's scary as shit. I didn't know what to do. Please don't tell my boss. I could lose my job over this...if I don't get killed first.'

Maybe he wasn't cut out for that job. Then again, perhaps no human was. Booths might be better operated by vampire staff at reception. I'd often thought it.

But I nodded my head because Sam was correct. Damion was formidable. I'd seen what happened to poor Ruby and Sherri. Sam could very well be killed over this. Still, this was my job. 'You need to up your game, Sam. You're being paid to do a job, so next time, at least alert your manager about what happened if you're too scared to enforce the legislation, hey?'

Sam nodded his head at me, relieved.

'Ye...yes, Sarina. I will.'

I started to leave but then stopped and turned back towards Sam. 'You *are* right to be worried, though, Sam. Please be careful, okay?'

He nodded grimly, and I left to meet Donny.

CHAPTER
FORTY-TWO

'I found John Martin in the register, but it didn't tell me anything I didn't know already,' Donny said as I opened the passenger door and slid in. 'You?'

Waving my notebook before him, I said, 'I've got two addresses that Damion wrote in the book at Grove. Plus, he took Will in there last night under a false name. Will used his full name, Will Foster, like a complete rube. But Damion used "Derek Loman".'

I grabbed the Refedex from between the seats. It contained thorough maps of the areas with an index of every street. Every one until its publication date, and that version was published in 1996, so I figured it would be pretty trustworthy. It only took me a minute to look up both addresses and find that one didn't exist. I began directing Donny to Aumond Street.

'So Steve sent Will with Damion to get a feed, ay?'

'What is so pleasing about that?' I asked. My feelings were brutally conflicted. Pain from Will's turn being taken out of my hands, his apparent hatred of me. Yet, the comfort that he'd eaten in a booth and hadn't attacked someone on the street? When did being dead get so damn complicated?

'Well, he could have just let Will feed from Lindsay, right?'

Bloody Lindsay, I thought before catching my subconscious and stuffing it down to remain out of Donny's earshot.

We rode the rest of the journey in awkward and bruised silence.

Twenty-four Aumond Street was in the west, butting up against the thick, rich rainforest. The blocks were set in sprawling acre-plus lots. The home itself looked uninviting. Ramshackle and unkept, despite being an easy-care brick built on a slab.

Donny parked down the street. Even if Damion or Steve weren't inside, it seemed possible that other vamps could be, and they would sense our approach more surely than a human would. We parked and advanced on foot through some trees that bordered the property. The smell of Lemon Myrtle and Night Jessamine tickled my nose pleasantly as we stepped mindfully through the undergrowth to get as close to the house as possible while remaining safe.

At ten metres out, we stopped and crouched to listen. I glanced at my watch. It was nearly four thirty, and I realised it was a dreadful plan. We didn't have enough time. I tapped Donny on the shoulder, flashed him my watch and grimaced.

'Ten minutes,' he whispered, and we settled back into watch mode.

The house had been quiet for seven minutes—I knew because I was watching the hands on my watch turn slowly.

Finally, there was a light knocking sound. It must have been on the back door, as no one had approached via the front.

I noticed a muffled sound. Donny looked at me, alarmed. That was the sound of at least one person gagged and struggling.

'Almost gave up on you,' carried a voice. The door opened and closed again.

The noise continued.

'Shud up, bitch,' said the first man.

'Got held up at the booth, mate. That turd Agosti was there asking questions.'

I know it wasn't mature of me, but I stifled a laugh. Donny flashed that lovely smile and rolled his brown eyes.

'I had to wait 'til he fucked off,' the voice said.

'That's Damion. Dammit, you just missed him,' I whispered.

'Win some, lose some,' Donny said, trying to make light of it, but I knew he was pissed off.

'You sure he didn't see you?' the second voice asked.

'Yep.'

I turned to Donny. 'I reckon the other guy's Steve.'

Donny's face scrunched up. He wasn't sure, but I was. We kept listening. I looked at my watch. We had two minutes until we'd decided to call it quits and only about twenty until the sun rose. I was glad we'd found Steve, but it happening so close to dawn was a frustrating conclusion to the night.

'We need to clean house before this whole thing gets messed up,' Steve said.

'Well, I did Ruby and that slut from the Line. Make John do some,' whined Damion.

Now we knew for sure. Damion was the murderous bastard who took out those girls. Anger about Ruby and Sherri boiled inside me, but I was also worried about who the other targets were. Who did they have inside there?

Steve replied to Damion venomously, 'You're a fucking idiot, mate. He's already underwater, isn't he? Someone had to get the message out. This one can wait 'til nightfall, anyway. She'll be fine.'

So, one girl was trapped inside, and John Martin had already taken to the ocean. I looked at Donny quizzically. He shrugged. I could only imagine Damion's face. I bet he didn't like being spoken to like that.

There was silence for half a minute before the men said something about bunking down. I heard "light", "forest", "get a move on", and "nest".

'Are they planning to bed down in the forest rather than the house?' I said.

'I think so.' Donny was nodding slowly as though he was thinking.

'You wanna go for them?'

'We're cutting it too fine,' Donny admitted. 'At least we can free the girl as soon as they leave.'

But would we have this opportunity again?

'They're right there, Donny,' I said.

'It's too dangerous.'

'I know you're right. We'll rescue her, and then we can try to make it back as early as possible tonight. Maybe we can ambush them on their return?'

Then the screen door slammed, and we heard someone, Steve most likely, call out. 'There's someone in the trees.'

Within seconds, the undergrowth was swishing and parting, followed by a second slam of the screen door. Both of them were coming for us.

Donny grabbed my hand and led me in an arc around the house, placing a few extra metres distance between us and the edge of the trees that lined the property. Once the vegetation changed, our hands dropped away from each other as we took off running through the rainforest.

The air took on a heavier feeling, dense with moisture and an earthy, damp odour. Steve and Damion were never more than two dozen metres behind us. We all moved with vampire speed, cutting a swathe through the undergrowth and disturbing nocturnal *and* diurnal creatures unused to so much action in the forest from vampires near dawn.

After what felt like a half-hour's running, though it was probably only ten minutes, I was tired. But I pushed myself forward at top speed because it seemed like, finally, Donny and I might be gaining. In another few minutes, I felt sure we'd escaped. I dared to turn my head mid-run to check. I saw nothing—no vampires, no movement of the trees, bushes, or brush behind us. It wouldn't be odd for a vampire to suddenly take to the trees in a plan to move in front of us and cut us off, but there was no indication from above, either.

We continued to run as Donny did his spot check. Then we slowed and came to a stop deep inside the Daintree.

My muscles ached, and I was desperate to sit and rest.

'Holy hell,' Donny said, his voice low. 'Wasn't expecting that!'

I couldn't help it. I started to chuckle. Then Donny began, too. His cheeks became shaking spheres on his face, and his voice cackled. We flopped onto the ground and leaned back on a tree with a solid metre-wide trunk. Our shoulders rubbed against each other lightly as we laughed over the situation. Our noise silenced the insect calls, but the hum started again as we finally settled down.

A minute or two later, and still keeping a lookout for Steve and Damion, my mind turned to a plan.

'We won't make it back in time.' I was worried about the girl.

'It's alright. We can sleep out here, easy. We just dig down a bit and cover ourselves in the dirt.

'Great,' I said, dripping with sarcasm.

'Oh, come on, Miss Sarina. Don't tell me you've never slept dirty before.'

'What is it with you? You make everything gross.'

'It's a gift,' he said, already moving on, looking at the ground for items he could use. Soon, he grabbed a long branch and began digging into the earth, using it as a spade. The soil was rich and moist, so it wasn't hard work, especially for a vamp.

Donny had chosen a spot behind a large log that looked as though it had fallen decades before. It was a secluded spot where we'd be unlikely to be found. Who am I kidding? The section of rainforest we were in was incredibly remote. So, barring Steve and Damion, who themselves would have to go to ground soon, and animals who had created paths through the dense forest, no one would find us there.

I had just decided to give Donny a hand when there was a rush of air and motion around me. Halfway up from my place resting against the tree, I was knocked back down again with a thump and a sharp pain in my head.

CHAPTER

FORTY-THREE

I tried to get my bearings as another blow came.

Get it together, Sarina. I knew it was severe. With another hit incoming, I rolled to the left and jumped to my feet. Blood was streaming down my face and across my eyes, but through it, I saw Steve. His vulgar expression showed me how pleased he was to have caught me unaware.

I reached for a branch and pulled myself up. Steve's face took on a red shade, and his eyes were angry slits. A very different look from the solid young man I'd met earlier.

I began climbing the tree, looking towards Donny as I went. Metres from where Donny had been digging our sleep nest, he was busy fighting Damion. They were locked in a battle that would be a blur to the human eye. I saw the piece of timber in Donny's hand come down hard towards Damion, but Damion wrestled it from him. He threw it off into the distance, causing a flutter of nesting birds to flap into higher branches.

Steve used my distraction to jump into the tree and start after me. I climbed from limb to limb, trying to move horizontally, but inched closer to the treetop with each move. There, branches were less secure and would expose me to the coming dawn.

'You made a huge mistake coming after me,' Steve called.

'Is that right?' I yelled back sarcastically, continuing my ascent.

But maybe he was right because there seemed to be no way out. I would have to fight him, and he could easily overpower me.

Leaping to a branch just above, the encroaching sun stung my eyes briefly. Then I came down hard on Steve with my hands together, fingers entwined, a double fist. I bludgeoned him with as much force as I could muster. It knocked him down the tree a few metres, and I kept going for him.

Eventually, he landed on the ground, and I jumped down on top of him again and ripped at his throat with my teeth.

'Bitch,' he yowled—from what I could make out, at least. Blood spurted from the tear in his neck. Since I'd caught a break, I kept biting him anywhere I could while trying to hold him down. After some seconds, my hands slipped in the gore, and he took the chance to flip me over, ending up on top. Smashing down on my head a few times with his fist, he started biting at my neck.

Having made what felt like a deep and gaping wound just underneath my chin on the left side, Steve paused to look down at me. His wounds were bleeding everywhere when he smiled suddenly. My skin crawled.

'The best thing,' he said, 'is I was the one who took your boyfriend and drained him, forcing you to make him a vampire. Something you'd been keeping from him, Sarina Massey.' He stopped still, eyes wide as though he were thrilled to deliver the news to me. 'Even if you live tonight—and you won't—Will won't ever forgive you for how things went down.'

'You can't wind me up with that. I know it was Mike.'

Steve hit his fist on the tree trunk next to us, laughing. 'Are you sure about that? I've been to Will's apartment. He broke that blue vase trying to fight me off. Knocked it down with his foot. With all the nice, warm blood I'd drunk from him, he was so dizzy by then. I left him there on the bed for you. S'pose I won't get a thank-you for that.' He grinned at me. 'He's got shitty taste in music, by the way. I expected better.'

The vase. The records. I had seen the broken pieces of blue china … and Will's records. They were out on the coffee table. Will had never been much for home decor, but tidy he was.

But Steve knew all of that. He knew.

My entire body shook with anger. 'You maniac. You are dead. Dead!'

Steve laughed heartily before his demeanour changed halfway through. He went from laughing at me to a look of pure, unadulterated evil. His eyes were soulless, and his mouth looked foaming, although I might have imagined that part.

Not content with the pain he'd already inflicted, Steve continued. 'He'll never be what I am, either. If I'd made him myself, I could have made him one of the strongest vampires to set foot here in Standfort. My blood's special, Little Sarina. But I kept that from him, so he'll always be a sad little immortal like you.'

'You think way too highly of yourself, wanker,' I spat back at him.

'Ha!' And Steve launched into full-blown laughter again. 'You really have no idea. I'm on the precipice of running this tragic but useful little town.'

'Rubbish!' I managed despite the struggle.

'You can laugh now, but you don't know the onslaught coming. You think this is bad for little old Standfort? Wait until my relatives arrive.'

What on earth was he talking about? I had to question at that point whether the boy was of sound mind. Was there such a thing as a clinically delusional vampire? So much was yet unknown about vampires as a species.

I would have trouble gaining the upper hand again. My exhaustion after the run exacerbated our strength difference, with being out at dawn compounding it. Even though the cover of the Daintree Rainforest was thick above us, sunlight was beginning to filter through in sections. Here and there, threatening rays of light, ready to attack us. All I could do now was hold Steve back, using my two hands flat on his chest. His arms were longer than mine, but I was limiting the damage he was doing to me as I searched for a way out.

In response, I sneered, 'Planning a family BBQ, are you, Steve? How thrilling and scary.'

'You can't tell me you haven't wondered why I'm so strong and powerful and why I was made a vampire? I'm just some young dude from a hick town. That's what you think, right?' Though he couldn't lean in, he bent his face as close as possible to mine to sing, 'Wrong.'

I didn't want to show him he'd bothered me, but it was impossible. I knew a flicker of concern had crossed my face. Damn it! My gut told me I *had* missed something important with Steve. Very important.

But the fight continued, and there was no way I could keep it up for much longer. Besides, if I did, the sun would soon rise fully, making us both sick.

'If you're so smart, Steve, do a girl a favour. What is it that silly me has missed?'

'It doesn't matter now. You were too stupid to work it out, and I'm about to show you the ultimate death. But my ancestors will be on their way very soon, Little Sarina. Even if I decided to let you live, you'd have to say goodbye to all you ever held dear. Except Will. Perhaps I'd keep him on as a slave or something. I kinda like the guy, ya know? He seems, I don't know ... useful.'

My face quivered with Steve's bitter taunting.

'He's pissed at you, isn't he? I mean, I can hardly blame the guy. Once, I pointed out to him that you had kept him from eternal life all that time, finally turning him only because I'd been kind enough to drain him and leave him for you to press the issue. Well, he felt very hurt when I put it like that.' Steve offered me a grimace before the corners of his mouth twitched upward.

That lit a fire inside me that felt like a literal bonfire, but I held myself tight, trying not to fly off the handle.

'If you're going to kill me anyway, tell me about John,' I said. 'Where's John right now?'

I was vaguely aware that Donny was still fighting back against Damion just metres away, unable to help me. I tried to hold Steve back with one arm in a sliver of light as I set my other fingers to work, searching the ground for anything I could use to take Steve out permanently.

'Someone had to get the message out—and we can't just make a phone call.' Not for those matters. Steve looked pleased with himself. He loved knowing things others didn't and holding it over them. So childish. And annoying.

'John's on his way to bring backup. Standfort will be ours soon. Once they arrive in Standfort...phwoar.'

If what Steve said was true, it was concerning. But my focus was on Steve, the nasty, barely adult, who had surprised us all by turning out to be *the* problem.

My fingers found only moist leaf litter and twigs that were next to useless, so I tried to scooch over a little closer behind the fallen log. Steve was reaching a fever pitch then. His face became a mass of blood vessels. I'd seen that only once before, and that vamp had acted like he was rabid. I knew then Steve would not give up. There would be no mercy for me. He would keep coming until I killed him, he killed me, or the sun took both of us.

My fingertips could feel the end of the fallen log we were next to. I wasn't close enough to tear a piece off, though. My hand slipped, and Steve roared toward my neck again, tearing a fresh part of it. I cried out and brought my hand from the ground up to his face in a rushed punch that stunned him for only a second.

But a second was all I needed.

I turned my torso toward the log and broke off a section, smashing it into the side of Steve's head. He fell off me onto the ground, but the timber crumbled with him.

It was an opportunity, though. I scrambled to a crouch, grabbing my neck wounds involuntarily as I squinted at the approaching day. Seeing Donny's timber "spade" nearby, I grabbed it and leapt onto Steve.

'Motherfucker!' I yelled as I raised the makeshift stake—pointy enough on one end—above Steve and struck it down. 'Die!'

It pushed through Steve's skin as he struggled. I leaned gently on the spade, and it slid in further.

'Go to hell,' I screamed at him as his body lost rigidity and turned into a floppy mess of parts. I waited a few seconds more to be sure I'd hit the mark. Steve's face told me he'd never expected it to end like this. He was so shocked he hadn't won that last bout. The boy was used to having his way.

I reached down and pulled the spade out, holding his body still with my foot. It came out super-easily after the ultimate death.

Turning to see Donny, bloody and battered but still fighting Damion, I screamed, 'Move, Donny!'

My voice echoed through the forest's canopy as Donny flung himself aside, and I came down on Damion. A slippery one, he moved just a few inches, causing me to miss him. Damion grabbed for the timber and wrestled me for it. I might have lost out had Donny not gotten himself together to give Damion a swift kick to the side of his chest.

Damion let go of my makeshift stake, and I had my chance before he could come for it again. That time, I hit the mark. Damion's hands gripped the stake, but he had no strength left. Besides, it was already too late. The timber was already partway through his chest. His fingers wrapped around the stake like a baby grabs a parent's finger. The ultimate death was the only direction he was heading.

A few seconds later, his hands fell limp, his arms becoming jelly. His face lost its chiselled rigour, and his cheeks, the colour draining from them, sagged.

Donny! I kneeled next to him. Both of us were losing blood. We couldn't heal each other if the blood was mixed with another vampire's, so first, we cleaned our hands as best we could in a small puddle, then wiped them on some dewy leaves. After that, Donny healed me, and I found a clean spot on my arm to puncture. I took my blood and smoothed it over Donny's wounds. Initially, he pulled back slightly as though it stung, but then he held still and took it with barely a wince.

FORTY-FOUR

I was so close to Donny that I felt his heart beating without touching his chest.

'You saved me.' He grinned at me as I touched my hand to his neck, then the back of his head, transferring my healing blood to his wounds.

'I had to,' I said. 'Otherwise, they'd partner me with someone like Janet. Or Marcus. Can you imagine?'

We were staring right at each other, crouched on the forest floor.

'Your eyes are so beautiful after a fight,' he said.

'Shut up,' I said, annoyed. I looked away into the forest, which sparkled in speckled light. But I was still so close that I could smell everything, from the blood drying on Donny's skin to the smells of nature he'd picked up during our flight through the rainforest and, afterwards, fighting off Damion. Looking back, I saw Donny's blood pumping hard and fast through the artery in his neck. By then, it was wholly closed up. And the curve of his biceps...

Donny grabbed the hair on the back of my head lightly and

pulled me back so we could make eye contact again. My chest heaved as I looked into his eyes, dark, reflecting the dappled light that shone down through cracks in the canopy, prickling our skin. His nostrils flared. My lips parted, and I kissed him, long and deep.

It was becoming hard to avoid the slices of light streaming down onto the forest floor. I knew we should find cover, but we hesitated. It's Donny, I reminded myself, knowing I should move away. But we had crossed a line, and there was no going back.

I pushed him back against a tree trunk, straddled him, and opened his shirt with one quick movement. Buttons flew. Damn. Donny's chest looked better than I had ever imagined. Of course, I'd tried very hard *not* to imagine it.

I ran my fingers through the dark hair that grew there, feeling the muscles of his pecs tauten. He grabbed my waist, his hands moving from there up under my shirt and over my ribs towards my breasts. Then he pulled my stretchy top off my shoulder with one hand. His fingers were cool and welcoming, even in the fresh air of dawn.

My fingers opened Donny's zip easily, but suddenly, he cupped my cheek with his hand. He looked hard at me. My head flooded with anxiety. He cared. Goddamn it, he cared about me. It was perplexing.

I turned, considering calling it all off. But I couldn't. I *couldn't* leave him alone. I needed his body against mine. I turned back, leaned in, and kissed him again. Our mouths were open, wanting. My lips moved down to his neck, and I felt his pulse on my tongue while his hands unzipped my jeans.

'Sarina,' he whispered, the sound deep yet breathy despite vampires not breathing. I placed a finger across his mouth. I didn't want to hear my name on his lips again.

I felt him harden where I rested on him. Meanwhile, his

hand readied me until there was nothing to do except let ourselves go.

The aftermath of our passion was cut short by the increasingly unbearable sunlight and the recollection that a human being was held prisoner back at the house where Steve had been hiding out. It was simply too late to do anything to help the human. All I could do was hope she would be rescued during the day or be okay until nightfall.

Relieved to have the pressing focus of where to bed down, we dressed quickly and began scrambling for a solution. Donny dug a half channel behind the fallen log nearby. I worried it wasn't enough, but we had so little time.

But Donny pointed to it, telling me, 'I've got this. Lie here.'

He eased himself in next to me. Reality hit. We'd just been together after all those years, and now I was going to be stuck in a hole with him all day, unable to run—and I *did* want to run.

As soon as we were settled, we scooped as much leaf litter on top of us as possible.

'It's not enough,' I cried.

'Wait,' said Donny and with that, he pulled a section of the rotted log—a sound metre and a half diameter—over the top of us.

He was right. We would be safe until nightfall.

All I could smell in the cramped rut of soft earth was soil and odd animal odours. It may have been the most awkward position I'd ever found myself in. And I wasn't talking about the physical position of sleeping in a hole in the ground!

Best to ignore it. Don't say a word. Close your eyes and hope he does the same.

Then Donny's voice rang out in the darkness we'd created to protect ourselves from the dawn.

'I know it was you,' he said.

'What?' I whispered, irritable that Donny wasn't allowing my plan to pretend it wasn't happening. In my mind, it was the *only* plan that could work.

Just keep your eyes closed, Sarina. Relax. Don't worry about Donny's ramblings. Just get through the night.

'The dead guy in the unit … you know. Wine and Cheese.'

My eyes popped open so quickly that I worried I might lose an eyeball.

What the … oh, no.

I felt his body move a little with a slight turn towards me.

Stay exactly where you are, Donny Agosti.

'Jennifer Gordon knew it was you, Sar.'

'Christ on a stick!' I said before I could consider how to play it. There'd been too much drama and too much emotion already that night. I wondered if I had energy enough to get through this new assault.

'Yeah, I was surprised, too.' He just let it hang there.

Is he waiting for me to spill my guts? Should I spill?

My mind began scrambling for excuses. Was there anything I could say to explain away that woman's belief I was the perpetrator?

'I think you're a vampire with more depth than I'd imagined, Sar, and I already knew you carried some turmoil. From your turning, to your difficulty committing to Will, to your problems with your dad. But I didn't see this one coming.'

Say something, Sarina. For heaven's sake!

'I…' Yeah, that won't cut it, I chastised myself.

'There's something else Gordon said, too.'

Great. Plum bloody fantastic.

'She told me that those nights she went over to drink with the Wine and Cheese guy, he tried it on a bit more than she admitted during our questioning.' Donny paused. He was waiting for me to fill in the details.

'He wasn't a good guy, was he, Sarina?'

'No, he wasn't,' I said, finally—my first admission.

'Is that why you did it?'

'Maybe. How bad is it?' My heart banged against my ribcage, something rotten.

'Well, she knows it's you, but I've done a little rearranging of her memories.'

Puhh. I expelled the air I hadn't even known I was holding in my lungs.

'She'll be right,' he said.

I had nothing else to say. I brushed aside what had happened between us, and we lay dead still. Our bodies were perfectly aligned there under the soil and decaying leaves. With the forest alive and chittering around us, we slept soundly until sunset.

CHAPTER
FORTY-FIVE

'You sure you're ready for this?' I asked.

Donny stood beside me, fresh in blue jeans and a white cotton t-shirt—his signature style.

'You must be joking. You know what a charmer I am. I've got this,' Donny said.

I smirked and knocked on Mum and Dad's front door. This would be the first time Donny had seen my father since the night at Mike's house several months before.

'Here they are,' said Mum as she opened our front door, arms outstretched for an awkward hug. 'Come on, Tom,' she called out. I immediately sensed she was trying her best. She'd dressed up in a bright blue pantsuit, and her hair, always permed into light waves, was pinned up on one side with a pretty tortoiseshell comb.

Dad arrived to greet us then, all neat in an ironed short-sleeve button-down and cargo shorts, his hair still wet from showering and combed neatly off his face.

Finally, we bundled inside and took a seat in the lounge room. How ... pleasant. We were celebrating. The internal review into what had occurred in Standfort with Steve, Damion, John and Mike had just been completed, and Donny and I had come out smelling like roses. Incredible, really. Then again, I *had* saved twelve humans from slavery, and Donny and I had put some career criminals out of action. It turned out that some people high up in the After Dark Department were grateful for how things had turned out.

Mike's death had even been blamed on Steve. I didn't have to add kindling to that fire ... oops, I mean, lie. It just took off on its own, like dry twigs on a windy day, when someone suggested Mike's murder could have been Steve attempting to cover his tracks. It was probably because the theory made sense. Plus, it was backed up by Donny and me telling what we'd overheard Steve and Damion discussing "cleaning up" and how we'd assumed it meant getting rid of anyone who could cause trouble for them. That part was genuine, at least.

It all worked out well for me. However, it set Donny, Dad, and me in a strange triangle of secrets. Donny said he had my back and certainly would not blab. No surprise. But Dad was also happy to keep my secret. Okay, so that's not a surprise, either. Seeing my physical prowess and what I was prepared to do with it when I took Mike out had put my father in his place.

Dad wouldn't tell anyone what he saw at Mike's place that night. Not when he'd be risking my wrath. But it hadn't healed our rift because his newfound tolerance for me was fear-based. I knew that.

'Well, I'll bring out the bubbly, hey?' said Mum brightly. 'Marinda! Come on, now, we're starting!'

'You should give her a hand, Dad,' I said. He started to turn, probably to give me a dirty look, but thought better. Instead, he got up and went into the kitchen after her.

Sure, I was pushing his compliance. I wouldn't keep it up forever. I was just enjoying my newfound power over him for a moment or two. Besides, this might teach him not to be such a bloody chauvinist. Though Mum always said she loved looking after us, caring for the house and having coffee with the girls after tennis, Dad could have been more helpful and supportive.

There was some thumping in the hall as Marinda and a friend came bounding through, spilling into the lounge room.

'Here she is. You sounded like an elephant coming down the hall, you know?' I responded inappropriately.

'I've told you not to wear those in the house, Mar,' called Mum from the kitchen.

'I'm trying to wear them in, Mum,' Marinda yelled irritably. 'Jeez. New shoes. Aren't they cool?' she asked me.

'I think I'd break my neck in them, and I'm worried you will too.' They were slip-on sandals with good two to three-inch platform heels. Why?

'You better not be dissing them.' She frowned at me and leaned in for a hug, her super-sized hoop earring thwacking me in the face before she looked over towards Donny.

'Well, I like them,' he said. I rolled my eyes, making sure he saw it.

Then I noticed the girl partially hidden behind Marinda. I knew the face straight away. It was Kimberly, the waitress from Mack's—but also the girl who'd been tied up at the Aumond Street address where Steve had holed up. The poor thing had been stuck there all day, and as soon as night fell, Donny and I had run back, double-time, to release her. Fortunately, she hadn't been tied in too cruel a position. The thought had kept creeping into my mind while I slept to give me anxiety every time I stirred in my rainforest nest.

Marinda said quickly, 'Guys, this is Kim. Kim, this is my sister Marinda and her boyfriend, Donny.'

Everyone held their breath for a second before Marinda burst out laughing. 'Only kidding. They work together.'

'Hi, Kim. Nice to meet you,' I said, giving her a nod. We hadn't seen her for a month or two. Not since she gave evidence during the After Dark-Standfort investigation. I had hoped she'd fall on her feet after that. Steve and his crew had taken her, intending to kill her to guarantee her silence. What had happened to her during that short time was unconscionable. Still, I couldn't very well pepper her with questions about how she was doing in front of Marinda and my parents.

Mum and Dad arrived back carrying a tray each. One contained long-stemmed crystal glasses and a bottle of sparkling wine. The other, held by Mum, had some shot glasses containing a red liquid. Blood. Mum was holding the tray as far away from herself as she could while still being able to keep it steady. Meanwhile, she smiled and tried her best to look like everything was dandy and that it was normal for her to serve up blood in little glasses in her living room.

'Look, Sar! Surprise! Human blood. They're doing this in Brisbane now, you know. It's so cosmopolitan, don't you think? Look at us!' Marinda shimmied her torso a little, revelling in the idea of being capital chic despite living in little old Standfort.

'It is rather swish, sweetie,' I offered, though I couldn't have cared less about being ultra-modern. Still, I appreciated the smell and looked forward to a nice little snack. 'Thank you.' I turned to Mum and Dad and thanked them as well. It couldn't have been easy for them to go along with that.

'Well, we couldn't have you going hungry now, could we?' said Dad stiffly, looking over Donny and me without letting his eyes settle on either of us.

Soon, we had all toasted the successful conclusion to what went on in Standfort and, in particular, Donny and I, coming out scot-free and heroes for many.

Marinda was resting on the lounge when she suddenly

asked, 'What I don't understand is who made Steve and why. He was such a little dweeb. Who would even want him as their progeny?'

My eyebrows raised to hear my little sister using such precise terminology. That girl was a bit too interested in and comfortable with vampires for her own good.

'We'll probably never know,' offered Donny, reaching for his third glass of life-blood.

One of the most intriguing things that didn't come out of the complete debacle and subsequent investigation was the answer to Steve. Marinda was correct. We still didn't know who or why. The Queensland After Dark Department remained concerned over it, though. Mainly because of the possibility of European vampires being involved in some way. They have so many old vamps and so much history, making them a formidable force compared with the numbers and ages of those in Australia.

I was still extremely young in my vampire years. I'd never had time to learn about the broader vamp community and its history. Busy with work, my extracurriculars, and Will, it always seemed like something I would get to, eventually. But naturally, vampires had their history. It hadn't been taught when I was in school, of course. But during the trial, I discovered vampirism was believed to have originated in Europe and had then spread swiftly across much of the world. I was fascinated by the thought of an old and powerful vampire community centralised in Europe.

Whether they were connected with Steve and in what way was the mystery we still hadn't been able to crack. But it was decided that given the months that had passed with no sign of trouble arriving from abroad, Steve's talk of his "ancestor" may have been part of his eternal boasting.

'We have one more auspicious event to toast,' I announced. 'Someone here has received a promotion.'

'You're taking Mike's position?' Marinda yelled, deafening us all. Mum frowned in her direction.

'No. Donny is taking it,' I corrected. 'Being stuck behind a desk all day, every day, is not the life for me. Donny's well-equipped and ready to take it on.' I turned to Donny with my glass raised. 'You've earned it, mate, and you'll be a great boss. To your reign over After Dark. May it be long and successful.'

CHAPTER
FORTY-SIX

Vampire Court is just as solemn as any other. Thanks to Donny and me, Steve Gorman and Damion Lau wouldn't need a day in court, but finally, Will's day had come. A crowd was there at eight p.m. sharp, and the court was filled with whispers and fluttering papers.

Vampires created against their will still underwent rigorous investigation. By law, "innocent until proven guilty" was supposed to apply to humans and vampires. But in reality, outside the court system, people were more likely to think of vamps as "guilty until proven innocent". It wasn't wholly baseless if I was being honest.

Will had a lot going for him, though. Steve's criminality was already well known while I was a respected After Dark Detective. After all, no one knew what I really got up to in my spare time. Thanks to Donny, I managed to make it through that very close call.

During the months after the Daintree Rainforest battle, I'd visited Will as he sat, biding time, in the Vampire prison in Standfort. It was a fair-sized facility for our small population, but necessary, with Standfort being the entry point for so many. The prison offered up jobs, too. Regional Australians couldn't ignore that.

Will was sullen each time I saw him, and he quickly shut down any bridge building offered. I left feeling sad and emotional every time. More than anything, I wanted him to understand me and what I'd done, even if things couldn't return to how they were. And he was unequivocal that he couldn't—and wouldn't. Even though I had given him back his life by making him vampire, he was completely stuck on the trauma of being kidnapped and attacked, and he seemed to focus the anger he had about it towards me for delaying turning him.

That I was one of the rare vampires whose progeny rejected her still burned me from the inside out. The turn is an emotional time that should have brought us closer. Even if he remained pissed off, he shouldn't have been able to ignore our connection—I was his maker! Instead, I made one of the few vampires who'd turned against the bond. Why did I have such dreadful luck? Was it to do with the fact that I'd never known my maker? Perhaps I was broken. It all made my blood boil.

On my last visit, it all blew up.

'How's Donny?' Will asked.

'He's fine. He's taking a promotion at After Dark, so that's something positive for him,' I answered casually.

'This whole situation wouldn't have anything to do with your obsession with Donny Agosti, of course?' he said, his voice ripe with the tang of sarcasm. Then, he left the idea to hang in the metallic ambience of the prison visitor's room.

'First, what do you mean by "this situation"?'

'You know.'

However, I didn't know at all.

'Waiting and waiting before finally deciding to deign me with your gift of immortality,' he explained.

'No. No,' I protested. My skin felt hot for a vampire. 'I carried so much anger about my situation, having been made against my will, that it caused me to be conflicted. I wasn't sure I wanted to do that to you. Surely you can understand that? I didn't want you to have this life because I hadn't wanted it. I never wanted that for you because I love you. But I was wrong.'

'Yet, in many respects, it's a gift, right? A gift you didn't want to hand over, even though you said you loved me and I told you repeatedly that I wanted it. Immortality. Strength. Speed. Health. You refused to give those to me until the last moment.'

'That's not fair. I had already decided to apply for the paperw—'

'Too late!'

Seeing I was getting nowhere with that explanation, I switched tack. 'I've never been obsessed with Donny, either. He's a big part of my life because we're partnered together for work. I can't help that.'

'It's more than that.'

'No. No, it's not.' *Was it, though? Oh, shut up, Sarina.*

'So you're telling me you've never slept with him?'

Oh, no. Nooo!

As it turns out, silence in prison feels more painful than elsewhere. Or was it just the sting of truth slapping me in the face?

'I did. It happened once.' There was no use lying.

'Thanks for that,' said Will. He sneered and turned away to gaze up through the barred window. 'The truth is something, I guess.'

'It was only after you pushed me away, Will. Just the once

after you rejected me.' There I was, being a heel again and trying to blame my mistakes on something else.

'Well, we've got that sorted, then.' Will wore a look as though he'd just tasted something bitter.

'Would it have made a difference to us if I hadn't done it?'

He fiddled with a book I'd been allowed to bring into the prison for him before answering. 'No. It wouldn't.'

I nodded. Some truth from Will as well. We were over, then. My work, dragging Will into a dangerous web, my choice to turn him instead of letting him die. My decision to sleep with Donny. Our relationship had unravelled, and I felt little hope of stitching it back together.

I left the prison that day and never saw Will again until the court case. Yet nothing would prevent me from attending that, even if I wasn't giving evidence.

During the proceedings, Will rarely turned to look at anyone seated in the gallery, but he was my progeny, and I could tell he knew I was there. Marinda went too; my dad even came for two days. Will's parents were in the court daily but avoided me. Once, I caught their gaze momentarily before they turned away, lips furrowed harshly.

When my time on the stand arrived, the barrister asked me, 'So it was through your investigation, which you kept a secret from your boss, Mike Thompson, that this criminal element, headed by Steve Gorman, looked into your life, found out about William, and then attacked him?'

'Yes,' I replied. 'It was gutting, bu—'

'That will be all.'

I glanced at Will, but he was staring at a blank sheet of paper on the desk. A pencil lay across it, but he hadn't used it.

Weeks later, the results of the case came in. The courtroom was filled with a nervous buzz. The cost of the wrong outcome would be Will's life. He would be transferred to Brisbane, where court-ordered ultimate deaths played out in a specially built facility, unlike the hands-on way that Donny, me and the other After Dark Detectives would dispatch illegals back in Standfort when necessary.

My blood pressure rose so sharply that night I felt panicked. That's rare for vampires who, perhaps through their build for the hunt, have a much greater threshold for agitation. As the Judge read the decision, I felt like my blood had frozen. If I'd been a breather, I would have held my breath.

'I find William G. Foster not guilty of any charges.'

Even as the words rang out across the courtroom, causing many to jump up in joy and shout, my brain couldn't fathom it.

'You did it, mate!' and 'I knew it would be okay,' filtered through eventually.

Marinda squeezed me tight. 'He did it, Sar. He's free!'

As it registered, all the relief pumped through my body, and I relaxed into the bench seat. Will was genuinely free. He would be allowed to leave prison and start a life for himself, and I wouldn't have his death hanging over my head. Well, not his ultimate demise, at least.

There was paperwork to be done. I wasn't sure why or if I should, but I loitered at the entrance to the courthouse for a while. Donny wasn't far away, and Will's parents were there, too, avoiding me. Finally, the heavy door swung open, accompanied by a tremendous commotion. Everything seemed to happen at once. The media, who'd waited impatiently at the bottom of the stairs, ran up and began firing questions at Will and his barrister.

Though I remained behind a column, in the night's shadows where the media couldn't see me, Will did. He whispered something to his barrister and made his way over. Donny, a few metres away from me, moved to give us space and prevent reporters from following.

Will made eye contact with me. His blue suit offered a slight sheen in the moonlight. 'I did it.'

'You did. I'm so relieved,' I said.

'Fresh start?'

I nodded before he quickly added, 'Not the relationship thing.' Even though it was too much to hope for, I still felt a pang to hear those words.

'I understand,' I said, wounded.

'But the bitterness. Let's move forward, hey?'

I nodded again at the best I could hope for. Then Will hugged me. I held on a bit too long and wrapped my arms around him a bit too tightly as I inhaled him in that little too much.

I wanted to grab hold of the past and stop it from floating away, but it was already gone.

In an instant, Will extracted himself from my grip and disappeared into the crowd.

FORTY-SEVEN

A *few months later.*

It was an important day.

I had been congratulated for saving more than a dozen young men and women from slavery at The Red Line, stopping Steven Gorman, and making Standfort a safer place for upstanding humans and vampires. Madame Shey was doing a ten-year stint for her crimes, and I was staying as a Detective with After Dark.

The promotion would have been a great honour—had I wanted it. My father had even told me how proud he was of me when he thought I might take the position. But that life was never for me. It wasn't part of my career plan to work behind a desk all day while my staff went out and solved the crimes. My place was on the streets at night, stake-outs, talking to witnesses, and even on the endless beach assignments. It wasn't talking and giving orders from behind Mike's old desk.

When Donny took the promotion instead, I had misgivings and told him as much. Not that I didn't think he would do a good job. I absolutely thought he had it in him. Not that I would miss having him as my partner either, although that was very much true. I'd always known him to be someone like me. Someone who would be happier pounding the pavement, interviewing suspects, and arresting the new arrivals as they walked up on the sand, exhausted and hopeful. The classic gritty detective lives for us was how I'd always envisaged it.

But Donny reached for something new—something higher. I was damn happy for him.

The day arrived for Donny's swearing-in ceremony. We were at the Standfort Town Hall, all smart and crisp in our formal uniforms. No hair was out of place, and no shoe was scuffed.

Donny looked handsome, dressed in his finest.

As he was handed the shiny new badge, his pride was unmistakable. It shone to where I sat in the third aisle from the front. I was seated with my After Dark colleagues. Applause broke out, and it was exuberant, with some of Donny's large family in attendance. I joined them, standing with loud applause.

Donny's eyes scanned the crowd, and when they settled on me, I poked my tongue out at him, causing his smile to widen even further.

At the reception afterwards, we had little time to speak. Still, eventually, Donny sidled up to me just as I thought of slinking quietly away.

'You should have taken it, you know,' Donny said. 'It was yours, and you'd have been bloody great at it, Sar.'

'No. This is how it should be. You've got this.'

'Well, naturally, I've got it. But you have everything the role takes, too.'

'Dumb bumb,' I said, rolling my eyes as they often wanted to do when dealing with Donny Agosti.

Donny was unperturbed, though I knew I'd have to pull up

my socks at work from then on. You can't be calling the boss names all the time. At least not in front of everyone.

'I need you, you know?'

'I'm still going to be there—bloody hell. You act as though I handed in my resignation. I plan to be your best employee, mate.'

'That's not what I meant,' he whispered.

Everything that had happened between us flashed through my mind. People say that can happen when you're dying, but for me, it happened right there, in front of Donny while surrounded by hundreds of people.

'I don't know what you want from me,' I said.

'When was the last time you heard about me being with another woman, Sarina?'

'Well, there was my sist—'

'That was dreadful. I know I was a selfish arse, and I wish I could take it back. But it *was* nearly four years ago.'

He was concentrating entirely on me, his broad features handsome even under the fluorescent light of the auditorium in the Town Hall.

'I haven't been dating—' he started.

It was my turn to interrupt him with a loud sigh and a look away.

'I'm serious, Sarina. I love you and haven't been with anyone else for over a year.'

It was so unexpected I felt like I'd been shocked. In a good way, though, it made little sense.

'I want to be with you. There, I said it.'

'I...I just. I wasn't expecting...' I didn't know how I felt. The guests were crowding us. Confused, I said quickly, 'See you on Monday, hey?' I turned, hearing Donny say, 'Take care, Miss Sarina,' as I hightailed it for the double doors at the front of the Town Hall's banquet room.

Pushing my way through the crowd, I saw Will across the room. Two dozen people separated us. I stared for a second, but he disappeared into the crowd again. I wondered if that was how Will and I would always be from that day forward. So little connection, despite him being my progeny. He was little more than a ghost—a ghost of my past.

WALKING into the After Dark office the following Monday, nothing appeared out of order. Why should it? We had a new boss, that's all. Well, I'd need a new partner too. I was a bit worried about who I might be paired with, but then Donny knew me well and respected my work, so I was unlikely to be paired with someone terrible at their job. Or lazy at it. That would be the absolute worst.

I greeted the receptionist on the way in. 'Sergeant Donny will need to see you as soon as you get settled,' she called as I punched my numbers into the panel on the door.

'Thanks,' I said without slowing. Sergeant Donny had a ring to it. I smiled at her, and we tipped our heads to each other in that nonverbal agreement way. Donny was going to be great in the role. I just knew it.

It didn't take me long to put a couple of files away and place my badge and keys in the desk drawer. I sighed long and slow and started for Mike's—oops—Donny's office. Passing the After Dark employees and investigators on the way, I greeted them all. They seemed more odd than usual. Marcus looked as though he found something highly amusing. He would soon realise his mistake if he thought I was pissed off that Donny was promoted instead of me. Janette looked like she felt sorry for me.

Bloody hell. Like working with them wasn't hard enough before.

'Knock, knock,' I said instead of rapping my knuckles on Donny's door.

'Sarina? Yeah, come on in,' Donny called back.

On entering, I found him looking picture-perfect as the new unit sergeant. His shirt fit to a tee. I was proud. It made me smile, but that faded quickly when the person sitting on the other side of Donny's desk turned around.

'Will!'

There were a few seconds when no one knew what to say. Not even Donny. Then he took control.

'Sarina, say hello to your new partner.'

TO MY READERS

You're the best! Thank you so much, and I hope you enjoyed *The Red Line*.

If you did, the kindest thing you can do for me as an author is to leave reviews online and tell your friends about it.

Just a sentence or two with a rating helps other readers find my books, which is so important to me. Thank you.

Join my mailing list at www.mncox.com so you'll never miss out.

GLOSSARY

I've done my best to balance being true to Australian English quirks while also writing a story that any English speaker worldwide can enjoy.

Where I've used a word or expression that I thought might trip people up, I've tried to provide clues within the text to help. But here is a super-casual glossary for you as well.

Not every expression listed below is solely Australian.

Glossary:

Arc up: To become upset or angry.

Brekkie: Breakfast.

Ciggie: A cigarette.

Croc: A crocodile. Both freshwater and saltwater crocodiles are found in the north of Australia.

Dob: To tell on someone or report someone for a wrongdoing.

Dunno: I don't know.

Faaark: It's just a drawn-out 'fuck'.

Fag: A cigarette.

Fluoro: Fluorescent light or a fluorescent light bulb.

Gaffa/Gaffa tape: A strong tape made of plastic and cloth.

Get stuffed: Telling someone to go away or get lost.

Gung-ho: When you're enthusiastic or throw yourself into something with zeal.

Gunned it: Moved fast.

Himbo: A male bimbo.

Keeping your trap shut: Not talking about something.

Kerb: The edge of the pavement.

Macca's: McDonalds. Yes, the restaurant!

Ocker: Refers to Australians who are rough around the edges or who have a strong Australian accent.

Pissed off: Angry. (Not to be confused with 'pissed', meaning to be drunk)

Pokies: Slot machines.

Prize prawn: A big idiot.

Refedex: A book of suburban street maps in Queensland, Australia.

Salties: Saltwater crocodiles.

She'll be right: It will be okay.

Stubby: A glass bottle holding a drink, most often beer.

The Hut: Short for Pizza Hut, a common pizza chain restaurant in Australia.

Tongue-in-groove boards: Strips of timber that slot together and are used quite a lot in homes in Queensland.

Whingeing: Complaining about something, often in a whiney fashion.

XXXX: A beer brand in Queensland, Australia.

Acknowledgments

Back in 2023, when I was still calling *The Red Line* "Sarina" (after its main character), the manuscript was shortlisted in the Queensland Writers Centre's (QWC) Publishable program. It's a development prize designed to 'strengthen, refine and polish' a completed manuscript. Winning one of just ten shortlist slots was an experience I won't forget.

The feedback and advice that came from QWC staff and beta readers helped me get an outside view of the story I'd been so focused on, and helped me tighten my plot.

Plus, Publishable offered me the opportunity to pitch to agents and publishers. What a rollercoaster ride pitching was! It came complete with all the excitement and nerves you might imagine. A fascinating and eye-opening window into the publishing industry and an opportunity from QWC that I remain grateful for.

To *The Red Line's* other beta readers (beyond the Publishable program), a special thank you. It was encouraging, constructive and exciting to hear what worked and what didn't from that early version of the story. Your feedback helped me make some major changes early on, that I believe improved the plot.

Finally, many thanks to the members of Noosa Writers, a wonderful novel writing group in my district. Their instructive feedback during the early chapters of what was only a second draft of my manuscript was very encouraging.

ABOUT THE AUTHOR

Morgan Cox, as M. N. Cox, writes mysteries peppered with supernatural events and creatures, and approaches dark narrative elements with a light touch. Armed with an eccentric personality and a Psychological Science degree—that she'll probably never use elsewhere—she writes flawed and quirky female protagonists in the first person point of view.

Shortlisted in Queensland Writers Centre's 15th Publishable program, Morgan was born, bred and proudly sets her novels in Queensland, Australia. Fluffy oddballs keep her company as she plots, writes and reads, powered by endless cups of tea. You can find her online at www.mncox.com.